Edward Bramfeld

in the
Name of
the Kimberley

a novel

ISBN: 978-3-9820520-0-7

Front cover image by Marie Macieszko

Cover design by J.E.C

First print 2018

www.edward-bramfeld.com

Kununurra
Kimberley
Cairns
Broome
AUSTRALIA
Quilpie
Brisbane
Byron Bay
Perth
Sydney
Adelaide
Melbourne

Introduction

____

Around a camp fire, late in the evening after a few beers or glasses of wine, you hear strange stories, the kind that haunt you all night. In northern Australia the stories are about crocodiles, or about people who get lost in the bush, trapped in the immensity of Australia's wilderness. The truth is that very few deserve telling outside the circle of a camp fire. But one of them stayed on my mind, to the point that I felt I had to get to the bottom of it.

But let's begin at the beginning. A few kilometres away from the Mitchell Falls, in the north-western part of Australia that we call the Kimberley, I heard part of the story for the first time. It was the 15th of June 2016, around 10pm. We were four people around a camp fire: three tourists from overseas, including me, and a tour leader, Bryce. Drinking his fourth can of beer, Bryce, who had himself been born in the Kimberley thirty-two years earlier, told us the story the entire region had been talking about for two years.

On a quiet afternoon in Sydney on the 12th of March 2003, a

terrorist group calling itself the Earth Warriors burned down the headquarters of a major mining company. While the building was still burning, the terrorist group sent its demands:

The company, A.S. Mining, must stop all exploration in the Kimberley region.

A young woman died in the arson attack. The entire country went into shock and the so-called Earth Warriors were compared to terrorist organisations like Al-Qaeda. Most environmental organisations rejected the violence and publicly showed their opposition to the Earth Warriors in a statement to all the major newspapers. But when it came to protecting the environment the terrorists weren't going to take orders from anyone. Here is their response:

We, the Earth Warriors, who burned down A.S. Mining's headquarters, have a short message to deliver to all the environmentalists who support non-violent action: You have ten years. Even though your actions have done nothing to save this planet over the last few decades, we give you ten more years to succeed. After that, it will be our turn to act.

The authorities never found those Earth Warriors. Nobody was ever able to identify them. However, they knew how to keep their word. For ten years we heard nothing from them, and they were almost forgotten. But, as you probably realise, this story doesn't finish in 2003.

· · ·

In June 2013, five people working for a small mining company left the city of Wyndham in three 4WD cars to explore a very specific area of the Drysdale River National Park. This area, at the heart of the Kimberley, is one of the remotest in Australia and access is very restricted. Only the native people of the region can go there without authorisation. In fact, very few people visit this national park and anyone who does tends to go to the same area. You don't expect to meet anyone there or to see any kind of human activity.

No one from the exploration team can tell us today what happened to them there, because none of them ever came back. No dead body, no vehicle, not a single thing belonging to the exploration team has ever been recovered. The authorities have never found anything, apart from a message from the so-called Earth Warriors received in August 2013 by a local newspaper based in Kununurra:

It is a matter of fact that the mainstream environmentalists, the so-called civilised ones, have failed to protect either the Kimberley or this planet. We are the real defenders of Mother Nature. We will keep the Kimberley free from any kind of mining, or any human activity that would damage its ecosystem. The mining company that dared to call itself 'Kimberley's Future Inc.' was our first victim. All the members of its exploration team have been executed in the name of the Kimberley, which we will protect at any cost.

The story could have finished there. But no, the most important part was still to come. In September 2013, Andrew Foreman, the husband of Rachael Foreman, a member of the missing exploration team, sold everything he owned to go to the Drysdale River National Park to find his wife, dead or alive. He didn't believe his wife had simply vanished. She had to be somewhere, and he was determined to find out. 'I will do whatever it takes. It doesn't matter if it takes me a month or twenty years. I won't leave the Kimberley until I have found my wife,' he told local and national media. The authorities, who had conducted searches using planes, helicopters and a whole lot of people on the ground, expressed doubt that a single man with no field experience would find anything in a wild and remote area like the Drysdale River National Park. But for most of the Australian media, Andrew was a great story: thirty-seven, good-looking, tall and broad shouldered, Andrew resembled a rugby player and he was ready to play the adventurer in front of the cameras.

In his first TV interview Andrew said, 'For weeks I tried to accept what reasonable people had told me. Rachael was gone and there was no way to get her back. "We did the best we could, using everything we had," the authorities told me. I'm here because my heart tells me to be here. I can't live without knowing where my wife is. Anything is possible. The craziest things happen every day on this planet. So, maybe my wife is still alive. I know that the chances are very small, but it is possible. I won't give up.'

Lots of people in Australia were fascinated by this determination, which seemed to respond to no other logic but that of the heart. For the first six months, Andrew was the lead actor in a new kind of reality show; the latest adventure to be followed on TV and the internet. It helped to finance the search for Rachael, so no one really dared to criticise it. But the show only lasted six months. The Kimberley is an amazing region to film but after a while you need some action so as not to bore the audience. Beyond the logistical challenges of life in a very remote area, there wasn't much to show or tell. But in June 2014, Andrew once again made the headlines by calling the authorities and telling them that he had seen some distant, very powerful artificial lights over several nights in the middle of the national park. 'The Drysdale River National Park is probably inhabited,' he concluded. The authorities sent a full team into the field to check those claims but found nothing at all. No artificial lights at night and not the remotest trace of anyone living there. Nothing.

But Andrew didn't give up. He was no longer the star of a reality show; now he was just a crazy guy living in the middle of the Drysdale River National Park. For most people, what he was doing made no sense. His story seemed to have come to an end and nobody thought he would make the headlines again. But he did.

In November 2014, Andrew gave the authorities a USB stick that he claimed to have found in the bush. It contained a file that appeared to be Rachael Foreman's memoirs. The authorities stated that if it turned out to be authentic, Rachael might still be alive and there might indeed be a group of people living in the Drysdale River National Park. The police conducted a five-month-long investigation into the document, which was never published. No journalists got to read it, but everyone knew that it was a lot more than someone's diary. The rumour had spread that Rachael could have been one of the so-called Earth Warriors. How was such a thing possible? How did Andrew find these memoirs? Where were they hidden? Why were they hidden? Who was Rachael Foreman, really? Where was she? For five months, a lot of Australians kept themselves busy asking thousands of questions, but they never came up with any answers. Neither the authorities nor Andrew shared any information about the ongoing investigation or the content of the document. What had happened in the Drysdale River National Park remained a mystery that fed the collective imagination.

But in April 2015, the federal officer in charge of the investigation, Jeremy Trotman, declared before the cameras that, after a long investigation, he and his team had concluded the so-called memoirs weren't genuine and had probably been written by the Earth Warriors in an attempt to mislead the investigation.

'I want to remind everyone here that this document is part of an ongoing investigation. Despite the high level of curiosity generated, its contents cannot be disclosed. We have told you everything we can. Therefore, we shall answer no further questions on the matter,' Jeremy Trotman said before leaving the press conference.

For Andrew, and for Rachael's family, this was just unacceptable. As far as they were concerned, no one else but Rachael could have written the memoirs. In an attempt to get public opinion on their side, they allowed a famous journalist working for a national newspaper to read them. What followed was a short article on the front page of the newspaper.

Two months ago, Andrew Foreman and his parents-in-law, Abigail and Randal Flowers, allowed me to read what they claim to be Rachael Foreman's memoirs. It would be tempting to write a long article about them. A lot of journalists in this country would love the chance to do this. Some have felt jealous. They would love to have been chosen to read Rachael's memoirs. But no, I'm not going to write a long article about this document. This is a serious newspaper. We are not sensationalists.

I did my work properly. I investigated, and I considered every eventuality. I would have loved to have a good reason to write a long article about all of this. But I think the only purpose of this mysterious document is to defame a lot of people, including Rachael Foreman. The desire to find her alive does not justify ignoring the truth. I do understand Andrew Foreman and his parents-in-law. In their position, I would probably believe in anything that told me Rachael was alive. But the journalists and citizens of this country shouldn't let a document like this make the headlines. Our only wish should be to see the author of this defamatory document in jail.

The Attorney-General's department welcomed the article but reminded readers that the so-called Rachael's memoirs were part of an ongoing investigation and therefore shouldn't be shared with or published by anyone. *The Attorney-General's department will sue anyone leaking, partially or completely, any document linked to the investigation,* the statement concluded.

Rachael's memoirs had lost their curiosity value. Now, only conspiracy theorists believed Rachael was still alive. For Andrew and his parents-in-law, giving up wasn't an option. One article and a government statement wouldn't change their minds. Rachael had written those memoirs. Nothing would shake their belief.

Having lost most of the financial support they'd been getting from people all around Australia, Rachael's parents decided to sell their beautiful hotel in Cairns and move to Wyndham in the Kimberley.

Bryce finished telling us this story. 'Rachael's parents are still in Wyndham. They have a small hotel there. And Andrew is still in the Drysdale River National Park, looking for his wife. He hasn't once left the bush in the last two years.'

Hearing a story like that, at night, in the middle of the Kimberley, would have an effect on anyone. But for me it was much more than entertainment. I had been waiting for something like this for months. I needed to know if it was true or just a story. I needed to find out what it was that Bryce didn't know.

<h1 style="text-align:center">Who am I?</h1>

<hr>

My name is Edward Bramfeld. This book is not about me or my life, but I think it's important to tell you a bit about me and about how and why I'm writing this book. I turned seventy today and I've lived in Australia for two years. Before that I was in Los Angeles, where I was a successful screenwriter. You've probably never heard of me but I'm quite sure you have seen a few episodes of my TV series.

I really loved my life.

Then my wife of twenty years decided to leave me for another man. And then while I was visiting my lawyer to prepare my divorce I had a stroke. Thanks to my lawyer, who called 911 fast, I didn't die but I did visit a place that I would define as hell. Twenty hours after my stroke I woke up unable to speak. I was like a newborn, unable to express myself through language. But worst of all I was no longer able to take care of myself. Without the ability to speak, most everyday tasks were a real challenge for me, not to say mission impossible. Surprisingly, I found the patience to learn the English language again. It took me two years to write my first sentence on a piece of paper. Two years, during which every single day was a challenge. Two very busy years… and then nothing. I could speak and write English but suddenly I had nothing to do. I was sixty-six and had just recovered from a stroke and no one was waiting for one of my screenplays. As far as all my contacts in the industry were concerned, I'd retired… and to be honest, I wasn't sure I could write a screenplay. At least not like I used to.

What bothered me most was not that I wasn't a screenwriter any more but that I wasn't able to do anything that felt useful. I am not the kind of person who can keep himself busy with a hobby. I need to do something that feels really useful. With my screenplays, throughout my career, I had the pretentious idea that I was contributing towards making the world better. I wanted that back. I wanted to make my little contribution to the world. So, first, I joined the Democrat party in my neighbourhood. I thought being an active citizen, being active in the political debate, was the best way to feel useful again. I met some very nice and interesting people there, but it didn't bring me the satisfaction I'd expected. I needed to do something creative. I needed to write again. It was obvious.

From that point on I thought of writing a novel, but about what? My stroke, Los Angeles, the movie and TV industry… no, I wanted to write something original and useful. It took me a month to realise that I had no amazing ideas at all. It hurt not only my ego but also my ability to imagine any kind of future for my little life. The lack of inspiration wasn't new in my life. I had experienced it many times during my screenwriting career. In 1996, I went into a deep depression because of it. But the good news was that I knew the cure: travelling. Just leave the everyday routine and experience a totally different environment. Australia had been on my list for a long time, so Australia it was.

For two months, I travelled along the east coast. Then I went for two months to the Northern Territory and at the beginning of

June 2016, I was at the south gate of the Kimberley, in Broome, ready to join a tour through the heart of the Kimberley. This region is in the north-west corner of Australia, an area of 423,517 square kilometres, which is comparable to California. Most of its territory is uninhabited, making it one of the best-preserved regions of Australia – probably the best place in Australia to meet Mother Nature.

And here we were, seated around a campfire in the middle of the Mitchell Plateau, hearing this story, or I should say this unfinished story. What was lacking from this story strangely filled the void of my life. This was it. I knew what to do. This time I didn't want to write a story, I wanted to capture one. This story, I wanted all of it. I felt there was so much more to be told.

Wyndham

Obsessed by this story, I didn't feel like a tourist any more. All I wanted was internet access to check the story's veracity. Unfortunately, or fortunately, there was no internet access on the Mitchell Plateau.

Here, far away from our so-called civilised world, Mother Nature offers one of her best shows. The spectacular Mitchell Falls are not only beautiful; their extreme remoteness gives visitors the feeling they are experiencing something very special. But my only concern was how to get internet access. I needed to know if this story was true. Looking at some of the most beautiful scenery on the planet, all I could talk about was our next stop at the Drysdale River Station, where there was an internet connection and a public phone. I was the only one who was happy to stay only twenty-four hours on the Mitchell Plateau.

Once at the Drysdale River Station, I hurried to get a Wi-Fi password, ignoring everything that was happening around me. My sole priority was to check the veracity of this story. The answer came quickly. The story that Bryce had told us was there on numerous webpages. Every major Australian media outlet had at least one page about it. The same story over and over, as if someone had copied and pasted the same text on a hundred different websites. They all talked about the memoirs, or what they called 'the document', without ever revealing any of its content. Even the website Rachael's parents had created was evasive on that matter. *Our daughter is missing. She is not dead* was written in bold. They did challenge the official version of the story by claiming that 'the document' was the authentic memoirs of their daughter but they didn't reveal any part of it. What made this document authentic? What was in it that made them think that their daughter was still alive? They didn't answer these questions. Instead, they went on about the light Andrew claimed to have seen several times in the bush. According to them, this was proof that there were people living in the Drysdale River National Park. I could have thought, like most people, that they were simply crazy, deeply disturbed by the loss of Rachael, but I didn't want to believe that. I was desperately hoping there was an untold story behind all of this. I wanted to believe in these people who had changed everything in their lives for a cause that sounded hopeless. And most of all, I wanted to read that document.

I could have used the form on their website to contact them directly, but I decided not to. I wanted to meet them right in the middle of their everyday routine and feel the atmosphere around them, hear what their neighbours had to say. I didn't want to play around with people who might be psychologically fragile or unstable. I definitely needed to see what sort of people I would be dealing with. However, I couldn't hide my excitement. I couldn't wait to leave the Drysdale River Station and go to Rachael's parents' hotel in Wyndham. I wanted answers to the millions of questions I had in my head. So, I booked a room in their hotel for four nights and took advantage of the station's runway to get a small plane to pick me up. It cost me more than eight hundred dollars for a forty-minute flight, but money was the last of my concerns.

I was airsick for the entire flight. Flying in a small plane is nothing like flying in an Airbus or a Boeing. This is something I learned that day.

Once in Wyndham, I discovered that the city hasn't got a lot to offer a tourist who doesn't have a car. I had more choice there than at the Drysdale River Station when it came to restaurants, but it was still very limited. Everything you need is on the great northern highway that crosses the city. It's not really like a busy road in a busy city. Here, downtown, you smell, you hear, and you see the wilderness. In Wyndham, you're just a little way from the bush. Just walk a few minutes and then it's all about you and Mother Nature. But, despite its very small size, Wyndham offers the basic commodities. You have a supermarket, looking like a miniature version of the smallest one in the US, you have a hospital that doesn't look like a hospital, a post office, two gas stations and a liquor store that, sadly, looks like how it should look like.

Rachael's parents' hotel, two storeys, made of concrete with a corrugated-iron roof, wasn't pretty but it offered twenty-four comfortable and spacious rooms, all equipped with air conditioning. Nothing in the hotel showed why the Flowers were in the region. Only a picture of Rachael and Andrew in the lobby hinted at what was really going on there. The Flowers did everything in their hotel, from making breakfast for the guests at six o'clock every morning seven days a week to the house-keeping. No extra hand was there to help.

During my first two days in Wyndham, I didn't try and talk to the Flowers but did my best to have a chat with everyone around the hotel. People in Wyndham are friendly, they like to talk. From the Aboriginal native of the region to the young German with his 'work and travel' visa, you meet lots of different people in this tiny town. But when it came to talking about the Flowers, they were unanimous. The Flowers were not crazy or psychologically fragile. On the contrary, everybody agreed that they were totally sane and had a precise idea of what they were doing. This was good news for me.

The Flowers

I had noticed that the Flowers were busy from early morning to late in the evening. Opportunities to have a long conversation with them were limited. But between 2 and 3pm they seemed keener to chat with their customers. So, at 2pm I was in the lobby. The Flowers were there, seated at their desks, staring at their laptops. On their beige work shirts were badges with their first names on them: Randal and Abigail. Both around sixty, they couldn't have been more different from each other. Abigail had a short, round body with an oval face while Randal was tall and thin with sharp cheekbones. When they saw me, they both displayed wide 'customer-friendly' smiles.

'May I help you?' said Abigail.

'Last time,' I said, 'I didn't introduce myself properly. I didn't mention that I was an author. I'm travelling around Australia looking for inspiration. I've heard about what happened to your daughter and I wondered if it would be possible to talk about it with you?'

The Flowers glanced at each other. Then Randal stood up and

said, 'What do you want to talk about? Everything's on the internet already.'

'The memoirs aren't on the internet, even though it seems to have been a game changer for you. I mean, if I understood well, you moved here because of that. It's what makes you believe that your daughter is still alive. Am I right?'

Randal glanced at his wife, who wasn't smiling any more. 'Mr Bramfeld, you have to understand that this is a sensitive subject. Our lawyer advised us to say absolutely nothing about the memoirs. We could be sued for anything we say about them. You have to understand that this document contains real names and real locations, all linked to real events…' Randal sighed before going on. 'A tool to defame, they said.' Randal sighed a second time. 'We can say we think our daughter is the author but we can't share the contents or describe it to anyone.'

Abigail stood up and said, 'If we hadn't shown it to that journalist, we wouldn't have lost most of the support we had. People would still have some doubts, that maybe the police didn't do their job. But the journalist destroyed that. We were so naïve. *So naïve!* We can't trust the system. We can't!'

Randal put his hand gently on Abigail's shoulder, trying to calm her down. 'We welcome anyone who wants to help us bring our daughter back home but we won't talk about the memoirs. I'm sure you can find your 'inspiration' somewhere else.'

Randal and Abigail went back to their seats, making it clear the conversation was over. I just couldn't accept that. I wanted to read the memoirs. I wanted to understand the story. I wanted all the pieces of the puzzle. I was obsessed. I simply couldn't let it go. After five months of travelling I'd had no inspiration. The last time I'd had trouble finding inspiration, a couple of weeks' travelling had been enough to turn the light back on in my mind. The idea of leaving Wyndham with nothing scared me. So I insisted. I said, 'I could help you. I could write positively about what you're doing in the foreword of my future book. I could be really helpful.'

Randal stood up again and said, 'Thank you for the offer, Mr Bramfeld. We'll think about it. If we're interested, we'll let you know. Have a nice day, Mr Bramfeld.'

I went back to my bedroom, closed the curtains and walked around in circles talking to myself. It's how I think. It's what I do when I need ideas.

There must be a way, I said to myself over and over, until an idea came to me. I told myself the problem with the memoirs was their very nature. We could legally argue about content since it was supposed to describe events that actually happened and real people. But if I turned it into a novel the legal issue would disappear. The authorities had said it was a work of fiction. So, let it be one. Change the names and the locations. I wouldn't tell the Flowers I was looking for inspiration from what they thought of as their daughter's own memoirs, but I'd tell them I want to rewrite them as a novel.

I thought I'd had a brilliant idea until I realised none of it made any sense. 'The very nature of the document is what matters. The whole debate is about that, you idiot,' I shouted to myself. 'It would be just a novel, nobody would talk about it. Nobody cares about the story. Maybe it's boring. This is stupid. I should leave Australia and leave all of this behind me. I don't have any inspiration any more. This is a fact I have to accept,' I said, and sat down feeling the last of my optimism draining away. But there was still a 'what if?' running around in my mind. 'What if it was all about the story itself? What if it was far more than a pile of facts, events and names... what if the story itself had a meaning, a message to deliver? No... it can't be. Don't dream, Edward. Don't torture yourself.' I stayed silent for one long minute, staring at the grey carpet that covered the entire floor of the room. I felt empty.

This was it. I wasn't an author any more. I wasn't anything. I was useless. Maybe it was time for me to accept retirement. 'Everybody goes through that. Everybody,' I said to myself in a very low voice. 'But what if…? What if?' I shouted as if I was having an argument with myself.

I stood up and went to the lobby. Abigail and Randal were still there, working on their laptops. 'How about I transform your daughter's memoirs into a novel? I keep the biggest part of the story and its meaning, but I change the locations, the names and the events. I'll add some characters, some dialogue and descriptions. It will be a true novel, but it will still have your daughter's spirit and message.'

Randal stood up and said, 'OK. You transform it into a novel and then what? What for? Our daughter didn't write a piece of fiction. That's the whole point. The situation is already complicated enough. We don't need this.'

'I understand. I understand,' I replied in a low voice and went back to my room.

I hurriedly packed my stuff. I had to leave. That was it. I wasn't going to torture myself any longer.

But then Abigail knocked at my door. 'May I come in? It's about your idea.'

From that moment, I knew that I was going to write this book. I knew those memoirs were more than a collection of events, names and locations. There was a story. A story that meant something. A story the Flowers wanted to share.

Abigail used the conditional a lot to express herself. We were still in the world of 'if'. Nothing was decided, and she made it clear that lots of questions still needed to be answered. They wanted to know more about me, to clear up any legal issues with their lawyer, and they wanted to think through the conditions of our co-operation. 'We haven't made our decision yet. I have to insist on that.' Then she said the only thing that mattered for me at that time: 'Two weeks. We will give you our final answer, and eventually our conditions, in two weeks.'

I wasn't planning to wait two weeks for an answer. As far as I was concerned, Abigail and Randal had already said yes, and it was time for me to do my homework, to prepare myself for the writing process. I had never put a location I hadn't physically been to into any of my screenplays. I needed to visit the locations where Rachael had lived, studied, and worked. I needed to feel what it was like to be in these different places. Then I would have the difficult task of finding other locations, the ones that would appear in the novel. Locations that would be different and similar at the same time.

'See you in two weeks!' I said to the Flowers when I left their hotel, heading to Kununurra airport. They'd already told me what I needed to know. I knew where Rachael had grown up, where she had studied, where she had met Andrew, where she had spent her honeymoon… I had the list of locations.

For two weeks I travelled all over Australia, to Sydney, Adelaide, Brisbane, Perth, and to some very remote areas at the heart of Queensland and Western Australia. It was very intense and very immersive. I had all the pictures that I needed in my head. I didn't know Rachael's story, but I started to imagine a character called Helen. Just some ideas, the first lines of a complex drawing. Inspiration was on its way. I was still an author. I was relieved.

Then came the phone call from the Flowers. 'We have to talk about your next novel,' said Randal in a friendly voice. This was it. Nothing was going to stop my next novel being written. My life wasn't finished yet. I still had something to do, a task to fulfil. I was happy.

The conditions

It was in downtown Sydney that I met the Flowers again. It was at the office of their lawyer, inside a pretty Victorian building. Everything looked expensive and like it came from the 19th century. The Flowers' lawyer, Scott Narain, around fifty, Indian, in an expensive suit and showing off an expensive Swiss-made watch, gave a good impression of someone who wasn't in the habit of sending cheap invoices. A bit overweight, with a round face and wearing glasses, he had a way of looking at you that offset his unimpressive physique. He fitted in well with the portraits that hung on every wall. Coming from another century, they stared at you, intimidating you. Here, serious matters were discussed.

They were all seated at the far end of a long wooden table in a small conference room that looked like a fancy library. Scott started the conversation in a very serious tone.

'Mr Bramfeld, before discussing the conditions under which you may read Rachael Foreman's memoirs, I would like to tell you the current situation concerning this document. If you have any questions, don't hesitate to interrupt me.'

Scott glanced at one of the papers in front of him and then

continued, 'What we claim to be Rachael Foreman's memoirs is still part of an ongoing investigation concerning the disappearance of five individuals in the Kimberley.'

Scott locked his eyes on mine and said, 'The authorities have been clear with us. Sharing Rachael's memoirs with anyone could have an impact on the investigation and could constitute an obstruction of justice.'

He looked away, glancing for a moment at the Flowers before gazing once more at the piece of paper in front of him. 'According to the authorities, Rachael Foreman's memoirs, found by her husband in the Drysdale National Park, can't be authentic. Their hypothesis is that the so-called Earth Warriors wrote them with the aim of misleading the investigation. They didn't share the elements on which this hypothesis is based. We refute the hypothesis.' Scott paused briefly, glancing around. 'Rachael Foreman's memoirs do give an explanation about what happened to the exploration team in the Kimberley. We don't believe that the authorities have any means to confirm or deny this explanation, since all the protagonists involved in it are missing or dead, *without a single exception!*'

Scott paused once again. 'Besides that, it's important to mention that most of the memoirs have no direct link with the investigation and match perfectly with what we know of Rachael Foreman's life so far. A private investigation by this law firm has confirmed the document's accuracy and shows it's highly probable that Rachael Foreman wrote it.'

Scott stretched his arms and readjusted his glasses. 'The authenticity of this document wouldn't matter that much to us if it didn't tell us that Rachael may still be alive. People are living in the Drysdale River National Park and Rachael could be among them right now. That is the most important thing in this precious document. The authorities have never made any comment on this, rejecting the document wholesale. According to them, every detail of Rachael's memoirs was investigated and led them to conclude that the document was written by the Earth Warriors.'

'They lie. They don't want to let people know what's going on in the Kimberley. Some people are living there, this is...' said Abigail before Scott threw his hands in the air and interrupted her.

'Abigail, please. We can't do that. You, Randal and I have read Rachael's memoirs. We know what it's about. We know every detail. Mr Bramfeld doesn't.' Scott gazed at me and continued, 'Mr Bramfeld, we believe that anyone reading Rachael's memoirs would have doubts about the investigation. This has been our conviction since day one and we have never changed our minds on that matter despite what has happened. The famous journalist who discredited the memoirs put us in a difficult situation. We don't know why he did it but if his goal was to discredit us, we can say that it's been a great success.'

Scott held a paper in front of him and read:

'*I do understand Andrew Foreman and his parents-in-law. In their position, I would probably believe in anything that told me that Rachael is alive. But the journalists and the citizens of this country shouldn't let a document such as this make the headlines. Our only wish should be to see the author of this defaming document in jail.*'

Scott put the paper back on the table. 'The husband and parents are seen to be ready to believe in any crazy story telling them their daughter is still alive. And let's be honest, our version of the story does sound crazy, as long as you don't know all the details. Their version of the story is simple and sounds reasonable. Despite what people think, we didn't stop talking to journalists after that. Five of them read the memoirs, all of them motivated to investigate. But one turned out to be a conspiracy theorist. He wrote an article that went way beyond the facts, bringing in theories that came from nowhere but his own imagination. His article was a hit among the conspiracy lovers. We lost the last bit of credibility we still had. The serious journalists were done with us.'

Scott glanced at Randal and Abigail with a smile. 'But we didn't give up. Randal and Abigail sold their beautiful hotel in Cairns to get closer to Andrew in the Kimberley and to have the financial resources to keep going. Rachael is lucky to have such parents.'

'Rachael is lucky to have such a good friend as you, Scott. We know you've lost a lot of money because of us,' said Randal.

'And he's put his reputation at risk,' added Abigail.

Scott remained silent for a few seconds and then said, 'It's been quite a ride so far, hasn't it?'

Randal and Abigail nodded. Then Scott gazed back at me. 'Mr Bramfeld, if I've told you all of this, it's to be sure that there's no misunderstanding between us. We're looking for credibility. Transforming Rachael's story into a novel has never been our goal and we don't want it to happen. Rachael's memoirs aren't a work of fiction. But we're not indifferent to your interest in Rachael's story. It's not every day a successful former Hollywood screenwriter contacts us. It wouldn't be clever of us not to exploit this. So, we're ready to let you read the memoirs, but under strict conditions.' Scott handed me a paper on which the conditions were listed. 'The first point is the most important for us. For the past three months, one journalist working for us has been making a documentary about Rachael's story. We've put all our resources into it. This documentary project is our last hope. You must give an interview to our journalist today. Then, and only then, will you be able to read Rachael's memoirs in accordance with the other conditions.'

I had worked almost my entire life for Hollywood, but I was no star. I wasn't used to giving interviews. I was just a name appearing in the end credits that most people don't read, and I was fine with it. But for Scott and the Flowers, I was something else. I was a communication tool. I was Hollywood having an interest in Rachael's story. This didn't amuse me at all. And there were of course the other conditions:

- I was only allowed to read the memoirs inside Scott's office under the surveillance of one of his employees for three sessions of eight hours. I wasn't allowed to take any notes or attempt to make a copy of the document.
- I wasn't allowed to quote the memoirs or to describe their contents in any of my future books.
- Any work of fiction or non-fiction inspired by the memoirs must contain this sentence in its introduction: *This book, though inspired by the so-called Rachael's memoirs, contains no quotations from them and cannot be considered as a faithful description of this document.*

I accepted all the conditions without complaining or asking questions.

In Scott's office, I spent hours in front of a camera, describing my career in Hollywood and what had led me there. I did everything they asked me to do. I was docile, waiting for my reward.

And then I read the memoirs, and I loved what I read. It went beyond my expectations. Sadly, I can't tell you any more about it.

I flew back to the Kimberley where I rented a bush hut within a small cattle station called Digger's Rest. There, with a stunning view of the Cockburn ranges, I could feel the atmosphere of the Kimberley and keep my inspiration alive. During the day, under the shade of a boab tree or in the evening under the roof of bush hut number six, visited sometimes by horses or by Marilyn the emu, I wrote my novel in less than four weeks. I had never worked that fast. Every word, every sentence came naturally to me as if someone was dictating it. I made no revisions afterwards. What I wrote at Digger's Rest is what you are going to read.

It is a novel

What you are going to read in the following pages is a novel, a work of pure fiction. This book, though inspired by the so-called Rachael's memoirs, contains no quotations from them and cannot be considered as a faithful description of this document.

From Quilpie to Brisbane

My name is Helen Anderson. I was born on the 12th of February 1982 at the Green River cattle station, forty-five kilometres away from the very small town of Quilpie in the south-west part of Queensland, in the middle of the outback. My brother Charlie was born one year after me, then came my other brother Stephan two years later and finally my little sister Lilly who was born four years later.

The station was owned by my grandparents who lived with us in our beautiful two-storey stone homestead. Our family station, with just 94,118 hectares and 300 head of cattle, was quite small by Australian standards but looked limitless to my young eyes. It was, for my brothers, my sister and me, a beautiful playground, a paradise where there were almost no restrictions. Wherever we watched there was this mix of gidgee trees and golden grasses that extended to a distant horizon. We lived away from what some people call 'society' or the 'civilised world'. We lived in our own world with its own schedule, its own rules. We were never bored. None of us went to kindergarten. It was way too complicated to get there and anyway, our mother wanted to spend time with us as much as she could. She didn't understand parents who sent their kids to kindergarten all day. Till I was twelve my mother was my only teacher and the cattle station my only school. Sometimes people visited from the Quilpie community, but I can't say that I really knew anyone outside our family. I was fine. I was happy there. We didn't need the outside world. We had our own water supply, our own power station, our own food. We didn't have TV and I was not interested in what was happening over the horizon. Strangely, I never missed seeing other kids. My two brothers and my sister were the only company that I needed.

But from the point of view of my parents the situation was different. My father had grown up on the same cattle station and had spent his childhood dreaming about the outside world. With no brothers and sisters, his days here were probably sometimes very boring. He was raised with the idea that his only future was here, on this cattle station, doing the same as his father had done all his life. All through his childhood my father had learned to hate this cattle station and to dream about the great somewhere else. At the age of nineteen he left the cattle station with the idea of never coming back.

His destination was Byron Bay, a pleasant town on the east coast. He had read a lot about this place during his teenage years and had always dreamed of living there, becoming a kind of hippy. At Byron Bay, he did find a lot of people who believed they were super-cool hippies, living the charmed life the books and the songs talked about. My mother was one of them, playing the perfect hippy during a two-week holiday. In real life, she was studying economics in Adelaide, a life that didn't provide her with any satisfaction. She was looking for plan B, the exciting life, the one that so many people talked about on the east coast. What sounded fake about my mother's behaviour for most people, sounded exotic to my father. She was the cliché he was looking for, the hippy from the books, the one that only existed in his dreams. Besides, my mother is a concentrate of kindness. Even her body seems to have been designed to express kindness. With her short, rounded body, her oval face and her luminous curly hair, there is nothing aggressive in her physical appearance. She isn't an intimidating beauty queen; she is an appeasing landscape made of gentle curves. I can't imagine a man who would resist her charms. My father, on the other hand, was to my mother a sexy stockman who seemed to have come straight from a movie, a true call to adventure. I don't know how a sexy stockman was supposed to look from my mother's point of view, but my father is tall and thin with sharp cheekbones and untamed hair, hidden most of the time under a hat. One day my mother said to me, 'Your father and I met each other within the same dream. We experienced true love, the kind that exists above reality, where everything seems possible. So it took me only one week to give up the life that I had in Adelaide. When you are living in a dream, you don't want to come back to reality.'

They lived above reality for three months, caring about nothing but the present moment. They had no problem working for restaurants or hotels for a low income. They didn't spend a lot and didn't need a lot. But this situation didn't last. Reality made its big comeback when my grandfather informed his son that he had broken his leg and needed his help immediately to take care of the cattle station.

My father was not enthusiastic about having to come back to the cattle station, but he is a real farmer from the outback, not the kind of person who would let down a member of his family or community. My mother, on the other hand, was totally excited about coming with him and experiencing life on a remote cattle station. This was a call to adventure that she didn't want to miss. Once there, she loved this unusual life. Here, my father wasn't the guy working in a hotel, obeying orders, serving other people any more. He was a stockman, a real one. The real stuff, the real adventure, was here.

My father loved the way my mother watched him at the cattle station. It made him feel that he was the right person in the right place. For his parents too, there was no doubt about that. Everything seemed to be where it belonged. There was a kind of virtuous circle making everything better, day after day. This is how my beloved paradise was born. For years, nowhere else existed. There was no other place to dream of. Paradise was right here, down on earth.

But when I turned eight, my grandfather was diagnosed with lung cancer. Needing daily medical care, he couldn't live on the station any more. My grandparents had to radically change their life, find a new place to live in the so-called civilised world, where the hospitals are. But for that they needed money, urgently. All my grandparents had was the cattle station. They had put all their money and their energy into it. So they offered my parents the cattle station, for a fair price. My parents accepted the offer and took out credit to finance it. This changed all our lives. Suddenly my grandparents didn't live here, and my parents discovered a kind of pressure that they had never really experienced before: the financial one. For my mother, it changed the way she saw the station. As long as my grandparents were here, my parents didn't have to care too much about finances. The station made more money than we all needed and so money had never been an issue. But with the debt, my parents felt a new kind of monthly pressure. My father felt the need to work harder, to get more cattle, exploiting every square metre of grazing area. But it didn't turn out as he expected.

For three consecutive years, we faced a severe drought, forcing us to invest in new expensive deep bores and kilometres of piping. The debt, instead of decreasing, just rose to a level that my parents hadn't expected. Then for the first time I heard my mother complaining about her life here. The cattle station wasn't an adventure for her any more. The dream of a better life somewhere else, somewhere shiny, marvellous and far, far away was back. My father didn't contradict her at any time. On the contrary, he shared her dream. The idea of a different tomorrow, an adventurous one, seemed to re-ignite their love to its highest level.

Each time we visited my grandparents in Brisbane we made a detour to Byron Bay. This was the place they dreamed of. Byron Bay were the two words to say to bring a smile to their faces. The only reason that we were still on our cattle station and not the great somewhere else was money. To sell the cattle station to pay back the credit wasn't enough for them. My parents were not ready to go to a 'somewhere else' where they would be any kind of employee. Not having a boss was the last thing that they still enjoyed at the cattle station and they had no plan to give that up. For years, they dreamed about a new source of money without having any kind of idea of where it could come from. For years, I thought that the 'somewhere else' would never be close to a reality. It seemed to be all talk.

But on the 16th of June 1994 I saw that it was about more than just talking. That day an exploration team from the mining company WUM came to the station. Their visit had been planned for months and hidden from my siblings and me. It was only when we saw those twenty-one men and women that the full story was finally unveiled to us. A year ago, my parents had been contacted by WUM who were planning a reconnaissance around Quilpie. My parents told them right away that their team was welcome at our cattle station. In reality, they were more than welcome. They could do whatever they wanted. They were treated better than the best friends of the family. For me it was like the invasion of a foreign army, with their strange, big trucks that seemed to come from another planet. For a week, the quiet of the mornings was replaced by an unbelievable noise, as if we were suddenly living in a city. My brothers and my little sister were fascinated by the trucks but not so much by what was really going on. On the other hand, I wanted to know what all of this was *really* about. I spent my time asking questions of each member of the crew. I learned a lot about how seismic exploration works. From the computer centre truck, to the vibe truck and the seismic cable truck, I saw everything and understood rapidly that these people were not my friends. For them my paradise was a potential oil field. My paradise was, day by day, becoming their paradise.

Two months later, on a sunny and warm Sunday afternoon, my father made a speech in front of the whole family.

'We've sold the station to WUM for an excellent price. Far more than any of us would ever have dreamed of. We're going to be able to leave this remote place and live another chapter of our lives. In this new chapter, you will be able to go to a regular school and have the same chance as other young Australians to build your own future. You got the best of the outback, now it's time for you to get the best of an urban life. Staying here has never been our plan. You can't get a proper education here. Besides, your mother and I have always dreamed of owning a hotel by the sea on the east coast. We will fulfil this dream and you will be able to build and fulfil your own. We have one year to leave the property. Just time for your mother and me to find out where we're going to experience our new, exciting life.'

My parents' dream was my nightmare. I didn't care about the

east coast and its beaches, its cities, its hotels. So, I decided to resist. The next night I went into the bush and set up my resistance camp. I had previously left a note on the kitchen table telling my parents that I didn't want to leave the station and, as long as the sale of the station went ahead, I would remain in my secret bush camp. My father was furious, and it took him only a few hours to find me. It took more for my parents to find our new home. Ten months precisely. They found the hotel of their dreams: twenty rooms in downtown Byron Bay, ten minutes from the beach, a little paradise for a certain kind of tourist.

For me, Byron Bay was hell. I hated that place from the moment I got there. The quiet of nature that I used to know was gone; it was busy, noisy, smelly. I couldn't breathe here. I felt like I was in jail, constantly observed by other people and unable to run wherever I wanted. I couldn't see or hear Mother Nature. And when night came, I couldn't even see the stars properly. All those artificial lights make the night sky of our cities so boring, so dead. The only positive point that I found about our new home was the presence of my grandparents. They moved to our hotel, living with us once again. I loved the idea of all of us being together under the same roof, as it used to be in the cattle station. But it soon became painful. Here, my grandparents looked small, bored, diminished. They weren't cut out for living in the city. My grandfather, once a great stockman, able to solve every problem at the cattle station, was a weak man here, recovering from his cancer, one less lung in his body. 'I am here to die,' he said almost every day. My grandmother was obviously bored. It wasn't her thing to go to the beach or downtown. She used to take care of the horses at the cattle station. All her skills were to do with horses. Here, she was like a light bulb that wouldn't switch on. There was no light in her eyes anymore. I am sure she hated Byron Bay.

Someone complaining about Byron Bay is not the kind of thing that people are ready to hear. For most people Byron Bay is a wonderful place, a little paradise that thousands and thousands of tourists from all over the world come all year round to visit. I couldn't share my complaints, not even with my brothers and my sister. They loved it. It didn't take them long to forget all about our little paradise near Quilpie. They were at an age when it was easy to turn the page. I was a young teenager; I didn't want to turn the page because I was trying to read my own life. The result of all of this was an extreme loneliness. Nobody wanted to hear me complaining about my awful life in Byron Bay. The problem was that I was so focused on my hatred of Byron Bay and on my good memories from our cattle station, that I didn't have any real conversation. With no friends, no real communication with my parents, my brothers or my sister, it didn't take me long to start to see everything in black and not have the will to do anything, including go to school. In short, I fell into a depression. Thanks to my parents, I didn't stay there too long. They found a excellent shrink who took good care of me. Her name was Gilly. I don't know if she was really old, but she looked old, at least from my thirteen-year-old eyes. I got the conversation with her that I didn't have with the others. What was great about her was her ability to understand my point of view. She really listened and that made all the difference. She helped me to put my complaints into words by asking me, over and over, to describe as much as I could what I disliked about Byron Bay. With her, I put my love of Mother Nature into words. With her I was able to describe how disturbing I found the attitude of our so-called 'civilisation' towards the environment. She helped me to understand that I was an environmentalist. The moment I got it, saw my vision of the world described in a dictionary, it changed everything in my life. I was not alone anymore, I belonged to a movement of thought, a philosophy, a way of life. To be an environmentalist sounded, to my ears, so exciting. I suddenly had the feeling that I was more than a teenager living in Byron Bay. I was someone with a mission, something that went far beyond the everyday life, the business as usual. I felt far more important than all those teenagers who only talked about movies, music, surfing and sex… All I wanted was to change the world.

From that point on, I didn't make new friends but at least I went back to school and gave people around me the impression that I had a kind of normal life. The city's library became my favourite location. Away from anyone who wanted to get me into "regular teenager activities", I built up my knowledge about environmentalism. Day after day I enlarged my vocabulary to explain who I was and what I wanted to do. But this didn't bring me any friends. On the contrary, I was even better at annoying everybody around me. My main problem was that I had no subject of conversation other than environmentalism and didn't see anything wrong with it. When life is in danger, you don't want to talk about music or sport. In my mind nothing was more important than environmentalism and I was not ready to accept any contradiction on that matter. I was not happy being alone most of the time but at least I thought that others were the problem, not me.

And then came Sarah. It was the 1st of April 1995. She was new at school and so knew nobody at all. But most of all, she had no pleasure being there. She thought that she had come from a paradise called Sydney. It sounds strange that a fourteen-year-old girl preferred Sydney to Byron Bay, but she had some really good reasons for that. She played violin at a very high level. All her conversations, her thoughts, her dreams were about violins and nothing else. In Sydney, she had the opportunity to develop her talent, to meet people like herself. In Byron Bay, it was all about surf and tourism, not really a hot spot for violinists. Unlike everybody else, I didn't see her monomania as something annoying. She and I were very different from many perspectives, including physically. She was a gorgeous, tall, redhead, with a beautiful, ivory silken skin. Wearing glasses on top of her dainty nose, she had this unique look that left nobody indifferent. Me, I was the kind of person who blended easily in the middle of a crowd. I am physically average in many ways. I am a brunette, 1.70 metres tall, thin but not skinny, with an oval face just like my mother. Next to Sarah, I was invisible. It was as if we weren't designed to be next to each other. The violinist and the environmentalist, one coming from a metropolis and the other from a cattle station. It was like everything was made to separate us, but our mutual rejection of Byron Bay helped us a lot in being open to each other. Besides, I liked to see someone being passionate about something, someone who wasn't satisfied with the regular, everyday life. Just like me, she wanted something more. Sarah and I became the best friends on earth.

She initiated me into classical music without making me into a violinist but she did become an environmentalist, a real one. Sarah was a perfectionist. She was not the kind of person to do half the job. She put all her energy and her free time into it, pushing both of us to be more than two teenagers talking about environmental issues. After six months of friendship, we became unofficial activists of the Sea Shepherd Conservation Society. We went to the beach, distributing flyers that we had made ourselves at the local copy shop, met most of the environmentalists in Byron Bay and annoyed the manager of the high school canteen into getting some vegan dishes. Sarah and I were always together, from Monday to Sunday, from sunrise to sunset. Sarah was my only friend and I was Sarah's only friend. We always did everything together and didn't plan to do otherwise in the future. After high school we both wanted to go to law school in Brisbane.

We wanted to become some kind of "eco-lawyers" and work together.

We both worked hard to make our near future in Brisbane possible. I worked a lot at my parents' hotel to finance my future studies and succeeded in persuading my parents that studying law was the right thing for me to do.

In July 2000, Sarah and I were in Brisbane, sharing a small apartment, sharing the same dream. But Brisbane was different from Byron Bay. Here, we had more opportunities to meet other environmentalists of our own age. At last we didn't feel alone anymore. It is so good to talk to people who understand you. We suddenly felt so strong, so confident. We loved this new experience so much that we tried to meet all the environmental activists in Brisbane. We visited all the environmental organisations, without exception, missing no event, no action, until we went to the meeting that changed every aspect of our lives.

It was the 10th of October 2000. The meeting was held by the Rainforest Saviour Association, and it concerned the construction of a tourist resort on the border of the Daintree National Park in the north-eastern part of Queensland. Several environmentalists were there to share their concerns about a project that would not only damage the rainforest but set a precedent in an area that had been successfully preserved until now from any similar project. The president of the association presented his plan of action which included direct dialogue with the company behind the project, Eastern Holidays. He used the word "negotiation" a lot, which irritated the young militants who were there.

'Trust us,' I heard a thousand times.

'Fuck you,' I heard twice. The first time it came from a twenty-five-year-old man called Brian, before he got the support of Sarah who, standing proudly in the middle of the room, repeated the insult. Glancing at Sarah with a smile, Brian found the strength to say a bit more than the 'f' word. He said, staring at the people in the organisation with an arrogance that I had never seen before, 'There is nothing to negotiate. We are going to protect this forest. We are going to live there as long as is necessary. We are more stubborn than those people.'

Brian's speech had been a hit. Most of the young militants there applauded. I didn't. My disapproval of Brian's behaviour went totally unnoticed. Sarah's attention was fully on this young blond man with tattoos on his muscled arms, his four days' growth of beard and his black dirty clothes, looking like an eco-warrior was supposed to look in Sarah's imagination. But what Sarah loved most in him was his leadership. He didn't just speak out loud, he always knew how to choose the right words at the right time. Brian wasn't a beginner when it came to activism. He loved to say that he was born a leftist environmentalist activist. It seemed that there was nothing in his life that wasn't political. Everything he did and said was a kind of activism. He used all his knowledge and skills to serve the cause that he fought for and he found it difficult to consider anybody else's opinion, including mine. He always spoke to me with an arrogance that I hated. Maybe I didn't have his experience, but I did have an opinion that deserved to be considered. Sarah, on the other hand, loved this man who was so sure of himself. She loved to listen to him and his ego loved her close attention. Sarah was a pretty and clever woman. To have a fan like her was probably the best reward he could get.

Their relationship evolved very rapidly. Less than one month after their first kiss, Brian moved into our apartment. From that point on, I was never alone with Sarah. Wherever, inside the apartment or outside, Brian was always with Sarah. They were a true couple in love. I was number three, the one that wasn't supposed to be there. I should have let them have some space, but I wasn't ready to let my best friend go. No other friend could replace her. She and I were supposed to do everything together. It was the plan, it was why we were living in the same apartment and studying at the same school. So, wherever Brian and Sarah were, I was there too. That's how, in October 2000, I found myself camping with them and forty-eight other activists next to the Daintree National Park, a hundred kilometres north of Cairns.

Free enterprise

October 2000. Instead of studying in Brisbane, I was in the middle of the rainforest with forty-eight militants, barely knowing what all this was about. The truth is that I was not there for a good reason. I was there because Sarah and Brian were there. I was an environmentalist; I did care about the rainforest, but I didn't feel that I was in the right place at the right time with the right people. My biggest difficulty was dealing with the fact that it was really hard to meet someone who wasn't politicised. By that I mean leftist. If you had nothing to say against capitalism and free enterprise, your contribution to the global conversation was then really limited. I wasn't comfortable that the preservation of our environment wasn't the main, not to say the only, subject of conversation. Though I had no political knowledge and had never really taken the time to think about politics, I had the deep conviction that environmentalism shouldn't be linked to anything political.

My discomfort reached another level when a majority of the group voted for the construction of a billboard on which would be written:

No to the destruction of our forest in the name of capitalism. The forest belongs to everybody. No company has the right to destroy it.

It took less than a day to build it and two days for it to be noticed by a local newspaper that made its headline:

Communist Group Threatens Local Economy

The article didn't say a word about the destruction of the rainforest itself. Nothing about the true reason for our presence. In the eyes of a lot of people, we were just a group of young leftists. From that moment, the political stance of the group really annoyed me, and I finally dared to talk about it in front of everybody.

That evening, around the camp fire, I stood up and said, 'I don't know about all of you, but I am not here because I belong to a political party or to defend an ideology. I am here to protect this forest and nothing else. Therefore, I am not comfortable with being seen as leftist or communist. Besides, I think we should keep our message as simple as possible if we want the support of a maximum of people. Personally, I think that environmentalism has nothing to do with politics. The moment we link it to a political movement, we seriously damage the idea that environmentalism is something universal that concerns every living thing on this planet. The fate of our planet shouldn't depend on the political orientation of the people at the head of our governments. If we want to save this planet we need everybody. Environmentalism has to be above politics.' All through my little speech, most of the people facing me had their attention focused on Brian's gaze. It was all about him, the leader, the one who had the right words at the right time. The guy who had the experience, rolling his eyes while the young, inexperienced woman was speaking. My eyes scanned these forty-seven immobile faces, one by one, looking for any kind of support. Nobody was here for me. Not even Sarah. Even more than the others, she couldn't take her eyes off Brian. I was alone. The only one standing while everybody else was seated.

Brian didn't bother to stand up to respond to me. He said, 'I understand your point. Why don't we just talk about saving this forest? Why don't we keep the message simple? Because none of us, including you, is here to only save this forest. If the world was fine, if our planet wasn't in danger, we wouldn't be here. We are here because all the forests of this planet are in danger. We are here because, more than ever, every single tree that we can save counts. And why are we in this situation? Because the attraction of profit in the short-term overwhelms longer-term considerations. Capitalism requires a very short-term view of the world, while environmentalism demands a very long-term view. This planet needs plans for the next decades and centuries, not only for the coming years. So, to keep it short and to really answer your comment, we aren't here to deliver a short-term message and pretend that it's just about a few trees. We are here to deliver the complicated message and fight the real problem. Capitalism is the problem.'

Brian got a big cheer, but I didn't give up. Staring at Brian I answered, 'I am here to save this forest. Not to discuss of the role of capitalism in our society. I doubt this is the right place to have this kind of debate. Besides, when you asked us to come with you, you didn't mention that all of this was about fighting capitalism. In fact, it would be quite strange to come here to fight capitalism. We aren't in the middle of a financial district. We aren't demonstrating, facing the cameras with anti-capitalist placards. Our physical presence here has only one meaning: to make sure that nobody cuts down these trees. Because if we aren't here for that, then I think we are quite stupid.'

Brian stood up and came very close to me, plastering on a smile. Everybody was silent, staring at us. Brian said in a serious tone, 'Helen, nobody wants to impose anything on anyone here. So, let's vote. Who is in favour of giving up any anti-capitalist message?'

Nobody moved. Brian walked slowly around the camp fire, glancing at everyone. 'Come on, don't be shy! You have the right to disagree with me. In fact, I encourage you to challenge my opinion. Helen is doing the right thing. Come on! Is there anyone who agrees with Helen?'

One woman said, 'Sorry Helen, but you are wrong.' Then someone else said, 'Yeah. Brian's right. Capitalism is the problem.' Then I heard a succession of 'Yeah's. Sarah didn't say anything. She remained totally silent and inexpressive. I thought that it was a question of time. At one moment or another Sarah would come onto my side. I knew her, I knew that she could understand my point. To push her to react, I left the group, announcing that I would continue to occupy the rainforest and protest against the construction of a tourist resort, but without any political stance.

I camped a hundred metres away from everybody, hoping for Sarah's visit, but it didn't happen. Nobody paid attention to me. I spent two long days alone before suddenly, something did happen. It was the 8th of November at 7am. All the police officers in the region turned up. It was quite spectacular to see all those policemen and policewomen dragging a bunch of militants out of the forest. It took them five long hours. But there was an exception: me. They simply didn't see me at all. I was so insignificant that I was invisible. At the end of the day I was totally alone. Nobody was looking for me or worried about what could happen to me in the forest. I hadn't told my parents about my presence here, too scared of their disapproval on that matter. They financed my study, not my activism.

My first night totally alone was not a pleasure. Without the presence of others, you are more attentive to everything else. I almost didn't sleep, scared of every noise. To sleep in a rainforest is totally different from sleeping in the desert. In the desert, you always see the sky and get lots of light from it. In the rainforest, you are under the canopy. You are overwhelmed by the million forms of life around you. A rainforest is alive like no other place. Day and night, life plays its biggest concerts here. When the sun rose, the only thing I wanted to do was leave. To stay here alone was no fun at all and served no purpose. Besides, I only had enough food in my backpack for the next two days. I had no choice but to walk the twenty-five kilometres that separated me from the closest pay phone and any kind of "civilisation". I didn't waste my time and left as soon as I was ready. The journey ahead of me was not an easy one. Most of the twenty-five kilometres I had to walk were on a dirt road where I had almost no chance of meeting anyone with a car. My chances of getting a ride were close to zero.

But after less than an hour's walking, I saw at least thirty cars parked alongside the dirt road. Not far away, I could hear people talking, applauding, laughing. After a night without sleep, I wondered if I was dreaming. All of this was so unreal. Driven by curiosity and my will to get a ride to the closest city, I walked through the forest looking for those people who seemed to be having a good time. After ten minutes' walking, I found myself facing at least forty people, all wearing suits, looking at two men holding two brand new shiny shovels. One of these men was Marty Koenig, the CEO of Eastern Holidays, a tall, skinny man with an elongated face, and the other was Sean Braden, the Premier of Queensland, a bulky, short man with a massive double chin. Both were around sixty years old and weren't in any way physically impressive. Their suits looked expensive, but as long as you didn't know who they were, there was nothing intimidating about them. Of course, I had no clue who those two men were, nor any idea of what was going on. But the most important thing was that two teams from two different TV news channels were here, filming the whole scene. Totally exhausted, physically and mentally, from my night alone in the forest, I spoke without any filter. My thoughts were my speech.

Marty Koenig stood in front of me, so I naturally asked: 'What's going on here?'

Koenig laughed and said to the crowd, 'Oh. Our first customer is already here!' Then he said to me, 'Sorry, we're not open yet.'

The crowd laughed. I didn't. I asked, 'Is this about the tourist resort that is supposed to be being built in the area?'

Koenig and the crowd laughed again, and he answered, 'Yes. We have a brochure explaining everything about it if you want. But, if you don't mind, the Premier and I would like to inaugurate the construction of our wonderful future resort.'

I replied without thinking, 'I'm against it. You're going to destroy the forest.'

Koenig laughed and said, 'No, we're not going to destroy this forest like you and your communist friends think. Now I invite you to leave. You made your point in front of the cameras. Mission accomplished.'

I replied immediately, 'I'm not a communist. I have nothing against capitalism. I believe in free enterprise.'

Koenig laughed again. 'OK, sorry, guys, but now I'm starting to get curious. If you don't mind, Mr Premier, I would like to ask our unexpected visitor what kind of militant she is. So, young lady, I give you five minutes to tell us what all of this is about. After that you will have to let us do what we're supposed to do. So, we're listening.'

I simply said, 'You're going to destroy this forest with your resort. Forests are precious. We can't afford to destroy them.'

After a speech like that, it was easy for Koenig to make fun of me. He said, after a long laugh, 'We're not going to destroy the forest. Just cut down a few trees. This has nothing to do with the Amazonian forest that is slaughtered 365 days per year. If you want to save the forests, you should be there, not here. So, thank you very much. You said what you wanted to say. Obviously five minutes was more than enough.'

But then a story I had heard from Brian came to my mind. It was kind of a standard response to people who say, 'We're just going to cut down a few trees.' I gazed at Koenig, locked my eyes on him, and said, 'You're right. Why save one square metre of trees while the Amazonian forest is slaughtered seven days a week, 365 days a year? The answer isn't hard to understand.

'Just imagine you're living in a neighbourhood where there are plenty of trees. You think that it wouldn't matter to cut down the one in front of your house. You cut it down. Then your neighbour thinks that he could do the same. There are plenty of trees in the neighbourhood and after all, you did cut down the one in front of your house. So why not cut down the tree in front of his house as well. He cuts it down. So does the neighbour of your neighbour, for exactly the same reason. And this goes on and on, until there are no trees left in your neighbourhood.

'Nobody thinks he or she is endangering life on our planet. We know we're doing some damage but most of us think that on the scale of the planet it doesn't make a real difference. Everybody cuts down the tree in front of his house. And yes, it's just one tree among many others. What is killing our planet, and so could kill all of us, is the accumulation of all the damage that we do to our environment, day after day, year after year, decade after decade.

'So, what I want to say is that every tree counts. Eastern Holidays is not planning to destroy the whole rainforest but it will be the first one to cut some trees down here. Then you know what could happen next. If Eastern Holidays can do that, why not anybody else? Why couldn't anybody cut down a few trees? So, you see things are not as simple as you describe. It's not about a few trees and, like I said before, it's not about communism. It's about common sense.'

Marty Koenig could have ended the conversation there, but he didn't. It didn't only surprise me, it surprised everybody else. He stopped laughing.

'I totally agree with you. Cutting down a tree in a forest like this shouldn't be thought of as something unimportant. I apologise to you for my previous response. It wasn't designed for a real conversation. But now that we have a conversation, I can share with you the concerns that we at Eastern Holidays have for the preservation of forests all over the world. We do plant more trees than we cut down. We have an entire department in our company that takes care exclusively of the preservation of the environment inside and around our resorts all over the planet.

'Through our label of "Sustainable Tourism" we can now certify that all our resorts are eco-friendly in many aspects. At Eastern Holidays we take environmental issues very seriously. It's why two members of what we call our "Green Team" are here. They will monitor the logging over the next two days, making sure that everything is done in the eco-friendliest way. I invite you to stay with them and see for yourself the reality of our commitment to the environment. You can really be our first customer!'

His last sentence made everybody laugh. I was then gently invited by three Eastern Holidays employees to join the rest of the audience. There, a journalist said to me, 'Don't leave before you give me an interview.' An hour later, I was facing a camera and several embarrassing questions. Who was I? What was I doing here? Which environmental organisation did I represent? I didn't have any long answers to those questions. In fact, I was embarrassed to expose the reality of my situation. I was barely a militant, representing nobody except myself. I hardly knew

Eastern Holidays and had almost no idea what its project in the region was about. I just knew that they were going to cut down some trees. I was pathetic.

But when I got the opportunity to say more about my claim to be pro 'free enterprise', I didn't lack inspiration. I wanted to be the opposite of Brian and his friends. I wanted to be the antithesis of those leftist environmentalists who had made fun of me and stolen my best friend. Driven by anger more than anything else, I didn't really know at the beginning where my own words were driving me. But sentence after sentence, I found a path, a real argument, something that I was proud of. I remember word for word the end of my little speech to the journalists. Here it is:

'I don't believe in state intervention because it lets people think that they are not responsible for the condition of the world they live in. With a strong government, you don't believe it's your duty to change the world or at least to improve it. We've already seen how governments are unable to take good care of our planet. But everywhere around the globe we see more and more initiatives coming from simple citizens, consumers, entrepreneurs.

'The real creativity, the real movement doesn't come from big structures. It comes from individuals. Therefore, we have to let each individual bring about change. Freedom is what we need. Free enterprise, instead of a heavy government killing any initiative.'

Once the interview was over, Marty Koenig didn't miss the opportunity to announce in front of the camera that his invitation to stay here for the next two days was real.

Then he introduced me to the two guys who were supposed to be part of the "Green Team". 'Take good care of her. She is our first guest,' he said to them in a serious tone.

Ninety minutes later, still not realising what was going on, I was sharing a campsite with a team of ten lumberjacks and the two guys from the "Green Team". Totally exhausted, I didn't even try to think about the meaning of my presence in such a camp. All I wanted was to rest.

Meanwhile twenty kilometres away, my ex-friends were taking on the police force. They weren't planning to give anything up. They had lost the first battle in the rainforest but not the war. They were counting on coming back and the police seemed to be having a real problem stopping them.

In the media another kind of battle was taking place. On one side Marty Koenig was being portrayed as a man with an open mind, the kind of person who could have an improvised conversation with a young environmentalist and agree with her.

'A conversation between two reasonable persons,' one journalist said on a national TV news network. 'The protesters are communists, not environmentalists' was the slogan of Marty Koenig, the Premier of Queensland, and supporters of the tourist resort project.

On the other side, few of the public figures who supported the protesters could resist taking the bait. According to them I wasn't an environmentalist, I was an advocate of capitalism being paid by Eastern Holidays. I had become a diversion, Miss Free Enterprise, a great way to take the environmental issues out of the debate. Koenig had scored a fantastic PR coup. It didn't matter whether it had all been improvised or prepared in advance, Koenig had used me in a very efficient way.

I knew nothing about it at that time. In the rainforest I had no internet, no mobile, no radio, no TV. It was my family who had to put up with all the madness. What shocked them the most was seeing Sarah's very short, well thought-out speech against me on the TV.

I read Sarah's speech days afterwards on the internet. Here it is:

We won't save this planet without a strong state. The citizen will change the world, not the consumer. The consumer has already failed. The consumer buys a price, a performance; the citizen votes for ideas, prepares the future, sees himself or herself as a part of a large community and not as a single individual. Consumers are focused on the short term; they are the murderers of this planet and you, Helen, you are more than their accomplice, you are their new champion. You defend their ideology more than anybody else. Shame on you, Helen.

And then came the heavy rain, forcing the protesters to give up their plan to come back to the rainforest. Most of the dirt roads of the region were flooded, including the one, fifteen kilometres long, giving access to the campsite where I was.

The battle in the field was over, making the one in the media tougher. While I was stuck in the forest, unable to contact anyone, Marty Koenig was still using me as a PR tool for every newspaper, radio and TV channel in Australia. He was a communication war machine who impressed everybody. But it lasted no more than forty-eight hours.

Just before the beginning of a TV interview, Marty Koenig had a few words with the PR director of Eastern Holidays, Rudolf MacQueen, who turned out to be Marty's best friend. Between the two guys the conversation was direct, with no filter. The problem was that Marty was already equipped with a HF microphone and the sound technician didn't miss a word of the conversation, recording all of it.

The subject of conversation between Marty and his friend Rudolf was me and women in general. Here is a small sample: 'It's a good thing for us that this girl stayed in the forest. You don't want her to give an interview to the press when she gets her period. I've already had enough of female hysteria in this company. No, leave her in the forest. At least she can entertain the guys there…' The conversation lasted more than ten minutes.

That audio recording changed everything. I was no longer a

puppet working for Eastern Holidays but a victim of sexism. Making fun of me was no longer acceptable. Nobody dared to say that I was ridiculous or stupid. But of course, the media were now more focused on Marty Koenig than anybody else. He didn't keep quiet; it wasn't his style. He still had a self-assurance that nothing seemed to shake. Marty refused to apologise for what he said was a private joke with a friend that should never have been recorded. He claimed that he and his friend Rudolf liked saying politically incorrect stuff for fun.

He said to one newspaper in Sydney, *Our jokes never reflect what we really think. It's just humour between two old friends who have known each other for more than twenty years. You don't do this kind of banter with people you don't know. Therefore, it was inappropriate to publish this conversation out of context. It was a private conversation. No newspaper or TV channel has the right to publish or broadcast it. I will personally sue anyone that does. It is simply unacceptable. To take my own words out of context is an attempt to defame me.*

Hardly anyone bought this version of the facts.

I was totally unaware of all of this. For three days, all I thought about was the heavy rain, which seemed as if it was never going to stop. I couldn't leave the camp and walk the twenty-five kilometres that separated me from the closest sealed road. Not in that weather. Waiting seemed the only reasonable option, even if every single second here reminded me of my own misery. *What am I doing here with these people? Why am I still here?* I wondered. I felt I had done nothing useful and I had no idea what to do next. Go back to Brisbane and meet Sarah again? Go back to Byron Bay and give everything up? I had no answer to these questions. In the early morning of my fourth day it was still raining, and I was still unable to make up my mind.

But then along came William Brotsky. He had been walking all night, a kind of forty-five-year-old Harrison Ford dressed like

Indiana Jones. He got my full attention before he'd said a single word. 'Good morning Helen,' he announced. 'I'm going to be very direct and very brief because we don't have much time. My name is William Brotsky. I'm the president of the John LaFleur Organisation. You've probably never heard about us but we're a very active environmental organisation. Like you, we care a lot about this rainforest and we believe you can play a major role in opposing the Eastern Holidays project.'

Then he showed me a series of recent newspaper articles that he had sorted chronologically. He wanted to be sure that I understood the role I had been playing indirectly over the past days. While I was reading, William said, 'Your absence has been as important as the words you said in front of the camera. As long as Koenig makes the headlines, what you do or don't do will have an impact.

'The question is, what kind of impact do you want to make? Or should I say, what kind of story do you want to tell? Do you want to be Miss Free Enterprise and a victim of sexism or do you want to be something else, something that has more to do with the future of this forest?'

Getting back at Marty Koenig was the first thing that came to mind. I wanted to be a feminist, someone who doesn't let men talk about women like that. But then William said, 'OK. You hate this guy. You want to punch his face. I got it. Nobody likes him. In fact, he is such an embarrassment to Eastern Holidays that he could be fired tomorrow afternoon by the company board of directors. The bad guy is out, end of story. Then you have no role to play because you aren't taking part in any story. My point is, you won't make the headlines by shouting at Koenig like everybody else. You can claim that you're a feminist, that you're outraged by what Koenig said. It won't take you anywhere except to the middle of the mainstream, where you have absolutely no influence.

'Don't misunderstand me, I don't want to stop you being a feminist. But it's a matter of fact that you didn't come here to defend the feminist cause. You're here to defend this forest. What I am proposing is for you to be part of a story where you could really do something for this forest. A story that could make the headlines and so give us the influence that we need to make a difference. The story could start this evening at Sydney airport. The media will be there waiting for you and here's what you're going to say.' He gave me a piece of paper.

Like I said before, I am not against the economy. I don't dream about a communist world where the government takes care of everything. I want to keep this world where everybody can choose his own way and where creativity is not blocked by the state. I believe in people. I believe in personal responsibility, in the ability of each citizen to bring his or her contribution to the world. I don't believe that this world is run by companies. A company doesn't decide anything, doesn't have a will or desires. A company is not even an object. It's a concept, something virtual. CEOs, top executives and employees make decisions, they have desires, they have wills, they have feelings… they are real.

I met a lot of people in the forest who were working for Eastern Holidays. Women and men, young and older. They all looked like the people that I come across every day. Most of them looked sympathetic and none of them said anything negative about what I have done against the company they work for. One man even showed me some support. He shared with me that Eastern Holidays planned to do some greenwashing to calm everybody down but had no plans to change anything when it came to building its resort. Everything was supposed to look green, but nothing really was. Stunned by what he said, only one thing came to my mind. I wondered how it was possible for such a nice man to work for a such a bad company. What was he doing there? His response was simple,

'I need my job. I have kids and I can't afford to lose my job. It's been difficult enough getting this one.'

But when I met Marty Koenig, I saw something else. Mr Koenig told me that he wasn't really the boss of Eastern Holidays, that he couldn't do what he wanted. He even dared to say to me that he would love the company to follow an eco-friendly path, but the shareholders wouldn't accept that. Besides, he said, what he is doing within Eastern Holidays is dictated by the laws of the market. I couldn't tell you how much Mr Koenig earns per month, but I'm sure you have some idea. You and I know that money isn't an issue for him. He doesn't need to be brave to change the course of Eastern Holidays. He has absolutely no excuse.

This careless society must stop. We've got to start caring about what we are doing. We should bring in ethics everywhere, at every level of our society. And this brings me to the real reason for my being here today. I can't require Mr Koenig to be more human, more ethical, if I don't require it of myself. I can blame Marty for a lot of things but not for being a sexist. I don't know Mr Koenig very well, but I have had some conversations with him on the phone over the past days. I can tell you that he likes to use humour to facilitate a conversation. He really does make these jokes where he likes to play the bad guy and say some awful stuff. I'm not saying it's always funny, but I can affirm without any doubt that it's always meant to be a kind of humour. Marty Koenig told me that tomorrow he's going to meet the board of Eastern Holidays and that he could lose his job because of that stupid audio recording that you, the media, have broadcast without any hesitation. I don't want to let that happen. I want to be fair, just like I want Marty Koenig to act with morality and responsibility at Eastern Holidays. Marty Koenig is more than a CEO. He is a human being just like you and me. He has a wife and three children. He deserves to be treated with respect and not be judged by a few sentences taken out of context. It is simply not fair. Therefore, I am here to show him my support and to bring the truth to light. Thank you for your attention.

At first, I was very uncomfortable with all of this. I had no reason to trust William. I didn't know him, and I had never heard of the John LaFleur Organisation. I said, 'No way will I say that. No way will I lie in front of the cameras. Sorry but I barely know you. You can't ask me to do such a thing.'

William replied immediately, 'Of course, you could say the truth. But what would be the result? For decades, we environmentalists have been talking about the state of our planet. And what has happened? Have people radically changed their habits? Of course not. Most people in the world don't feel they're living on a dying planet. You can tell them a million times how bad the situation is, you won't change anything. We won't change the world by sharing some facts. But most of all, we won't save the world by saying that tomorrow will be a nightmare if we keep everything like it is today.

'Instead of talking about a dark tomorrow, we have to share our vision of a bright tomorrow. In 1995, I saw hundreds of people camping in front of computer stores in the US to be the first to get Windows 95. We're talking about an operating system, not about a cure for cancer. Rationality is not the human engine. Passions, emotions drive us, move us. We need more than facts. We need more than the truth. We need great stories. The kind that bring emotions.'

I interrupted him. 'A lie isn't a great story. I don't want to be part of these people lying all the time, trying to manipulate us through our emotions. I despise these people. I believe in honesty. I don't believe one second that there is a good reason to lie. No way.'

William locked his eyes on me and said, 'The truth is that Eastern Holidays really does do greenwashing. An employee of this company gave us some documents proving that. The problem is that we can't make the headlines with it. Greenwashing is too common and most of the time it's legal. It's not the kind of story that attracts the big media. But *you* could make the headlines. The speech I wrote for you, it's just about embedding the truth in the story to attract people's attention. You shouldn't focus on the small lies in the speech but on the important truth, the one everybody will remember. You should keep in mind that right now, you're in a position to get a lot of attention and do something that really matters. It's a lifetime opportunity. The organisation will give you everything you need in the coming days until everything is settled. After that we will pay for you to go wherever you want. If we fail and you want to come back, we'll bring you back here, no questions asked.

'Of course nobody is going to force you to do anything. It's all up to you. But as you know Sydney isn't exactly close. You don't have to decide immediately whether or not to come to Sydney with me, but you do have to decide quickly whether or not you want to leave this forest. Even if you don't want to go to Sydney, I can still offer you a ride to Cairns airport. Whatever your choice, I have to drive there anyway. I'll give you thirty minutes to decide. I'm going to walk away a bit, to let you think in peace. If you have any questions, just ask.'

William really did walk away and gave me thirty long, uninterrupted minutes. I looked at my own situation from every angle possible and always came to the same conclusion: when you have a bad plan A and a bad plan B, you don't close the door on an eventual plan C, whatever it is.

During our long walk and then drive to Cairns airport, William said just one thing to me. 'I'm not going to talk to you until you make your final decision. I've already told you what you need to know. I want you to have enough time to think. It's important to me that you're comfortable with your own decision. I don't want you feeling that I pushed you to do something. Once we're at Cairns airport, I'll leave you alone for ten minutes. Then you'll have the choice between leaving without having to tell me anything or flying with me to Sydney.'

Once at the airport, I could have been "reasonable". I could have chosen to go back to Brisbane or Byron Bay, back to a kind of regular life. But just looking at a rubbish bin next to me was enough to remind me how unreasonable this world was. Plastic bottles, plastic bags, paper coffee cups... a world of single-use items made for our convenience, coming at a huge environmental cost. This world had no regular life to offer to me. There was no daily routine waiting for me somewhere. When you don't accept the world as it is, you do everything possible to change it. That day at Cairns airport, change had a name: William Brotsky.

William

I read the speech William had written for me three times during the flight. By that time, I knew every word of it. I hated and loved it at the same time. I hated being part of an invented story, the tool of an organisation that I had never heard of. But on the other hand, I loved being able to speak like that to the media, the feeling of doing something useful, something that mattered. On the plane, totally ignored by the other passengers, I couldn't imagine what was waiting for me at the airport. It didn't feel like I was going to be right at the centre of things.

It was only when I looked through those sliding doors separating the area where you pick up your luggage from the arrival hall that I realised that all of this was not about giving a speech to one or two junior journalists. Behind the sliding door a crowd waited for me.

'You can still change your mind,' William said, 'but once you cross the threshold of this door, there's no turning back. I'm with you wherever you choose to go. You make the move.'

It took me some time to take that step, to go beyond those sliding doors. I could still stop everything. I was supposed to be a student in Brisbane, not an activist speaking directly to the national media. I hadn't planned that at all. It hadn't even been my idea to go to the rainforest and protest against Eastern Holidays. Everything I said and did seemed to have consequences that went far beyond what I could predict or even imagine. Everything seemed to be accelerating at a crazy pace. To stop all of this and get my life back under control sounded the reasonable thing to do but, deep inside myself, I knew that going back to Brisbane and having a 'regular life' there wasn't an option. Behind those sliding doors, my life had a purpose. I had an opportunity to be more than just a passive inhabitant of this planet. Behind those doors, I had the feeling that I might change the world. Nothing was stronger than this feeling.

The fear disappeared the moment I started to speak to the journalists. I said what William had written exactly, word for word, but I didn't feel at any time that I was reciting something written by somebody else. I didn't respond to any of the journalists' questions. I told them with an assurance that surprised even myself that I had nothing else to say.

William and two other men from the John LaFleur Organisation helped me to get out of the airport, where a black Mercedes was waiting for us. I told William I felt like a movie star and he answered, 'What you just did and what you will do tomorrow have more to do with show business than anything else. Right now, it's all about the story.'

A few minutes later, we stopped downtown in front of a luxury hotel. Before leaving the car, William said, 'Be sure that everybody is going to wonder how you can afford to stay in a hotel like this. It's important they believe you and Koenig have a kind of agreement. It's going to give more weight to every word you say to the media. You're going to spend the night alone in this hotel. Dinner will be served in your room. Everything has already been paid for. I will pick you up tomorrow morning at ten to go to Eastern Holidays' headquarters. You're supposed to meet Marty Koenig there. I don't know if it will really happen, but this is what the media have got to believe. Have a great night, Helen. You deserve it.'

A few minutes later I was alone in a gigantic hotel room. Being alone again gave me a strange feeling, as if all of this was just a dream. I was confused, and it took me some time to accept what was happening was real.

I called my parents that night. They totally disapproved of what I was doing and urged me to go back to Byron Bay. I loved my parents, but I couldn't quit this adventure.

The next day was even more extraordinary. We went to Eastern Holidays' headquarters and, according to the media, I did meet Marty Koenig there and had a long conversation with him. The reality is quite different. I remember word for word a conversation between Koenig and William but not between me and Koenig.

Here is the conversation as I remember it:

Koenig: So what's all this about?

William: What if what Helen said yesterday was the truth? Could you be this person? Somebody ready to hear and to consider what Helen has to say. It's all about what kind of person you want to be.

Koenig: Don't bullshit me. Get directly to the point. Tell me what you really want from me.

William: Marty, you've already given us what we needed. We've been in this building for forty minutes. You made us wait, your secretary offered us some coffee, we've talked a bit about the weather with a few people working here. But the story we're going to tell when we leave this building will be a different one. It will be about the long conversation we had with you for more than forty minutes. Everything is already written down. Of course, you can deny it. Tell the world that Helen is a liar, but who will believe you? Besides, in our story, you are quite a good guy. But of course, if you want to be a total arsehole, it's up to you. Now, if you want to excuse us, we have to meet the media. We have a story to tell.

And that was it. I don't remember saying a word. A few minutes later, I was standing in front of Eastern Holidays' headquarters reciting to the cameras a speech that William had written.

'Marty Koenig has agreed with me that the practice of greenwashing is not acceptable. He has told me that he is committed to ending this practice at Eastern Holidays. No more green labels that don't match the reality. To show his goodwill, he took the risk of sharing with us some internal documents that show the lies behind the green labels that Eastern Holidays uses in its resorts around the globe. I hope the board will keep him on as CEO and that I will be able to discuss with him the cancellation of the construction on the border of the Daintree National Park in Queensland. As far as I am concerned, I'm not planning to give up on that matter. As long as this project is on the table, I will be here to defend the rainforest.'

This speech didn't excite me. I still didn't understand the big picture. William was fully aware that I needed a much better explanation than the one he had given me. I needed to know more about him and the John LaFleur Organisation.

After our stop at Eastern Holidays' headquarters and a quick lunch, William gave me three hundred dollars in cash. 'If you want to know what all this is about, including who I really am, I suggest you buy a dress and come with me tonight to the Opera House. Then I'll tell you the whole story about the vision behind the John LaFleur Organisation.'

I accepted the invitation and a few hours later, I was in the Sydney Opera House, sitting five metres from the stage. The concert hall was packed. The orchestra arrived onstage, then came the hundred members of the choir and finally the conductor was welcomed by generous applause.

Silence.

The philharmonic orchestra played its first notes. I heard Vivaldi's music in a way I had never experienced before. Most of my life I had heard music through speakers, headphones, but very rarely from the instruments themselves without any electronic devices. Sarah's violin had been the only instrument to directly reach my ears. Hearing one instrument is a very different experience from hearing a full orchestra. One violin sounds so different from ten violins playing together. It is a kind of magic. To hear a symphony orchestra is to get one of the most basic lessons of life: Working together is magic. It brings you to another level.

Then came the choir's first notes: 'Gloria, gloria…' I was dazzled by the sound of a hundred people singing at the same time in all their diversity. It was the most beautiful thing I had ever heard in my life. During the intermission I couldn't speak. I wanted to stay in the middle of the magic of the music. I stayed in my seat, willing to keep the emotion intact and not pollute it with anything coming from our world. My mind was floating in another universe.

When the music stopped for good, I did everything I could to remain silent and walk as slowly as possible, avoiding physical contact with anyone. Then William invited me to a wine bar. 'After that concert, you're ready to hear the story behind the John LaFleur Organisation,' he said.

The wine bar was impressive at first sight. It was divided into many, roped-off areas. Each was designed like a private lounge, with two small leather couches separated by a low wood table.

The lighting was low, and no sound seemed to escape from any part of the bar. The atmosphere was incredibly hushed. This place was an invitation to murmur. A suited waiter showed us the way to our little lounge. Once seated on the leather couch we couldn't hear or see anyone else. I couldn't tell how many customers there were in the entire bar. Everything was designed to make you feel you were the only ones. The wine list was impressive, not to say confusing for someone like me who wasn't used to drinking wine. 'A glass of Henriot, please,' said William to the waiter. 'The same,' I said without knowing that Henriot was a brand of Champagne. 'Excellent choice,' William said with a smile.

Once we'd taken the first sip of Champagne, William leant towards me and spoke in a very serious tone. 'It's time now for you to know how the John LaFleur Organisation was born. Knowing its beginnings is essential to understanding what it's all about. Ten years ago, I was a militant like many others, participating in demonstrations, chaining myself to anything you could put a chain on. It was the same story over and over with very poor results, not to say no results at all. It didn't matter how hard I protested or how long I handcuffed myself to a bulldozer. In the end, almost nothing changed except the file that the police had on me. There was always some guy telling me that what we were doing was all about communication, that it was a kind of long-term strategy.

'After a while, two of my best friends and I got sick of hearing that. We didn't want to communicate about the destruction of life on our planet. We wanted to act and not wait for a few people to change their minds. So, we acted. We did a lot of tree spiking and a lot of sabotage, or monkeywrenching as we eco-warriors called it. But after six months we'd become disappointed with the results. We hadn't stopped anything. At best, we had slowed the damage being done to the environment, but no more than that. We couldn't win the war by monkeywrenching. It was obvious to us.'

William stood up, looked around, checked the couches behind the ropes and sat down again. His mouth curved into a smile. 'It isn't just a feeling. We really are alone here.' He had a sip of Champagne, leant towards me and spoke in a very low voice, almost a murmur.

'So we thought about what to do next. The most efficient thing. The answer came not from us but from the authorities, who chose to call us "eco-terrorists". Real terrorism makes the headlines and has impact on a global scale. So we considered becoming real terrorists, spreading terror among those who terrorised the wilderness. We didn't want to target what was replaceable, what could be seen as an additional cost rather than a real problem. Bulldozers don't make decisions. When you destroy one, you don't damage the ability of all the other bulldozers on the planet to work.

'But to kill the CEO of a mining company… None of us were murderers and we found the idea pretty disturbing. Still, we thought that it was the most efficient solution. How many people died because of the indifference of companies to the pollution they created? How many disasters, how many mass murders were there in the name of immediate profit? The wilderness was being destroyed and the poor were dying in silence every day because of the bad behaviour of some companies. Why not strike back? Does the life of a CEO have more value than that of a child working in a tannery in Bangladesh, surrounded by dangerous chemicals? What is right and what is wrong? It took us months to make a decision but we made it. One name haunted us. One person was known to be a mass murderer of landscapes, of biodiversity and, indirectly, of people: John LaFleur, CEO of WUM. He was the guy we wanted to kill. He was the guy we hated.

'The moment we said "let's do it", we gave up any kind of private life, spending every second we had preparing for the murder of John LaFleur. We did our best to get hired by WUM whatever the job, as long as it was inside WUM's headquarters and not far from LaFleur. We followed him night and day, getting to know everything about his life so we could hit him at the right moment. He was rarely alone and very difficult to approach. This seventy-six-year-old man mainly focused on his work and didn't really have a private life. Inside WUM's headquarters, it was almost impossible to get to his office. The old man didn't fear for his life but he did fear industrial espionage at a level close to sickness. After four months of hard work, it was still impossible for us to get to him. When we were following his car or waiting outside his house, we always had a gun on us, waiting twenty-four hours a day, seven days a week for the opportunity to kill him.'

William leant back on the couch, took a breath and rested his hand on the table. He glanced at my empty glass and said, 'We need more Champagne.' I nodded. He stood up and came back an instant later with a bottle of Champagne in an elegant ice bucket. He filled my glass and leant once again towards me.

'One evening I got that opportunity, the moment that we'd all waited for. LaFleur was at a classical music concert in a church. It was the first time I'd seen him without one of his employees, in a place open to everybody. I managed to sit just behind him. My right hand was in my jacket pocket, one of my fingers on the trigger, ready to shoot. But then, a miracle! The philharmonic orchestra which I hadn't even noticed, although it was just a few metres in front of me, played a note like a warning or an announcement. Then the choir sang "Requiem," like a message coming directly from the sky. It was Fauré's *Requiem*. A pure moment of poesy and beauty that I listened to until the very end, putting aside my intention to shoot LaFleur. Thirty-five minutes of Fauré's *Requiem* and I was in love with this humanity that I had hated so much a few minutes before. This humanity, so destructive, so selfish, so violent, can be beautiful, creative, transcend its animal status. Music like that had nothing to do with nature, it was supernatural.

'Those few minutes of music were enough to disturb all my beliefs and seriously damage my militancy. I couldn't hate John LaFleur any more, not this man who was listening religiously to this music, to a moment of pure beauty. To harm that man had suddenly become unacceptable to me. I couldn't touch a man who was able to appreciate such beauty. Someone who took the time to listen to that music couldn't be all bad.

'I left the church without even looking at LaFleur. I am not a murderer, I told myself all evening. But the next day, I hated myself. I couldn't understand what had happened. I was deeply disturbed by it. How could thirty-five minutes of music have done this to me?'

William drank some Champagne, glancing at the ceiling as if he wanted to avoid looking at me. He took a deep breath and then spoke again. 'I didn't share all of this with my comrades. To have missed the opportunity to kill LaFleur was embarrassing. I couldn't let that happen again. I couldn't let music do that to me. So, I decided to renew the experience, to somehow face the problem and try to fix it. I attended every performance of Fauré's *Requiem* in Australia. Four concerts in one year. Not one more, not one less. One in Darwin, one in Melbourne, one in Adelaide and the last one in Perth. Four miracles, each time in the presence of John LaFleur. He was never late and was always one of the last to leave the concert hall, just like me.'

•　•　•

The front door of the wine bar slammed. Suddenly the laughter of a man and a woman disturbed the quietude of the place. We heard the calm voice of the waiter inviting the couple to sit on the other side of the bar. William waited for their voices to disappear before continuing.

'The fourth time, in Perth, just after the concert I walked up to him and asked him why he was always here. He smiled and told me that it was probably for the same reason as me. And then, I don't know why, I told him the entire truth. And when I say entire truth, I really mean it. I told him literally everything in less than ten minutes. After this express confession in the middle of an empty concert hall, LaFleur took one of my hands and said to me, "We are in paradise, my friend, where enemies speaking to each other and contemplating the beauty of the world surrounding them finally understand that the grievances they had with each other were just misunderstandings."

'He took a deep breath and said, "Let's stay in paradise. Let me invite you to a restaurant and let's talk about our misunderstandings." We went to the first restaurant we could find downtown before spending the rest of the night at the bar of the five-star hotel where he was staying. That night, I learned a lot about the mistakes we environmentalists make all the time. We spend too much time talking to the people who already agree with us. It's so easy to say that others are stupid, greedy, inhuman, but it's counter-productive.

'When I asked John why he'd built an empire in the mining business and didn't care about the environment, he answered, "I've been in the mining business all my life. WUM *is* my life. And yes, I didn't care enough about the environment and I probably didn't care about some people either, including my own family. I didn't do that because I'm selfish. I did it because all I know is the mining business and nothing else.

'"I never met anybody like you, even though I've met a lot of different people in my life who've had something against me. People insult you, judge you before talking to you. But who am I? Am I the devil? The truth is that I'm like anybody else. I have three children and a wife I still love. You heard me, I said *love*. God knows I have lots of anger against those environmentalists who attacked my company and my honour. I don't want to listen to them. Why would I, anyway? For what purpose? Destroy my own company? And then what? A competitor comes and does the same thing as my company used to do before! It's so easy to be against us."

'He calmed down for a few minutes, glancing at me and remaining silent and then said, "It would have been so easy to kill me. It would had been so easy to come to this church and not listen to the music. The journey you took, William, few people on this planet do it. I haven't done it. Not yet. But I can tell you that, from now, I'm going to listen to you very carefully."

'So that night I told him everything I knew about the state of our planet and how bad the situation was. Then he said, "William, please, understand my ignorance. Just look around you, see the world that I see every day. It's a world of abundance. You go to the supermarket and you get all the food, the appliances you want. Switch on the TV and environmentalism is just a subject among thousands and thousands of others. What you told me tonight is that we are on the Titanic and what I'm telling you right now is that the orchestra is still playing."'

The loud popping of a Champagne cork scared both of us, as if someone had opened fire with a gun. Our fear was quickly replaced by a laugh.

William filled our glasses. 'The Henriot is an amazing Champagne, isn't it?' I responded with a smile.

William leant back on the couch, drinking slowly. His eyes were scanning the bottles displayed on a shelf. 'I don't know why they call this place a wine bar. Most of the people come here to drink Champagne. It should be called a Champagne bar,' he said in a detached tone, as if we had spent the evening talking about superficial topics. I remained silent. I didn't have anything to say about Champagne or about wine in general. I just waited for the rest of the story. William noticed it. He put his glass back on the table, took a big breath and gazed at me.

'So, where was I? Oh yes, at the bar with John LaFleur. We drank some Champagne that night too! But I'm digressing from the main subject. Let's go back to what is essential. By dawn, John had changed his mind about environmentalism but not about environmentalists.

'"You were an idiot like me before tonight, my friend. But now it's going to be different. We're going to see each other and speak to each other regularly. I want to see you in my office when I get back to Sydney in three days," he said. He looked really tired. But that night I was so full of hope. The founder of WUM had spent the night listening to me and wanted to hear more. It was like a dream.

'But the dream didn't last long. John died two days later. A stupid heart attack, normal for his age, the doctors said. But his death wasn't the end of the story that linked John to me. Because my name was in his personal calendar and address book, his secretary called me just after his death and two days later sent me an invitation to his funeral.

'It was at that moment I decided to paint again. I'd given up when I was eighteen, thinking that the militant's life was more important than the artist's. I thought art couldn't save the planet.

In my mind, only direct action made sense. But twenty-four hours before John's funeral, all I wanted to do was paint. I did a very subjective portrait of him from bits of memory about his face and all the thoughts I had about him. I painted John smiling and crying at the same time. Two feelings, for a man who was responsible for so much damage to the wilderness but who had also taken the time to listen to me and was ready to change in the twilight of his life. He didn't have the time to really change, but in an indirect way he had changed me.'

William paused to take a breath. 'Three hundred people were at his funeral. Most of them were from the mining business – CEOs, engineers, geologists, managers, the whole business was represented. I went up to his grave when everybody else had gone. I put my artwork in front of the grave and said my last goodbye to John. His daughter, Sheryl, was behind me. Just as I was getting ready to leave, she came up and asked a lot of questions about my artwork and the relationship I'd had with her father. I told her everything without missing out any details.

'She was thirty-eight, attractive and recently divorced. Her former husband was the chief financial officer of WUM. He'd cheated on her with the head of the HR department. With no children, she was at a point in her life where she was open to everything, ready to hear the different sounds and vibrations of the world. So the conversation between us lasted more than a few minutes. We quickly became good friends, calling each other every day, spending most of our weekends together. After four months, we couldn't deny the love we had for each other. The two best friends became a couple and, just months later, we were married.'

William locked his eyes on mine to attract a bit more of my attention. 'This is when the entire philosophy of the John LaFleur Organisation was born. Thanks to Sheryl I had access to a lot of people in the mining business, but also from other industries or sectors of the Australian and world economy. None of them showed any interest when I talked to them about environmental issues. But Sheryl helped me to see my own mistakes. I was here next to her because of Fauré's *Requiem* and the portrait I'd painted of her father. Art is an amazing and powerful proxy, the most efficient vehicle to deliver understanding. So Sheryl pushed me to focus completely on my art and introduced me to Sophie Brooks, a friend of hers who had an art gallery. Thanks to her I became a professional artist, selling to the richest and most influential people in Australia and around the world. As an artist, people were suddenly more open to my speeches about environmental issues.

'But the most miraculous moment came when I realised that I was able to put environmentalists in the same room as the CEOs of the most polluting companies and get them communicating. In two years I became an expert, knowing how to make people speak to each other; how to gently bring up a difficult topic and keep everybody calm. Through all this process, a lot of changes were made. Some companies got greener, some even gave up projects. An invisible wind of change was really blowing over Australia, giving me a faith and a hope that I had never experienced before.

'Even in the LaFleur family. Jeffrey, Sheryl's youngest brother, a twenty-nine-year-old professional photographer and owner of 15% of WUM shares, became a passionate environmentalist, creating with Sheryl a 30% shareholder environmental front within WUM. Bill LaFleur, the oldest brother and CEO of WUM, gave up two mining projects just because of Sheryl and Jeffrey. Janet, their seventy-one-year-old mother and John's widow, was always sensitive to her youngest son's arguments. She was always on his side, giving Bill absolutely no choices. Environmentalism had a majority of shares inside WUM – it was simply a revolution. And made with what? Love and understanding. But on the 2nd of

February 1997 at a quarter past two, the wind of change lost its engine, its inspiration, its matter.'

William closed his eyes and remained silent for a minute. When he opened them again he said, 'That day, Sheryl was in a car accident. She lost her life. I lost my light, my sun, my tomorrow. Then everything got complicated. Sheryl left me all her WUM shares in her will. In fact, that was the only thing she specified. "My little contribution to the planet," she had written. This made Bill LaFleur furious. Less than a week after Sheryl's funeral, he tried to invalidate her testament. For a year, Bill made my life impossible. He used his cousins, his uncles, his own children, trying to influence his brother Jeffrey and his mother to testify against me. Jeffrey never gave up on me, and even today is still an environmentalist, but Janet, his mother, couldn't resist this family war. She gave up by selling all her shares to foreign investors. These investors were all in favour of Bill and not very pleased to hear Jeffrey and me speaking of environmentalism. Even so, my contacts in industry were intact and still very useful.

'But Sheryl's death forced me to face my own mortality. My network, my contacts had to be used by something larger than me, something that could survive me. That's how I got the idea of creating the John LaFleur Organisation. I used John's name instead of Sheryl's because I wanted, from the very beginning, to keep a minimum distance from this organisation. I couldn't afford to be emotional about it. Besides, John had been the spark that made all this possible. To use his name was like going back to the origin. I also gave the organisation all the WUM shares I'd inherited from Sheryl.

'The organisation was officially born on the 2nd of June 1997 at Sophie Brook's gallery. Sophie played a big role from day one, pushing artists to join the organisation, keeping the idea of using art as a proxy, a bridge for a better dialogue between environmentalists and the industries. A year later, it was the world of sports that I invited inside the organisation.'

He paused once again and then said: 'What I think the most important thing for you to understand is that you won't change the world by being some sort of full-time militant. Don't be one of these people that nobody wants to hear. Get a real life with the real people. Be in contact with every part of society. Don't lose contact with your family and your friends. You won't change the world without them.'

God knows I had a lot of questions to ask William, but he interrupted our conversation at midnight, saying that I needed to process everything I'd heard before going any further. He drove me back to my hotel and told me a friend of his would pick me up at noon.

I was woken up by a well-dressed forty-year-old Bangladeshi woman called Salima. Thin and short, Salima wasn't physically impressive but her large brown eyes expressed a confidence that I had never encountered before. She knew how to look at you, showing no sign of doubt and giving you the impression that she perfectly knew what she was doing. She inspired respect at first sight. You couldn't be indifferent to her. The moment she entered a room, she became the centre of attention.

So, when she spoke to me for the first time, I paid attention to every word she said. She told me William had asked her to take care of me for the next few days. I couldn't stay on at the hotel, not only because it was too expensive for the John LaFleur Organisation, but mostly to make it harder for the journalists to find me.

'Some journalists are already waiting for you in the lobby. It's not official yet but it seems that Marty Koenig is going to quit. We must hurry. The longer we stay here, the more difficult it will be to avoid the journalists. William thinks it wouldn't be a good idea to say anything to the media right now.'

I followed her without asking any questions. An hour later, I was at her apartment with her husband and two kids. Again, my mind didn't have time to process anything. I knew nothing about Salima, but she immediately treated me like an old family friend. There was no time for any explanation. It was all about this little piece of rainforest north of Cairns and this company, Eastern Holidays. For two unbelievable weeks, Salima and I spent almost all our time together, two weeks during which I didn't have time to think about what I was doing.

It all started with Marty Koenig quitting his position as CEO of Eastern Holidays but staying on in the company as an adviser. This happened without a single word from Koenig. No press conference, no interview; the journalists didn't even know where he was. He had simply gone. But his seat within the company wasn't empty for long. Cathy Stromberg, fifty-six years old, in charge of the successful North American subsidiary of Eastern Holidays for more than ten years and well known for her perfect discretion, replaced Koenig on the day he left. She didn't speak much to the media. It was not her style and nor was it in the interests of the company to feed the noise around me about Koenig and the greenwashing affair.

On our side, things were different. We wanted Eastern Holidays to give up its project near the Daintree National Park and to kill the greenwashing within the company once and for all. So, we did all we could to feed the noise around Eastern Holidays, using the documents that we had about the greenwashing that the company had been doing for years. I talked a lot to the press, under the supervision of Salima. She was always at my side, ready to intervene any time I had problems answering a question. Salima was a successful lawyer, a loving mother, and an environmentalist member of the John LaFleur Organisation. According to all the people I met within the organisation, William trusted her more than anybody else. It was also true the other way around. She considered William to be a member of her family.

Salima didn't count the hours she spent working for the John LaFleur Organisation. When she was needed, she was there, ready to give all her time, all her resources. I don't remember much about the interviews I gave, or what I really said. I was her puppet, saying what she wanted me to say. But I do remember her indestructible faith in the John LaFleur Organisation and its philosophy. She was ready to give her life for it.

Nine days after Koenig's departure, Eastern Holidays announced that its project in the Daintree National Park area had been put on hold indefinitely. The company had seen all its communication plans ruined by the 'Koenig Story' and needed to turn the page as fast as possible. Without Koenig or any project in the rainforest, Eastern Holidays could focus again on communicating with its customers. Then it was time for William to play his discreet role with them: making sure behind closed doors that the resort project would never reappear in its original form.

Suddenly, I had nothing to do any more. I hadn't exactly gone back to the situation in the rainforest because, this time, I convinced myself that I had accomplished something, though my mind was still full of unanswered questions. After an experience like that it's difficult to imagine yourself living a regular life. You want to keep up the adrenaline, you want to hang on to the feeling that you're doing something that really matters, that you're changing the world. Aware that I was facing a difficult "landing", Salima and William didn't let me have a day to myself. They spent a full afternoon talking to me about my future.

I remember how William started the conversation. He said, 'It's important that you study, get through the complexity of one domain. Only ignorant people think that fixing the world can be easy, that there are easy solutions waiting for us somewhere. Whether you choose to study law, or biology, or computer science, you'll experience the long journey that separates a problem from a solution.'

He insisted that what had happened with Eastern Holidays should only be a parenthesis in my young life. 'Be a real adult before being a militant. Get some experiences, open your eyes and your ears before you judge this world. No one should be a militant before turning thirty and getting some real-life experience. It takes time for all of us to discover our own imperfections and to lose our arrogance. The biggest misunderstanding you want to avoid is the one with yourself. Understand who you are before judging others.

'That's why I want to emphasise that what happened to you over the past weeks was an exception. You're a great person but you're only eighteen years old. You need to take time to process what happened. I'm sure you'll be a great member of our organisation in a few years. You have great potential. But right now, I want you to focus on your education. I'll make sure we stay in touch, but you won't do anything for this organisation before you're ready.'

Hearing you're too young and inexperienced to be part of the game leads to the kind of frustration that you get all through your childhood and adolescence. Once you're eighteen, you don't expect to hear it any more. You think this is it, nobody is going to tell you you're too young for anything. It's very difficult to accept that you belong to a sub-category of adulthood. It was difficult to accept that I wasn't immediately going to be a member of the John LaFleur Organisation. After all I'd done, I thought it was totally unfair.

To calm me down, William invited me to the organisation's

three-monthly network meeting that was taking place three days later in Sydney. He concluded our conversation by saying, 'At the network meeting, I can guarantee you that you will feel your age. We'll finish this conversation there. Until then, I advise you to really think about your future. Next time we won't have a full afternoon, so be ready.'

Salima seized the opportunity of this conversation to tell me that I was welcome to stay in her apartment until the meeting, but no longer.

Three days later, on the evening of the 8th of December 2000, I was at the meeting, held in a conference room of a hotel downtown. Around sixty members of the organisation were there. None of them was under the age of thirty-five. During the first hour, I met a lot of people who were very interested in my little adventure in the rainforest. I understood what William meant by saying I would feel my age. All the people who talked to me had knowledge and experience I didn't have. They knew what they were talking about, each of them having expertise in one domain. That day, I realised I knew almost nothing and hadn't much to tell.

What had I really accomplished? Being, by chance, at the right place at the right time, reading two speeches that William had written for me and following Salima for two weeks. That's it. That evening I learned to be humble.

Then came William's amazing speech.

'Over the past years we've done our best not to be a conventional environmental organisation. We don't fight, we don't have enemies, we blame no company, we humiliate no one. We are positive people. We don't talk about the possible darkness of tomorrow, we talk about the light of tomorrow, this bright future in which everybody can make a positive contribution. For us, tomorrow is not the status quo or a diminished version of today.

'The problem is that we are an exception. People don't dream any more about tomorrow. This is why it's so difficult to improve our world. Our politicians are not the creators or the engineers of the future. They are simply the managers of today. They improve small stuff, fix small problems. Nothing to be excited about, nothing to dream of. We are not living in the future that people dreamed of thirty years ago. We are not a multi-planetary civilisation and we still drive cars with combustion engines. Computers, internet, cell phones, haven't changed the main status of our civilisation. We're stuck on this planet and we still rely on its limited resources. We're destroying our beautiful planet because in the last thirty years we've been keeping our heads down, dreaming of nothing but business as usual.

'Dreams are the best engine of change. Dreams accelerate everything, make possible what seemed to be impossible. To save this planet we need big dreams, ones that can change the status of our civilisation, ones that don't taste of déjà vu, ones that transport you far away from your everyday life, ones that change your vision of the world. Becoming a multi-planetary civilisation is the kind of dream that can change the entire world, moving what seemed to be unmovable.

'We environmentalists should talk about space exploration. We're the first to tell everyone that we have only one planet, a fragile one with limited resources. It is true as long as we are stuck here. How long are we going to tell ourselves that space exploration is not a priority? We landed on the moon forty years ago. We could already be mining on Mars instead of here. But no. Space exploration has never been in the environmentalists' vocabulary and now look where we are. Mines are everywhere in Australia. We're stuck here, taking all we can get from our beautiful planet. We should all be ashamed of this. If our ambition is to keep this planet alive and in good shape, then space exploration should be our priority. Humanity won't stop growing and already the resources of our planet aren't enough for all of us. This is obvious.

'Of course, we can lie to ourselves and think there's a way to live on this planet in harmony, without any extra-terrestrial resources. We've been doing that for the past forty years, but we can't afford to go on doing it for forty more years. Dear members of the John LaFleur Organisation, whatever your choice for the future of this organisation will be, I know mine. I won't stay behind the scenes any more, building secret networks. That time is over. More than ever, I have the feeling that it is time to rescue tomorrow. Business as usual has never been so strong, so threatening. Coal is making a comeback. You heard me, I said: *coal*. The present is managed with the recipes of the past. This world is going backwards. That's why I think that our organisation should change its strategy. Communication is now more important than action. We won't achieve anything if the majority of the world's population thinks tomorrow is just a small evolution of today. It's time to get out and switch on the light of tomorrow.'

The audience remained silent for at least five long seconds. Everybody, including myself, was stunned. Nobody had expected such a speech. We all needed to process it. But at the end everybody applauded.

When William finally took five minutes' break from answering questions to talk to me, he said: 'I know that we were supposed to finish our long conversation tonight, but it isn't going to be possible. Let's do that another time, just you and me, somewhere we can speak in peace. I'm going to China tomorrow. I'll stay there two weeks. I'll contact you when I get back. Until then, go to your parents in Byron Bay. Take the time to think. Don't rush anything and do consider what your parents have to say.

'There are two things you should keep in mind. First, like I told you before, you can't be a full-time militant. It's definitely not recommended. You need to have a life that connects you with others. And when I mean others, I mean people who aren't environmentalists yet.

'Secondly it's important that you're in contact with the complexity of this world. Be an expert in one domain. It will help you to be humble and acknowledge that you know almost nothing about almost everything. The more you learn, the more eager you are to learn more. So, when you and I meet again, we won't talk about the environment or the John LaFleur Organisation. It will be all about you.'

Then he gave me a CD of Fauré's *Requiem* and said, 'Have a merry Christmas and a happy new year. Spend some time with your family. We will see each other next year.' And those were his last words.

I didn't go back directly to Byron Bay. Most of my belongings were in Brisbane, in the apartment that I rented with Sarah. No matter what, Sarah and I needed to speak and find an agreement. I took a night train, arriving in Brisbane at 9am. At a quarter past ten, I stood in front of the apartment's door. It took me more than ten minutes to decide to use my own key to open the door. Sarah wasn't there. The apartment was in total chaos, but my room seemed to have been left untouched. I started to pack my stuff as fast as I could. I wanted to be ready to leave the moment Sarah came into the apartment. I didn't want to have a long conversation with her. I was afraid I wouldn't be able to stay calm, that I would make everything even more complicated. I played the scene over in my head a million times. I expected her to be aggressive and prepared myself to be insulted and to not respond.

And then she came in. My heart was beating at a speed I had never experienced before. Every part of my body was shaking. It lasted few seconds, just time for Sarah to open the door and walk the few metres that separated the entrance from the living room.

The moment my eyes met her gaze, I calmed down immediately. She was embarrassed. 'I'm not with Brian anymore. It's over. It was a mistake.'

She tried to apologise for what had happened in the rainforest, but I didn't let her go on. I almost regretted that she didn't do her anti-capitalist speech. It would have at least given me the impression that she hadn't sacrificed our friendship for a short adventure with a guy called Brian. I had more respect for her when she sounded like a hard-core activist. Now she sounded like a teenager who had played the militant, as if everything that had happened in the rainforest was just for fun.

Sarah did all she could to have a friendly conversation with me, bringing up any possible subject that had nothing to do with what had happened over the past months, but it didn't work. Our conversation lasted no more than fifteen minutes. I stayed focused and did my best to reach an agreement with her about the apartment. I had until the end of December to move my things. After that, Sarah was on her own, able to share with anyone she wanted.

Once outside the apartment, I got the first bus to Byron Bay. At 9pm, I was outside my parents' hotel. I knew a lot of questions were waiting for me but I had never been so happy to be home. I needed a pause in a place where I could feel at peace. With my parents, my brothers and my sister, I couldn't be in better company.

I took the time to think about everything that had happened. I listened to the concerns of my parents about my future and took good note of their advice and warnings. But no matter what, all I had in my head was William's story. It didn't matter if it was a true story or not. The philosophy behind it fascinated me, obsessed me. I couldn't think about anything else. I listened to Fauré's *Requiem*, imagining William listening to it, seated just behind John LaFleur. My mind couldn't rest as long as my conversation with William wasn't over. I couldn't wait to see him again.

Without William

On the 29th of January 2001, I was still at my parents' place, my future still on hold and the patience of my parents reaching its limits. I had nowhere to go, no plan for tomorrow. All I was doing was waiting for an e-mail, a phone call, any sign coming from William. That day, I did receive an e-mail but not the one I'd expected. It was from Salima. She had written *Call me ASAP* above a forwarded message from the vice president of the John LaFleur Organisation, Sophie Brooks. Here is the forwarded e-mail as I remember it:

Dear Members,

I have some very unpleasant news to share with you. William is right now in prison in Beijing. He is accused of raping a young woman. None of the elements of the accusation match with any of the facts. William can prove his innocence with documents and witnesses. But the Chinese authorities have already shown that the truth doesn't matter. Some officials came to William a few days ago to suggest to him that our organisation should sell its share in WUM to investors linked to the government. They also made William understand that he won't leave China as long as those shares haven't been sold to the right people. His lawyer received this clear message as well.

Two days ago, I went to China and I have been able to talk with William. He gave me a letter to share with you. This letter is attached to the e-mail as a pdf file.

In this situation, as vice president of this organisation, I took the decision to arrange a meeting next week in Sydney. You will receive a second e-mail regarding the meeting in the coming hours. We have to make some tough decisions in the fastest way possible. William's life depends on us.

Sincerely,

Sophie Brooks.

Here is William's letter to all the members of the John LaFleur Organisation:

My dear friends,

Our organisation is not limited to my simple existence. In fact, I think more than ever that the John LaFleur Organisation should have no link with me anymore. Our organisation, like any other environmental organisation, shouldn't be dependent on certain personalities, names or political parties. The John LaFleur Organisation is an idea, a philosophy, a way to save our planet. It can't fulfil its mission if it depends on me. I am not the John LaFleur Organisation. I am not and shouldn't be important. Our goal is to save this planet.

I know that some of you are going to be tempted to use the means of our organisation to help me, but it would be totally wrong to do so. We can't let a few corrupt people have a negative impact on the John LaFleur Organisation. I don't believe in violence. I refuse to accept its power. We can't let it work. We can't let it be efficient. We have to send a strong and clear signal to anyone who uses violence as a means. Let's say loud and clear that it doesn't work. This brings me to the main point: Don't help me, don't spend your time and your money on me. Don't make the headlines with me. It would be the worst thing to do. Lots of people in China are working on my case. I have no doubt that those who are behind my incarceration will be in jail soon. Your time, your money, your passion must be focused on this planet. Nothing is more important than to save life on earth.

One day after getting this e-mail, I was back in Sydney in Salima's apartment. Staying at Byron Bay was unbearable. I love my parents, my brothers and my sister but they couldn't understand what was going on in my life. I didn't want a regular life. I didn't want 'business as usual'. I couldn't pretend that everything was fine on this planet, that the real choices I had to make were about where I wanted to study and then where I wanted to work. William had told me that I couldn't be a full-time militant, that I needed a real life, but I couldn't have a real life if I wasn't somehow, somewhere, a militant, an environmentalist. I couldn't be inactive while William was held in jail.

But Salima hadn't informed me about William's situation and then invited me into her apartment so I could be any kind of activist. On the contrary, Salima kept me close to restrain me.

'You could be tempted to use your little bit of fame to bring William's situation to the attention of the media, but it would be totally wrong. I want you to take the time to understand the situation before thinking about doing anything,' she said in a professorial tone before reminding me that the members of the John LaFleur Organisation were no activists. 'They discuss, they listen, they understand. They don't demonstrate, 'name and shame', or talk negatively about anyone.' She even pointed out that within the organisation most people thought that the future of environmentalism was in China, mentioning that more than half of the Chinese identify themselves as environmentalists. To say something negative about that country, even in this particular situation, was unthinkable.

Before going to the meeting at which William's case was going to be discussed, Salima reminded me once again that I was here to understand, not to participate. I was frustrated even before anything started.

The meeting, organised by Sophie Brooks, took place in the conference room of a fancy hotel in downtown Sydney. Fifty-six members of the organisation were there, seated in front of a small stage where Sophie was standing behind a lectern. The room with its thick blue carpet, its dropped ceiling light boxes and its elegant wood panels didn't allow any sound to travel too far. In this kind of room, unless you hold a microphone, you have almost no chance of being properly heard.

The audience, elegantly dressed, didn't seem like a band of undisciplined rebels. Here, people murmured politely. Sophie Brooks, a tall, slim, thin forty-year-old, looked like a retired top model. With her long, shiny blonde hair, her tight black dress that fitted perfectly with her black and elegant shoes, she seemed to come from a fashion catalogue but definitely not from an environmental organisation. I have to confess that I liked how her appearance didn't fit with what she was supposed to be. Finally, an environmentalist that doesn't look like one, I told myself, thinking that Sophie was the kind of person who could reach the ears of those people who normally don't tend to hear environmentalists. I couldn't wait to hear what she had to say, hoping to hear an eco-warrior dressed like a hot businesswoman.

After the usual greetings, she said: 'We are all here today, because our organisation is the victim of an attack by some members of the Chinese communist party. William, the creator and president of this organisation, was jailed for eight days in the Masanjia labour camp, probably one of the worst jails on the planet. People who have been there describe it as hell on earth. William was tortured and forced to work, until a public servant authorised his transfer to a better jail in exchange for a thousand US dollars. You all know that William hates corruption and has always been eager to fight this cancer that makes life so miserable for people everywhere on this planet. But his suffering was acute, so unbearable that he accepted the deal. Moved to a more conventional prison in Beijing, he was then able to get a lawyer and to contact me.

'I went to Beijing as fast as I could, calling all my contacts in the government to get a visa in less than twenty-four hours. When I finally met William, I had difficulty recognising him. His face was covered in scars and his weak voice was barely audible. Probably on drugs, I couldn't really speak to him. He seemed out of it. During my second visit, the next day, he was in better shape and was able to speak. It was during this visit he gave me the letter I sent to all of you by e-mail.

'William tried very hard to persuade me it wasn't worth fighting his case with members of the Chinese communist party. For him, no one outside China should intervene in his case. He is persuaded it would create problems for the Chinese officials who are helping him. He told me he was confident the people behind his incarceration would be in jail one day. He refused the help of the Australian consulate and he has been crystal clear about the fact that our organisation shouldn't do anything for him either.'

•   •   •

The buzz of conversation in the audience forced Sophie to interrupt her own speech. The emotion was too high to be stifled by the acoustics of the room or by the politeness these people seemed accustomed to.

Sophie stayed immobile and silent for a few minutes, waiting for the audience to find its own path to silence. Once the attention was back on her, she went on.

'But then, let me tell you a bit more about his current situation. Every two days, William has to pay five hundred US dollars to be treated with a minimum of respect. Even his lawyer, who is used to dealing with cases involving foreigners, told me that he had never seen a such thing. William told me he was ashamed of all the money he had already given to those corrupt public servants and that he was planning to stop paying. That's what he did three days ago. Now he lives in terrible conditions, sharing a cell with twenty other prisoners and getting only one meal per day. And trust me, you don't want to know what this meal is made of.

'Meanwhile, the authorities have informed his lawyer that William will be transferred back to the Masanjia labour camp in ten weeks. And don't see in this ten-week delay any kind of clemency from the people behind all of this. Those ten weeks are not for William. They are for us. Just the time that we need to sell our WUM shares to a Chinese company that already owns eight per cent of WUM. The CEO of this company has been perfectly clear with me. After the sale of the WUM shares, William can be back on Australian soil very rapidly. The deal is simple and clear. The price offered for the shares is fair. Our organisation shouldn't lose money on this operation. So, I'm going to be clear and direct with all of you. I want to sell those shares. I want William back with us. I don't care about WUM but I do care about William. This is my opinion. Now it is time for you to give yours. William's future is in your hands. You have two different voting options. You vote in favour of my proposal and we sell our WUM shares. You vote against my proposal and we keep them, but God knows what will happen to William. If you want to make any comments before the vote you are of course welcome to do so by coming up onto the stage.'

After a few seconds' silence, a man of around forty stood and went up to the stage. Short and thin but with a square jaw, long beard and large forehead, he had a face that expressed a strength that his body didn't. But the biggest contrast was probably between his good-looking, and probably expensive, suit and the large tattoo on his neck. Beyond his physical appearance, this man expressed a strong confidence. Nothing in his gaze, in his way of moving or in the tone of his voice expressed any kind of doubt. He knew exactly what he was doing.

'Hello! For those who don't know me, I'm Christoph. I have a lot of respect for William and for his philosophy and the way he manages this organisation. Like him, I'm an environmentalist and I do know what's going on in northern China, where WUM is helping some corrupt people destroy the environment and millions of people's lives. Those who know the details about William's visit to China shouldn't get the idea it's OK to negotiate with those people. I don't go along with this disgusting idea. Just thinking about it makes me sick. William is totally clear on that matter in his letter. He doesn't want negotiation. He doesn't want the organisation to play the game of corruption, whether it's in Australia, China or anywhere on this planet. I understand every word William wrote in his letter. It makes sense and it fits with the philosophy that pushed him to create this organisation.

'I do think he's going through hell right now, but he's alive. He still has hope. Even in these terrible conditions, he still believes in the people of China. We won't save him by acting against his will, against who he is. We'll murder him by doing something that goes against what he fights for, by not believing in him in the way he believes in other people.

'He and I have talked of China a lot in the past. There are so many complaints. Especially about their human rights. But he and I have always thought that our best chance to save this planet will come from China. He told me one day that going to China is like being a speleologist visiting a beautiful cave where nobody's yet thought of switching on the light. Beauty and hope are there, waiting to be lit up. We should respect William's will, even if it is difficult to understand. I don't understand how it would make sense to sell our WUM shares. How does it fit with William? How does it fit with the philosophy of our organisation? I tell you what I think. Selling WUM shares is like killing William.' Christoph left the stage.

Nobody in the room made a sound. I have never experienced such deep silence in a room full of people. But after a few seconds someone broke the silence. A man of around sixty got up and went onto the stage. At first, he didn't seem to know what he wanted to say. At last he spoke.

'I am Aaron Sigman. William is an old friend. A precious friend. Far more precious than those WUM shares we should have sold years ago. Only a very few of you know why we still have these shares. So, I'm going to tell you what this is all about.

'One year ago, WUM got the authorisation to conduct mineral exploration in the eastern part of the Kimberley, having secured the mineral rights. Some geologists inside the company think they've identified an area that could be rich in rare earth. William tried to block the process by using the power that our shares give us. He somehow succeeded in slowing down the full process but didn't stop it. The stakes are simply too high. Rare earth in the mining industry is like the Holy Grail. It's why he worked with our precious Salima on a plan B.'

He waved at Salima, who responded by waving back, and then continued, 'I'm sure she'll share all the information about it with you, when the time is right. But now it is time to take care of our friend, William. It's time to save his life, whatever he said or wrote. I will listen to him when he's free on Australian soil. I'm ready to fight against corruption but not at the price of William's life. We have to get him out as soon as possible. If selling WUM shares is the best way to get William out of there, let's do it. We don't need these shares. We should have sold them a long time ago, because then we wouldn't be in this situation. Let's not waste any time. Let's sell those shares. Let's bring William back home.'

Most people applauded. Then Sophie came back on the stage. 'I want to quickly respond to Christoph by saying that there is almost no chance of getting William out any other way. I don't believe the Australian government could do anything useful. It could take years. We have to be realistic. Selling WUM shares is the only possible way. There is no credible alternative way to save William. I'm quite surprised to hear that our organisation could be more important than William's life. I won't sleep properly till he is back among us. I have no time for this organisation as long as he's not here. Right now, I care about William, not about the John LaFleur Organisation.'

Once again, most people applauded. I didn't. I couldn't accept what I had heard. The people who were torturing William mustn't win. This was the red line. I cared about William. I cared a lot about what he had done and his philosophy. I did understand his letter and the decision he had made. It made sense to me. William didn't accept the world as it was. He was not the kind of person to give up at the first inconvenience or real difficulty. Changing the world was his only priority. I couldn't imagine him accepting the Chinese government deal. Christoph was right. It was all about the encounter between John LaFleur and William at the concert. It was about that murder that didn't happen.

So, I stood up and went on stage without any authorisation from anyone. 'What William wrote from his cell sounds like him. We can't let the violence win. The idea that the communist party could get this organisation's WUM shares by force terrifies me. We can't encourage this kind of behaviour, we can't make it work. Where will this path lead? I don't know William like most of you, but I think I understand the meaning of what he has done. None of you really think that his letter is the work of someone who's lost most of his common sense or ability to think. What he wrote makes sense and all of you know it. From the first word to the last it reflects the William that I know and with the few things that I know from this organisation. If we care about William, then we should respect his wishes.'

Christoph stood up and applauded alone. I went back to my seat under the disapproving watch of Salima. Sophie Brooks took the opportunity to say I wasn't a member of the organisation, just a guest who didn't have the right to vote in this assembly. Only Christoph voted against the sale of WUM shares. I would have loved to talk to him but Salima didn't give me the chance. She made it clear we had to leave and then have a serious conversation. I didn't play the rebel with her. Our disagreement of the day couldn't offset the deep respect that I had for her.

Back at her apartment, Salima told me to go into the living room; she stood in front of me, I sat on the couch and she made no attempt to hide her anger. She spoke in a loud voice and never stopped moving. It was clearly not the right time for me to say anything, so I kept quiet.

'Who do you think you are, with your eighteen years in this

world? Do you think you've already got enough life experience to give lessons? To explain to all of us what the John LaFleur Organisation is about? I know William told you his story about John LaFleur but I guess he didn't tell you who Christoph is, did he?'

I answered quietly, 'No. He didn't tell me.'

Salima raised her hands and said, 'Of course not.' She went on, 'Christoph was one of his friends who wanted to murder John LaFleur. He is a part of William's dark past. When Christoph talks about William, it's not the William we know. Not the one who founded this organisation. What you did today was so wrong! So wrong!' Salima pressed her hands to her cheeks, breathing loudly. She closed her eyes for a few seconds. When she reopened them, she looked a bit calmer. In a low voice she said, 'Build your own story before going onstage. Eighteen is very young. God knows, I was confused at your age.' She paused and said, 'Do you want something to drink? Tea, coffee, water, juice… rum?'

'A tea will be great,' I answered.

Salima came back from the kitchen a few minutes later with a tray that she put down on the low table facing the couch. On it was a cup of tea, an empty glass, a bottle of rum and a packet of my favourite chocolate biscuits: Tim Tams. 'Tea for you, Tim Tams for both of us, and a glass of rum from Bundaberg for me,' said Salima with a smile, before sitting down on a comfortable armchair next to the couch.

After a glass of rum and two Tim Tams, Salima leant back in her armchair and, staring at the ceiling she said, 'You see, I wasn't born in Australia but in Dhaka, Bangladesh. My family has owned a tannery there for more than five generations and despite the fact that I was born in one of the poorest countries on earth, I've never been poor or felt that I was short of money at any time. However, I never felt comfortable being rich in the middle of desperate poverty, having everything I needed when my father's employees were working twelve hours a day and earning just enough to survive.'

Her eyes left the ceiling, aiming now at my gaze.

'The worst part was that some kids worked in our tannery. My father always told me that, for those kids, working there was better than anything else. It sounded like we were helping them by giving them the opportunity to work for us. While they were working around dangerous chemicals without any protection, I was studying and preparing my bright future. The only future that I dreamed of was to get out of Bangladesh as soon as possible. At eighteen, I applied to different universities in the United Kingdom, USA and Australia. The first answer came from Sydney and immediately became my first choice. I didn't wait for the other answers. I just wanted to get out as soon as possible.'

Salima stood up. 'We need a bit of fresh air here'. She opened one of the living room windows and then came back to her armchair. She poured a bit of rum in her glass, drank a sip and then continued her narrative, twisting the ring on her finger.

'So, six months later, I was in Sydney studying geology. The mining business was already booming, and I thought geology could be a good option for getting work in Australia and not having to go back to Bangladesh. I didn't leave Australia for a whole year. I was enjoying a fantastic life, forgetting almost everything about Bangladesh. I was really happy to live in a world without deep misery in every corner, where people did so much more than just survive.

'Back in Bangladesh for a family reunion, the shock was really powerful. The most difficult part wasn't crossing the slums. It was seeing my own family exploiting kids at the tannery, giving them no protection, seeing all those workers from seven in the morning to eight or nine in the evening earning just a few dollars, while my parents were making thousands. How was this fair? It was clear in my mind that I couldn't approve or even close my eyes to what was going on in the family's tannery. So, I talked to my father and asked him to improve the security of his employees, to pay them more, not to hire any kids and to give a maximum of our money to charity, to make that country a bit better.

'My father answered, "You wouldn't be here to tell me that if these people were not working like they work every day, providing cheap leather for your friends in Australia who spend their Saturday afternoons in those big malls, never wondering where and how the leather for their shoes or jackets was produced. In the name of *what* do those people, who never worry about anything except their little lives, judge our way of life? Why is it they have their great houses with all their gadgets, and we do not? Do they care more about others than we do? I don't think so. I've been to those rich countries. I've seen how they waste everything, while most people worldwide go without the essentials. So yes, my dear daughter, I'm not Superman, I'm no better than those people you met in Australia except that, unlike them, I have to see the shit of this world every day and deal with it."

'This answer was far from acceptable to me. It was the usual denial of our responsibility in this world. I thought, and still think, that it's too easy not to do better just because others don't. So, I told my father he had no obligation to hire kids in his tannery, that maybe we didn't need so much money. But then he got very angry with me, telling me that he had always given me everything I wanted, including my expensive studies in Australia.

'He said, "If you have no respect for the money we make here, then you have no right to spend it. I'm not going to pay for your studies in Australia any more. You stay here. We're going to find you a husband and stop all this madness."

'I didn't waste a single second. I had a return ticket to

Australia, which I was able to change cheaply, and enough money in my bank account to live on for at least a month. What I needed was to run away as fast as I could. I didn't risk leaving the family house with my suitcase; I just went out with a very small bag as if I was going for a walk, and then I called a taxi. Once at the airport, I took the first flight that had a connection to Sydney. My main concern was to get out of the country as soon as possible.'

Salima glanced at the empty Tim Tam packet. She said, with a big smile on her face, 'I have more in the kitchen if you want.' I told her not to. I had a Tim Tam issue. I didn't know how to stop eating these amazing chocolate biscuits. Salima laughed for a few seconds about my Tim Tam problem before becoming serious again. She drew a deep breath and went back to her story.

'Once back in Australia, I changed everything in my life. I gave up geology to study Australian law. To study something that has no value anywhere except Australia was like saying out loud I was planning to stay here forever. My first year was quite tough. I had to move to a cheaper apartment, to work all weekend and to give up any kind of private life. But I was happy and felt free, more than ever. During my time at the university, I met my first husband. I married him in a hurry, not paying too much attention to who he really was. This wedding was my chance to build a future in Australia. It helped me get Australian citizenship and lowered the risk of having to go back to Bangladesh. After university, I worked for different lawyers before becoming one myself. Then I divorced, found a new husband and had my kids. I was happy, everything was fine.

'The story could have ended at that point, but you can probably guess that all of this goes beyond my little life. Six years ago, William came to my office and before introducing himself or even saying hello he said, "Do you want to make the world better, Salima?" Believing it was a kind of joke, I answered with a smile,

"Yeah sure, right away." But as you can guess, William wasn't there to make jokes. He pulled a huge calendar out of his bag, put it down on my desk and said, "Mark with a pen when you can come with me to Bangladesh to meet your father and make this world a better place."

'Then I started to freak out, asking him who he was, and who he worked for. He answered that two months ago he'd met my father and they had reached a deal to improve the working conditions inside the tannery as well as fix the environmental problems caused by using chemicals such as Chrome VI. An American company, whose CEO was a member of the John LaFleur Organisation, had agreed to buy leather from the tannery for a fair price, making all of this economically neutral to my father. But this didn't explain why I was supposed to go to Bangladesh to meet him.

'Then William said, "Your father is a great man! I visited thirty-five tanneries and only your father accepted our offer. He definitely has the will to make the world better. He could really help to change the mentality in the leather business. I feel he could move mountains if he had more confidence in his ability to do so. But the misunderstanding that he has with you stops him setting the example, being the leader of opinion he could be. How can a man contribute to changing the world when he doesn't even know where his only daughter is? He's in pain, Salima. He would really like to see you again, to make peace with you. By what he told me, I can assure you that what's separated you from him all these years has been a big misunderstanding."

'All of this was very hard for me to hear. I'd tried during the first year to communicate by post, giving my parents my new address, my new phone number, but they never responded. After that I just gave up and never kept them up to date about where I was or what I was doing. In fact, I spent more than fifteen years totally removing them from my life. I never talked about them and my two kids had no knowledge of the existence of their grandparents in Bangladesh. So I told William to leave my office and never come back. I didn't want to hear any more about Bangladesh or anything related to my father.

'But William was not the kind of person to give up. So he left on my desk a recent picture of my Uncle Peter who'd been living in the US for more than thirty years. He'd always been someone I appreciated but I'd never been able to get his address and phone number after I left Bangladesh. On the back of the picture there was a US phone number. William simply said, before he shut the door of my office, "Call your uncle. He knows, and most of all understands, what happened between you and your father."

Salima stood up to close the window, obviously annoyed by the noise coming from the street. She went to the kitchen and came back with a bottle of water and two empty glasses. She filled the two glasses with water and slid one of them in my direction without saying anything. She drank a full glass of water before looking back at me and telling me the rest of her story.

'It took me several days to call my uncle. I'm not going to tell you everything he said but let's say he helped me understand what had happened between my father and me. "It's easy to criticise your father's behaviour at work when you've never had to make the choices he has to make every day," he said. "He blamed you with your clean hands, because you judged him from your very comfortable situation. He worked hard to keep that tannery and to earn enough money to give you the opportunity to study what you wanted. And one day you come to him and tell him that what he does is unacceptable. You didn't tell him you wanted to help him improve the working conditions at the tannery. No! You didn't get your hands dirty; you just judged him without trying to understand his situation, and then ran away. I don't know a single person who's in favour of children working but I do know one person who really did something to stop that, and that person is your father."

'Two months later, I was with William on a flight to Dhaka. "You're ready to change the world when you are yourself ready to change," William used to say all the time.

'Through William's eyes everything looks different. William doesn't judge. He observes, tries to understand every person he meets. Whoever you are, criminal or hero, he wants to know the path of your life, what led you to where you are. Some people think he's naïve, but I think he's a genius. We can't afford to leave him in jail. We need him back as soon as possible, whatever the price.'

Salima gazed at me for a few seconds, expecting a reaction. But I had nothing to say. Her story, though impressive, hadn't succeeded in changing my mind. There were some principles I wasn't ready to give up. I didn't like people who wanted to make others happy against their own will. William had been more than clear in his letter. What he had written fitted perfectly with the few things that I knew about him and his philosophy. I could understand the situation; my youth didn't stop me being right.

But this doesn't mean I was indifferent to Salima's story. On the contrary, it made me think a lot about my own situation. It's difficult to convince other people when you don't yet have a life story to back you up. It's very frustrating. *Who do you think you are?* is a question that hurts, especially when it comes from a lawyer like Salima. She was totally wrong about William but she had the credibility I didn't have. She had a great life story to tell. A story that had brought her somewhere. I was nowhere and I didn't know where to go. Only one thing was sure in my mind: I had to stop following other people.

• • •

The first chapter of my own story, as an adult deciding for herself, has been to make the decision to live in Sydney. Most of the members of the John LaFleur Organisation lived in Sydney. It was the place to see them and go to any meetings they organised. Besides, Sydney is a pleasant place to live, full of opportunities. It is a great place to build your future.

I started my new life as a waitress in an unspectacular pizzeria downtown, living in a very cheap apartment in the suburbs. It wasn't impressive, but it was the beginning of something.

When I came to wonder about my long-term future, the only thing that mattered was what kind of environmentalist I was going to be. What kind of militant, activist, eco-warrior? What was my impact on this planet going to be?

Salima thought that she had an answer for me. My lesson wasn't over yet. The ignorant young woman that I was still needed to discover what the 'real world' was made of. She invited me to a small meeting that she'd organised. It was all about WUM's mining projects in the Kimberley. 'It's going to be an opportunity for you to see that things aren't as they seem. Reality is a complex thing that requires experience and patience to be understood,' she said, in her usual professorial tone.

The meeting took place in a small conference room at Salima's office. At first sight, I felt I wasn't in the right place. Among the ten people there, Salima and I were the only women and I was the only person who seemed to be under forty. Salima started the meeting by introducing us to Lenny Bedford, a man of fifty-six, a Njarinjin from the heart of the Kimberley. He was a short, dark-skinned man with glasses and hair cut very short. Wearing a suit, he didn't look like someone from the Kimberley. On the contrary, he seemed like one of those sophisticated people you meet in the big metropolises of this planet. He was an experienced geologist who had worked for many mining companies, including WUM.

Once he'd been introduced, Lenny stood up and said: 'The region of my ancestors is in danger. WUM has identified an area that could be rich in rare earth. For the ones who aren't familiar with this term, it refers to a group of seventeen chemical elements in the periodic table that tend to be found mostly in the same ore deposits. They can be found almost everywhere on earth but are rarely concentrated enough to be exploited, making rare earth a truly rare raw material. Two additional problems arise from that fact: The first is that rare earth minerals are essential key raw materials for the high-tech industry. The second is that almost all the rare earth minerals are extracted in China. The consequence of this is that the world is craving for new rare earth deposits.

'With rare earth, people tend to be even more crazy than for oil. I doubt that the government will put any obstacle in the way of the extraction of rare earth.'

For Lenny, the best way to protect the Kimberley from the mining industry was to be part of it. His idea was to create a mining company owned and run by the indigenous people of the region. He gazed at all of us, one by one. 'We, the native people of the Kimberley have been done over by big mining companies countless times. Which is all the more reason to enter the industry ourselves. Nobody can take better care of the Kimberley. Nobody else can make sure that money generated by the mines comes back to the region and into protection of the environment. We live in the Kimberley, this is our home. We don't want to pollute our water, our air, our wilderness. There is no one in this country better placed to undertake the mining of Aboriginal land responsibly, ethically and using best practice, than the first peoples themselves.'

I had no problem understanding the idea behind that and could almost agree with it but we were talking about the Kimberley, one of the green jewels of Australia, one of the last almost untouched regions. It was impossible for me to give up the idea of saving it from more mining. Besides, I had a problem with hearing someone tell me the mining industry was unstoppable. I wasn't in an environmental organisation to hear this kind of stuff.

But the worst bit came from Salima. She explained that William had tried to stop the WUM project in the Kimberley over the past year, by using the organisation's influence as an important shareholder in the company. This strategy worked well but, according to Salima, William had never believed that it would work for more than a year.

'The stakes are simply too high. A shareholder, even an important one, can't act too long against the interests of the company. What we need is a long-term solution like Lenny's project. Something different from a direct confrontation with the mining industry, that gets us nowhere. Let's be part of the mining industry with a responsible project that will set a new benchmark in terms of sustainability and ethics. It's a project that perfectly resonates with the genes of our organisation,' said Salima in that professorial tone.

I didn't dare give my opinion this time. It was obvious that no one thought like me. Everyone was smiling; I was the exception, the intruder, the one who couldn't understand. Salima kept looking at me, checking my reactions. I knew this time I had no right to protest. I hated this meeting. I hated this version of the John LaFleur Organisation. I left the meeting angry and confused.

And then came the three days that made me lose any hope in the John LaFleur Organisation. On the 16th of February 2001 the John LaFleur Organisation officially had no shares left in WUM. On the 17th of February 2001 William was free. The people behind his incarceration had given him a bit of money and a ticket for a direct flight to Sydney. William never boarded the flight. He informed

Sophie that he didn't plan to come back to Australia any time soon. He wrote:

I didn't suffer all that time to let them win that way. I believe in the future of China. I believe in all the people here who fight corruption. I can't let them down. I won't leave China as long as the people behind this ignominy are not in jail. We can't let them win, whether in China or in Australia.

On the 18th of February 2001, William was at Beijing airport with two Chinese friends, planning to fly to Shanghai where other activists were waiting for him. According to his friends, William was so exhausted and so diminished from his harsh incarceration that he was barely able to move. Just before boarding the plane, William collapsed on the ground with a heart attack. Paramedics couldn't bring him back to life. It was over. William Brotsky died at the age of forty-five.

I can't describe my anger and sadness when I learned about all of this. One thing is sure, the anger took over in a matter of hours. I hated Salima, I hated Sophie, I hated all the members of the John LaFleur Organisation, except for Christoph who, just like me, had understood William and voted against the sale of WUM shares. I knew nothing about Christoph and had no way to contact him. My loneliness made my anger worse. I didn't try to understand the situation. The reasonable world of William was dead. It was all about violence. We, environmentalists, had real enemies, the kind that torture and murder.

Sophie wrote in an e-mail to all the members and friends of the organisation that we had to turn William's page, not try to remake what had already been done. According to her, we had to move on, to focus on the future. But what future? She had no word to say about WUM or about the fight against corruption. Not only was

William dead, his vision had disappeared from the John LaFleur Organisation.

I didn't go to William's funeral. I didn't want to meet Salima or Sophie. It could have been an opportunity to meet Christoph, but I know today that he wasn't there anyway. I could have fallen into depression if I had not decided to rejoin the Sea Shepherd Conservation Society. Within this organisation I played a very minor role, helping the guys in charge of the logistics, but I felt I was with people who were really fighting for the planet. I met some wonderful people, ready to go anywhere on this planet to save our oceans. Peaceful people, who have often been arrested for non-violent actions. Some of them have been beaten, humiliated, spent months in jail in the worst conditions. What happened to William was not an exception. Day after day, I discovered an ongoing war whose scale was far bigger than anything I had ever imagined. An unbalanced war in which we, the environmentalists, were always the victims. We were the non-violent, the moderate, the reasonable, the ones trying to overcome our emotions. On the other side, there were those companies, governments or individuals who showed no sign of restraint of any kind. Polluting the air and the drinking water of thousands of people was not a problem for them. Generating nuclear waste that was going to last hundreds of thousands of years didn't disturb them. We were in the situation where insane people demanded that we be reasonable and condemned us strongly any time we protested. How could we tolerate that? I wondered many times, until I discovered that some of us weren't so tolerant any more.

The 5th of June 2001 was a turning point in my life. On that day the biggest WUM copper mine in Queensland was massively and expensively sabotaged. On several of the sabotaged vehicles was written 'ELF', meaning, Earth Liberation Front. This was the answer for me. All I wanted then was to get my hands on one book: *Ecodefense*. This book, forbidden in Australia but easy to find, is all about monkeywrenching, or ecotage – sabotage in the name of the defence of life on our planet. It's not about protesting or negotiating anything anymore, it's about direct action. I didn't want to be polite, to be respectful, to be reasonable with these criminals who were slaughtering our planet every single day without any restraint. I wanted to act, to strike back.

Eco-Warrior

I did my best not to show it, but I thought of nothing except monkeywrenching, from early in the morning to late in the evening. Discretion is the first requirement of any eco-warrior who's into direct action, so I left the Sea Shepherds and cut myself off from all "green" organisations.

My first step as a real eco-warrior was to choose a target. For my first act of sabotage, or I should say *ecotage*, I needed a straightforward target. My first action would be more about training than real sabotage. After several days of reflection, I decided on tree spiking, which is a good way to start. It doesn't involve complicated preparation, it's not technically difficult to execute and the risk of being arrested is very low, especially in remote areas where your "masterpiece" will be discovered a long time after its execution.

There are two kinds of tree spiking. The first is preventive. You spike lots of trees in an area that you think could be the victim of logging companies one day. Then you inform the authorities (anonymously) that you've done some tree spiking in this area, which will make logging both risky and expensive. This is a way to really save an area from logging.

The second kind is defensive. You know an area of trees is going to be logged because it has already been sold to a logging company. You know tree spiking won't stop the process, but it will do some expensive damage, destroying the blades in the sawmill. Your goal is to make logging as expensive and unattractive as possible.

I chose prevention for two main reasons. First, if you tree spike in an area that has been already sold, you know that your nails have lot more chance of encountering a chainsaw. So, to avoid accidents, you drive your nail into the top part of the tree where a chainsaw has less chance of meeting it. You also improve your chances of making more damage because a sawmill blade is more expensive than a chainsaw. But driving a nail into the top of a tree is more complicated and riskier than driving it in at the bottom, where you need no special gear or skill to do it. The second reason is that it's safer to operate in an area where you're not expected and where you don't expect to meet anyone working for a logging company.

I spent a lot of time in different internet cafés deciding where to do my first monkeywrenching, avoiding using my own computer and my own internet connection at home. I chose the Blue Mountains National Park, where the government of New South Wales was considering allowing logging to ensure the viability of the timber industry. Nothing was supposed to be decided for months, giving me the time to do proper preventive tree spiking. The Blue Mountains National Park also offered the advantage of not being too far from Sydney.

My first step was to buy a cheap car, then I'd do several reconnaissance trips to the Blue Mountains without being restricted to bus companies and their timetables, to help me to identify the places where I had the least chance of running into anyone. It turned out to be easier than I expected. The only challenge was not getting lost.

I remember Thursday the 20th of September 2001 like it was yesterday. That was the day I decided to do it. I went to a building supply store to buy a hammer and some bridge timber spikes.

I parked my car a few blocks away and had a story already made up in my mind in case anybody in the shop asked me about those big spikes, which most people never use. The story was about a tree house I was going to make for one of my nephews. In my bag I even had a book explaining how to build a small hut for kids. Before entering the shop I took a big breath, as if I was going to rob a bank. I easily found the spikes, taking fifteen of them. My heart was beating like crazy. I tried to calm myself, remembering my story and all the technical details about the construction of a hut. But the young woman at the checkout didn't care much about what was going on around her and didn't seem to have a clue about anything related to construction. Texting on her phone with one hand while scanning the spikes with the other, she didn't even look at me. This little experience helped me to understand that the hardest part of the job took place in my head.

Once in the Blue Mountains, I walked through the forest for more than three hours before reaching my tree spiking area. I met nobody and encountered no problems. Then came the technical moment, when I realised that to drive a twenty-centimetre nail into an eucalyptus is not the easiest thing on earth. In fact, it requires quite a lot of strength to do it. Besides, it is far from discreet. The shrill sound of the hammer hitting the nail was echoing all around and I couldn't hear anything else. Once my first nail was completely driven in, I paused and wondered if it really was reasonable to keep going like this, alone.

It took me thirty minutes to make the real decision, the one that made me a true eco-warrior that day. I beat my fear with my determination. I took my hammer and, until nightfall, I drove in all the nails I had. My hands were hurting, my ears were ringing, but the letters ELF were in front of me, written on one tree with nails. The Earth Liberation Front had a new member.

Back in Sydney, 'the job' was not yet finished. To really protect the forest where I'd done the tree spiking I had to inform the authorities. I wrote a letter on a cheap second-hand computer that had never been connected to the internet or any network. I described where to find the ELF sign made of nails so the authorities could prove to themselves that this was serious and not just words. I finished the letter with, *It is just the beginning, we will never give up. ELF.* I printed four copies of this letter using an old printer I'd bought for ten dollars. Three copies were for local newspapers and one for the New South Wales government. I sent the letters from four different and distant locations. It took me four weekends to complete this task. Travelling by car, train and bus, avoiding any kind of transport that required ID or credit card payment. Unlike the tree spiking itself, which couldn't be linked to a specific date, those four letters were a different story. It was possible to know where and when the letters had been posted, so I was very careful. But my tree spiking was never reported in any newspaper or website, making me wonder if my letters had reached the right recipients. That tree spiking was frustrating in terms of results, but it motivated me to do something riskier, more direct, with immediate effects.

It didn't take me long to look for the next target. I just had to go inside my memories. As fate would have it, the company that had destroyed my childhood paradise near Quilpie was WUM.

This time I wanted to do it quickly. No reconnaissance, no long-term preparation or research. The plan was just to go there one night and do as much damage as possible. The fact that I knew the area very well gave me unreasonable confidence. Gone were the rationality and prudence I had exercised in the Blue Mountains.

On Thursday the 8th of November I hit the road very early with a 1,321-kilometre journey ahead of me. I was fully aware that it wasn't reasonable to try to do it in one day, but I wanted to get as far as I could. At 8pm, totally exhausted, I decided to stop. I had driven more than 750 kilometres and was a bit north of the small city of Bourke. I was less than 100 kilometres from the Queensland border but already in the middle of the real outback, 800 kilometres away from the east coast. It was easy to park my car out of sight on a dirt road. Here, the noises, the smells were very similar to our cattle station. Spending the night here reminded me and strengthened my determination even more.

I left in the early morning. The idea was to get there before nightfall. After more than 500 kilometres of driving on sealed roads, I finally reached one of the dirt roads that used to belong to my parents' cattle station. The sun was already low on the horizon, but I still had time to drive slowly and not create a cloud of dust that could be seen kilometres away behind my car.

I parked four kilometres from the oil field. At 11pm I left the car. I carried a small flash light that I planned to use as little as possible, a pair of cloth gloves so I didn't leave fingerprints behind, a cheap plastic funnel and a crescent wrench. After an hour walking in the dark without using my flashlight, I reached the oil field. It took me a few seconds to climb over the ridiculously low fence. From that point, I walked very slowly, stopping every five minutes to listen. My goal was to do some damage to something which had no direct link to the oil extraction. An oil field is not the best spot for direct action. You don't want to risk touching any of the derricks, pipes, valves, anything that is in direct contact with oil. It would be more than stupid to be the source of oil leaks.

It took me more than thirty minutes to find my first target. It was an articulated loader, a massive one. It took me at least fifteen minutes to find its tank in the dark. I didn't want to use my lamp and ruin my night vision. I had to be able to run away in the darkness at any time. Once I'd found the fuel tank, I filled it up with sand and anything I was able to find on the ground. I did free style, crazy monkeywrenching, removing every part of the vehicle I could, messing up the hydraulic system, breaking everything that was breakable. After twenty minutes of craziness and making a lot of noise, I walked fifty metres away and hid myself behind a fuel barrel. I waited there ten long minutes, glancing in every direction. Seeing and hearing nobody coming, I looked for some new victims. I found five other heavy vehicles and accomplished a real machine massacre. At 1.30am I was back in my vehicle, so happy, so excited by what I had done, that I didn't feel the need to sleep. I drove for six hours until I reached the New South Wales border. I slept there from 7.30 until 11.30am and was back in Sydney at 11.30pm, totally exhausted but happy.

The Ghost of Quilpie, a local newspaper called me. The police never got a lead. I had been invisible. My free style monkeywrenching cost WUM 70,000 dollars. I was so proud. But my action was only one small piece of a big puzzle. Other eco-warriors had hit WUM far harder than I had done. Just two weeks after my "Quilpie coup" a WUM mine in Western Australia was the victim of a major monkeywrenching campaign. There was two million dollars' worth of damage, including the destruction of a small jet plane.

WUM handled the situation as if it was a communication

problem. They never thought the sabotage was meant to stop them. They thought it was about delivering a message. So, they did everything possible to make us the official bad guys. 'There is no eco-terrorism, there is only terrorism. Violence has nothing to do with environmentalism or any kind of defence of the planet,' they repeated on every TV channel. But of course, it had no effect at all. We weren't looking for any kind of communication. I didn't want a debate or even to explain myself. I considered myself at war. Monkeywrenching was a retaliation for WUM's attack on nature. When you do tree spiking, you're not sending a message, or opening a conversation, you do it to save trees. Period.

I didn't stop. In fact, I was more motivated than ever. The more I heard about monkeywrenching in the media the more I wanted to do it. My last action seemed to me to have been only partly successful. On the one hand, I had done a lot of damage, but on the other, the oil field was still running. The only acceptable result to me was to stop all activity in the oilfield. All this meant I had to do more. I had to harass this site, to give them no respite.

It was obvious I couldn't do the same thing again. WUM had done more than communicate; they had also improved the security on all their sites, including the oil field in Quilpie. I needed to find another kind of direct action. I found the way to do it in chapter 4 of *Ecodefense*: road spiking.

Road spiking has a lot of advantages. It is quite safe to do. Companies can protect their heavy and expensive vehicles as long as they are parked somewhere, but they can't secure the kilometres of roads along which these vehicles are driven. Tyres are expensive to replace, but the spikes for destroying them are easy and cheap to make. And road spiking can be done easily by a single person.

My goal was to shut down the Quilpie oil field, so I went to a building supply store and bought a lot of rods, the kind used for concrete reinforcement. I paid cash and, like the last time, nobody asked questions or paid me any attention.

Then I hit the road, heading to Quilpie. But this time I didn't go through Bourke. I took a longer way through Longreach to reach Quilpie from the west side instead of the east. On the way I stopped in the middle of nowhere, 200 metres from the deserted sealed road between Longreach and Quilpie. There I prepared my rods to make them sharp, ready to kill some tyres. Then I buried a fifth of them, saving them for next time. I didn't want to just do short-term damage, I wanted to create a real disturbance, to be more than a one-time problem. I took note precisely of the location of my rods and drove back to the road. Twenty kilometres on I stopped again; I buried another fifth of my ready-to-puncture tyres.

I repeated that procedure twice more on the road south to Quilpie, the Thargomindah road. Then, in the middle of the night, I parked my car near the dirt road that goes to the oil field. I knew that dirt road perfectly. I had spent my childhood learning its curves, its trees, the little rocks beside it, so that night I was very relaxed as I walked along it. I was the only human being around; the oilfield was two kilometres away on a straight line. I took my spike driver (made to drive the rod into the ground without blunting the sharp end), my hammer, and the first rod from my backpack. I said, 'This is for you, William and for you, beautiful paradise of my childhood' and then hammered the spike driver. It took me less than five minutes to do it. That night I set twenty-four rods on one kilometre, a real tyre-hell-on-earth.

Two days later my twenty-four rods were on the news. The damage wasn't impressive, just two trucks immobilised for twenty-eight hours on the dirt road, as well as three 4WDs. But the headline was *WUM once again victim of eco-terrorism.* The manager of the oilfield told a local newspaper, '*For now we will check every morning the 3.6 kilometres of dirt road that leads to our oilfield.*' In my mind this little sentence meant only one thing: I had to do the road spiking during the day. To do it that way was far riskier, but I didn't want to give up. Shutting down that oilfield was my new reason to live.

Less than one week later, I drove to the Thargomindah road to pick up some of my rods, slept there and left the next day around 10am. On my way to the oilfield, I passed four cars coming from Quilpie. In a region like this, everybody knows everybody else's cars, making me a bit nervous, checking the rear mirror constantly, especially on the dirt roads where it's difficult to see what's behind you beyond the cloud of dust produced by the four wheels of your vehicle.

I hid my car a few kilometres from the oilfield, in the middle of the bush. The ride had been tough, I'd nearly got stuck a few times, but I was almost sure nobody would find my car here. In forty-degree Celsius heat, I walked four kilometres to reach the oilfield's dirt road. Once there, I scrutinised both sides of the road every ten seconds to be sure that no car was coming. I managed to put eight rods in before getting exhausted and annoyed with the heat.

Just when I allowed myself to have a rest, two 4WD cars came past at high speed. The eight tyres of the two cars simply exploded. Both cars finished their trajectories in the bush. One of the cars came very close to me, less than two metres. I didn't have the reflex to run away instantly. I stayed put for three or four seconds. It was like an eternity. One passenger saw me and said, 'Here!! One of them is here.' Then I ran like I've never run in my life before. I thought about nothing else but running as fast as possible. I was sweating like hell, with my heavy backpack full of steel rods. I ran without checking behind me to see if someone was following. I just ran for fifteen minutes until my body told me to stop. I was close to losing consciousness; my vision was darkening, my strength was entirely gone, my body ready to collapse on the ground.

I crouched down, hiding myself behind a rock. I stayed still and totally silent, listening out for any unusual sound. Nobody seemed to be around, but I didn't want to get up so quickly that someone watching with binoculars could easily spot me. Here, the scenery is flat and there aren't a lot of trees. It's easy to see someone a hundred metres away. I waited an hour. Then I walked on, very slowly, pausing every 400 metres, checking the surroundings with my binoculars. I didn't want to miss anything. I couldn't afford to be surprised. I had to know what was ahead of me.

For more than an hour I encountered nothing, even though I scared myself many times with trees or rocks that looked like human silhouettes. But then came the moment when the silhouettes were real. I saw them first without my binoculars. I couldn't see any detail, but there were definitely two people. My heart was racing. I stayed still, my eyes trying to capture the two human shapes. They were immobile too, like statues. I wondered if they were real before I took my binoculars and observed the two men who were observing me with their binoculars... Those two men weren't wearing any kind of uniform, on the contrary they looked like hikers. We didn't smile or wave to each other. No. We observed each other for ten long minutes. None of us acted normally. We were all suspicious at first sight. To be observed that way terrified me. More than someone who had broken the law, I was a young woman alone in the middle of nowhere. As long they didn't move, I didn't want to run away and give them the impression that I feared them. You don't run away when facing a lion. You show that you are not prey. But then one of them took a piece of paper from his back pack and wrote something on it. He turned the piece of paper towards me so I could see it. On it was written:

HELEN?

To see my name written on that piece of paper was no comfort. The fact that those people who didn't look familiar knew who I was, worried me a lot. I didn't move and my face was expressionless. The last thing I wanted was to give them any kind of answer. I just stood there, unable to make a decision. Thankfully, the guy wrote something else on his piece of paper:

CHRISTOPH
John LaFleur Organisation

I felt so relieved when I read it. Even if I couldn't really remember what Christoph looked like, I did remember his speech and his vote against the selling of WUM shares. He was the guy I agreed with. I was almost happy to finally meet him and have a conversation with him. It wasn't just one of the strangest moments of my life, it was a turning point. Without this encounter, my life would have been radically different.

'Hello, Helen! What a nice surprise,' said Christoph, once we were finally facing each other. He introduced me to his friend, Gordon, a tall Aboriginal man of around fifty with long hair and huge snake tattoos on both arms. I didn't know if he was a tough guy in real life but he certainly looked tough. Besides, the fact that he did his best to remain silent made him even more intimidating.

Then a stupid game started in which Christoph and I each tried to work out what the other was doing here, trying at the same time to say as little as possible. At the beginning of the conversation it was like we'd all come here hiking. Of course, I had the story about my childhood in the region, but Christoph didn't seem quite satisfied with that. On his side, Christoph's story wasn't good either, trying to make me believe that his friend Gordon and he had a special interest in the region.

Then Christoph started to talk about the backpacks and their weight. He shook mine, hearing the noise of the rods hitting each other but also felt their weight. At first, he laughed, pretending he didn't understand what it was about, and then he tried to open my backpack. I did my best to prevent that, but Christoph wouldn't stop, pretending it was a game.

When one of his hands reached the rod driver, he stopped laughing and said, 'You don't want to keep that in your backpack. They're looking for you. Anyone in this area who has a walkie talkie or any kind of radio knows that a young woman did some road spiking two hours ago.'

Without taking the conversation any further, Christoph and Gordon helped me to bury my rods, my hammer and rod driver. Then they helped me to figure out the safest way to leave the area. At no time did I get the opportunity to ask them what they were doing there. It was all about me and the current situation.

Christoph said, 'Today is not the day to have a real conversation. But I promise you that we will have one. Give me your number and I will call you in three months. Until then I advise you to keep a low profile. Of course, we never met here.' I gave him my number and went back to my car without asking any questions.

It was already dark; I drove slowly back to the Thargomindah road, scared of damaging the car and getting stuck there. The tension rose as I approached the road. In the middle of the night, far away from any city or any kind of artificial light source, the headlamps of a car can be seen from a great distance, like a lighthouse on the ocean.

As Gordon and Christoph had advised me, I drove south on the Thargomindah road and then east on the Bulloo developmental road heading to Cunnamulla. I didn't pass a single vehicle but, even 400 kilometres away, I was afraid of meeting a police car.

I waited before I'd left the state of Queensland before thinking about sleep. I slept five hours south of Bourke before the heat woke me up. Then it took more than nine hours to reach Sydney.

Back home I slept for a long time. When I woke up, I got straight away on to the internet looking for anything related to my little adventure in Quilpie, but there was absolutely nothing. It was like nothing had happened.

Indeed, nothing had happened. The flat tyres were replaced. WUM had lost some money, but that was it. Nothing had changed. WUM was still WUM.

I was frustrated but didn't plan to give up the fight. If monkeywrenching didn't work, then I had to try something else. But what comes after monkeywrenching? What is the next step?

The next step

On Saturday the 7th of June 2002, around 11am, my mobile rang. It was Christoph. 'This phone call is not meant to be a conversation,' he said. 'Listen carefully and then hang up. I'm calling from a public phone, so don't try to call me back on this number. WUM is poisoning an area in China that used to be protected. The people who live there now have polluted water, full of toxic chemicals and radioactive elements such as thorium which cause cancer of the pancreas and lungs and leukaemia. Who is going to stop WUM and all the other terrorist organisations ravaging our planet? Not the governments, not the mainstream organisations, not even monkeywrenching eco-warriors.

'Right now, there are people in northern China who fear for their lives because of WUM. Maybe it's time for Bill LaFleur and his employees to fear something too. Maybe it's time to take the next step. On Sunday June 30th at 15.10h, I will be at the Hamburg café. Come with the will to really change the world or don't come at all.'

I didn't think fully about what the next step might be or what

Christoph really meant. All I knew was that nothing I'd tried so far had worked. I was desperately looking for the 'something else', the next step that would make a difference.

On Sunday the 30th of June 2002, I went to the Hamburg. Christoph was sitting in a corner of the café, away from the other customers. I sat opposite him. He slid an MP3 player towards me.

'You're going to listen to a recording and at the end you will say yes or no. There'll be no questions, no answers, no debate. Just yes or no. So now put the earphones on and listen carefully.'

It was Christoph's voice. 'Just like you, I went monkeywrenching last year, with three other people. Because we didn't get the results we wanted, we all agreed to go one step further to protect this planet. This means that we're ready to take more risks. We won't operate in the bush or in remote mines but downtown, where the headquarters are, where the people who make decisions live. We accept the idea that our actions could hurt some people indirectly, or even kill them. Even if we do our best to avoid any casualties it will never overshadow our primary goal. Earth comes first.

'If you, Helen, want to join us, you have to fully accept these terms and to give a response immediately. Say yes or no, now.'

I removed the earphones. Christoph said, 'I'm leaving in one minute,' then he gazed at his watch. I didn't like this, but I understood it and, as I said to Christoph later, I knew the answer before I went into that café. The status quo wasn't an option for me. I was ready for the next step, whatever it was. After I'd said yes, Christoph slid a piece of paper towards me and said, 'Be there next month with all the necessary gear and food for two days. And don't forget to bring a water filter.' The paper was in fact a map with a cross in the middle and a date and time: 10/08/2002 at 10am. The cross showed a location in Queensland, sixty kilometres south of the small city of Boulia.

On the 10th of August 2002 at 10am, by the side of the narrow Diamantina developmental road, in flat and deserted scenery, four 4WD cars parked side by side. Christoph got out of his car and came to tell me to follow it. 'We have a one-hour off-road drive from here,' he said.

One hour of off-road driving turned out to be two. During the first hour, the scenery didn't change much. The view was the same whichever way you looked; flat and covered in brown grass ready to ignite at the first spark. But then the landscape changed radically. We were facing some hills and could see escarpments in the distant horizon. The ground was full of rocks of different sizes, making the driving slow and complicated.

We finally stopped at the bottom of an escarpment that looked at least a hundred metres high. For most of us, getting out of our cars was our first opportunity to see how many of us there were and what we looked like. We were five and I was the only woman. Gordon, the Aboriginal guy I'd already met during my failed road spiking, was there. He didn't seem keen to talk, as in our last encounter. He just waved at me briefly when he got of the car, without saying a word. Then there were two other guys: Ralf and Bruce. Both were more talkative than Gordon and introduced themselves.

Bruce, twenty-five years old, a tour leader working for a company operating in the wildest parts of Australia, including the Kimberley, spent his life in the bush, driving an all-wheel-drive bus on the most deserted dirt roads in the country. He had no home and didn't plan to have one. With his long beard, his athletic body and clothes tinted by the red dust of the outback, he was what an Australian adventurer might look like in a Hollywood movie.

Ralf seemed to be an older version of Bruce crossed with a computer guy. A forty-two year-old with no wife or girlfriend, married to computer science and Mother Earth. Just like Bruce, he liked to describe himself as a free man wanting a very simple life. Unlike most people of his age, he hadn't really settled anywhere. As a freelance Java programmer, Ralf worked for different companies all over Australia, never staying in one place more than a year. Burly, tall, with sharp cheekbones, Ralf had an imposing physical presence that didn't match the computer guy cliché.

I would have loved to know more about him and Bruce but Christoph said, 'We have no time to waste. We have a thirty-minute walk in front of us. Be sure not to forget anything. Especially not your flashlight. You're going to need it.' We walked for fifteen minutes along the escarpment among the big rocks that made driving here impossible. Walking with our heavy backpacks was quite exhausting but that wasn't the most complicated part of our little hike.

Standing in front of a very narrow cave Christoph said, 'It's time to switch your flashlights on. We're going in.' It was complicated just getting into that narrow cave. The entrance was only forty centimetres wide and the ground was uneven and slippery. The walls of the cave were far from smooth. Some bits were like razor blades, grazing any skin that came into contact. We walked for forty minutes in this hell before we came to somewhere that looked like a little paradise.

It was no wider than fifty metres but it looked gigantic in comparison with the cave we'd come from. It was like a hole in the middle of a gigantic rock formation. Direct sunlight reached only the top of the walls, giving the place a pleasant temperature and the right amount of light. Camping chairs and a large table were already there waiting for us.

'Welcome to our conference room,' said Christoph, before showing us the 'facility' in detail. Five caves were connected to this place. Three of them would be used during the next forty-eight hours. There was, of course, the one through which we had arrived. 'This is our only exit. In case of emergency don't even try to use one of the other caves. In case of flood they will be the first to fill with water,' he said before showing us the 'toilet cave' where a camping toilet was already installed. Then there was the third cave, the one that led to a stream. 'Our water supply and our potential source of problems if it rains heavily. But it's pretty unlikely at this time of year.' Concerning the two other 'useless' caves, Christoph said, 'Go there if you want to die'.

Christoph invited us to sit around the large camping table. He didn't want to waste any time. I sat next to Bruce, facing Gordon and Ralf. Christoph was seated at the end of the table, like anyone pretending to be the leader would have done. None of us questioned this situation. We just accepted it. He sorted out some documents lying on the table while we sat there empty-handed, waiting for our leader to tell us what to do. We weren't a group, we were Christoph's team.

Once he was done sorting the documents in front of him, Christoph lifted his eyes and scanned our faces one by one. He slammed his hand on the table and said, with energy, 'Alright. Let's get started!' He paused two seconds and then said in a normal voice, 'I suggest that, before we talk about our next actions, we define who our enemy is. What are these big companies, these multinationals?'

He glanced at each one of us, expecting a reaction, but none of us was ready to say a word. A bit annoyed by the situation, Christoph raised his voice a little. 'All they are is an assemblage of capital and human resources. Remove one of those elements and the company dies. Through monkeywrenching, we all tried to attack the capital of these companies. We cost them some money.

But with what results? We didn't stop anything. Ten times more monkeywrenching wouldn't change anything. I think it's time to accept that monkeywrenching isn't for attacking big companies. The cost to them is ridiculous compared to the profits these companies make every single day. I think, deep inside ourselves, we already knew this.'

Christoph stood up and kept talking while circling the table. 'Deciding on the next step after monkeywrenching isn't the easiest thing to do. It's time to stop lying to ourselves, and admit once and for all that threatening a human being has more effect than threatening a bulldozer. We are the first to say that life is the most precious thing. So why don't we target the most precious part of a company? Why don't we challenge this taboo against violence? I propose that we put everything on the table. The authorities define us as terrorists. So, let's see how we can terrorise for good! Let's look at all our options, what we can do. Kidnapping, murder, let's talk about things that could have a real impact. Once it's all on the table, and only then, we can talk about what we want to do.'

Nobody said anything. Murder, kidnapping didn't sit easily with us. We weren't criminals. But Gordon broke the silence. 'We don't need to kill anyone. We just need to scare them enough. Fear can be very disruptive.'

Christoph went back quickly to his chair, glancing at all of us several times without saying a word. Then he finally broke the silence. 'Guys, you scare me a bit. Are you ready for the next step or not? It's not too late to give up.'

'No,' we all responded. Giving up wasn't an option.

Then Bruce said, 'We could burn down a company's headquarters.'

Christoph immediately responded, 'It sounds like a kind of hard-core monkeywrenching but not like the next step...'

Gordon interrupted, 'We don't burn down an entire building,

but we carry out an arson attack during the day, when everybody is still inside. We can do it in a way that nobody gets killed but is scary enough to let people think that we're ready to kill. Then we have the psychological effect of death without actually doing it.'

Then Christoph said, 'I think this could be a good start. But this kind of idea can only work if we all accept that accidents can happen. Burning down a building occupied by hundreds of people is far from being safe. It's not pointing a gun at somebody's head, but it could be just as lethal. Just because we don't want to kill anyone doesn't mean that nobody is going to be killed.'

A long silence followed. This could have been the end of what was supposed to be our next step. We all wanted to do something hard-core, but we had trouble accepting what it would take. But the silence didn't last too long. We all wanted to go further, to do something that really mattered, that made a difference. Gordon said loud and clear, 'I'm ready to face the possibility of someone getting killed.' Then Ralf repeated the same sentence, then Bruce, and then came my turn to say it. I was probably convincing when I said it in front of the group, but today I can say I lied to myself. I wanted to burn down WUM's headquarters, to hurt this company as much as possible, but not to see anyone die because of us.

For hours, we worked on the idea. First, we made a list of our possible victims. We didn't lack enemies. It took us twenty minutes. From Eastern Holidays to WUM, the list was very long and covered all major Australian cities.

Finding a name for our group wasn't difficult either. None of us was eager to spend too much time on finding a name. So, we took the easy way. We were the Earth Soldiers.

Then came the technical issues. Our main problem was to get inside the building of one of our enemies and stay there long enough to set up the incendiary devices. None of us had a clue how we could break into a company's headquarters. All our potential victims were big companies with huge office buildings, under constant surveillance. It wasn't just about breaking a window and climbing in. We could have spent hours thinking how to do it without having the beginning of a solution.

Thankfully, Ralf avoided us wasting our time. 'We don't need to break in. In fact, I think it would be stupid to do that. Every time I work for a big company I'm always amazed by the number of technicians working for external companies who get access to the offices. Plumbers, electricians, AC technicians, the guys maintaining the photocopiers and fire extinguishers, and so on. All those people spend hours in offices under the surveillance of no one. They go from one floor to another with no questions asked. All these technicians could install an incendiary device without any problem at all.'

Then came the question of how we could pretend to be technicians and have access to our victim's office building. Once again, Ralf had an answer. 'It's all about the appliance you're supposed to maintain. Get a serial number, call the company maintaining it and then you'll know everything you need to know, like when the maintenance is normally done, who does it, who inside the headquarters knows about it and so on... we can pretend to be any kind of technician as long as we get the right information about the appliance we're supposed to be checking or maintaining.

'At work, I get it all the time with the company taking care of the photocopiers. When I have a problem with a photocopier I call them and all they ask me to do is to read the serial number on the appliance. Sometimes there's a sticker with a number or a kind of code to read but the principle is the same. They never ask me to identify myself or to prove anything. It's all about the appliance. So, from my point of view what we need to do first is find a way to get a few serial numbers.'

From that idea came another question. How do we get these serial numbers? After an hour of reflection, we worked out an answer: apply for a job. The goal wasn't to get hired, but to get an interview. We only needed to get into the building for a few minutes and gather as much data as possible. We didn't need that much. A photo of a sticker on a photocopier could be enough. It didn't sound that complicated. All we needed was to send fake résumés and wait for interviews. We thought it was an easy solution, expecting to get a lot of interviews. Our only concerns on that matter were about security. We spent hours thinking about how to hide our real identity, how to change our appearance with wigs, glasses, make-up… but also how to get an anonymous phone number or e-mail address.

In fact, security took up most of our time and energy. That was the thing that concerned us the most. Christoph said, 'We won't achieve anything more serious than we've already done if we're not strict about security. This is the first thing that's going to impact directly on our everyday life. Your official life is your shield, your first security layer. If you feel you can't hide who you really are, then you shouldn't consider going further. Tell me your life. Show me you're not a terrorist who spends all her or his free time planning attacks.'

Christoph took two camping chairs and said, 'Ralf, come with me. We're going to check your life.' They walked to one of the caves that were supposed to be dangerous. Before going in, Christoph said, 'It won't take long. In a few minutes, Ralf will be back and he'll tell you who's next'. They disappeared inside the cave. For fifteen long minutes we heard nothing from them.

It was the middle of the night. The gas lamp that partly lit our camping table helped create the strange ambiance and the noises of the outside world resonated inside the wall of this big mineral chimney. Here, insects and the wind made a weird background sound that Bruce, Gordon and I couldn't drown out with our words. None of us had the will for any kind of small talk, or serious conversation. I think we were all processing what had already been said.

Ralf came back from the cave and said, 'Bruce, you're the next one.' Bruce stood up and walked towards the small cave from where the warm light of Christoph's flashlight glowed. Fifteen minutes later came Gordon's turn.

When my turn came, I felt nervous, like someone going to take an important examination. With Christoph, I didn't feel like an experienced eco-warrior who had already done serious monkeywrenching. Without him there was no group, no next step, nothing more than the frustrating status quo. Like the others, I wanted something more. Something that worked. Something that had a chance to make a real difference. I didn't want to disappoint Christoph. I wanted him to feel that I was the right person in the right place.

'Tell me a short version of your life story. Show me that your life has nothing to do with hard-core eco-warriors,' he said in a serious tone before settling into a deep silence that nothing seemed to disturb. I didn't manage to speak for more than five minutes before falling into an embarrassing silence. I had no life story to tell. At least, not the story of a normal person. My past was Miss Free Enterprise and my present seemed to be the very definition of emptiness. I had no friend, no hobby, no dream for my future. I was just a waitress in an Italian restaurant.

'You sound too much like a full-time eco-warrior, Helen. It can't work. You can't be one of these asocial monomaniacs with no life. Not only because it makes you an easy suspect but because it is the path to insanity. Get a life, Helen. A real one.'

Christoph and I spent more than an hour in that little cave. I didn't want to give up and he didn't want to see me leaving the group. So, we worked on my life, looking for a way to improve it.

'Be a student, get a future,' said Christoph before pointing out that it was quite strange that a person like me, thinking about the long-term fate of our planet, hadn't any plan for her own life. The problem was that I couldn't imagine myself studying or working in any field that didn't connect with the environmentalist that I was. I wasn't the kind of person who was easily able to have two different lives. I needed more than a cover, I needed something right for who I was.

Christoph suggested I study geology. He pointed out that I knew almost nothing about our biggest enemy, the mining industry. Studying geology was, according to him, a way to understand this industry and see what was at stake. Besides, this would give me a very good cover without feeling totally detached from the eco-warrior I thought I was.

'Your official life will have a direct link with our fight. It will give you valuable knowledge about the mining industry. Get to know the people who could be working for the mining industry in a few years. People who could be our future informers. See yourself as an undercover agent,' said Christoph in a calm, low voice. I don't know if he really believed it, but it worked. I did believe that studying geology would help me to understand the enemy. I simply loved the idea.

We slept only a couple of hours before going back to work. We hadn't got a single minute to waste. We were all glad to be here and to have a chance to consider the next step after monkeywrenching. This meeting had to be the successful beginning of our group.

I had the shortest breakfast in my entire life. Our meals weren't the highlight; they were seen more as an inevitable annoyance than as a convivial moment. On this Sunday morning, all our thoughts were concentrated on one essential element for our future success: communication.

Working and living in different places around Australia, we needed a reliable and safe way to communicate. This was the key to everything. Thankfully, Ralf had worked on that before attending our meeting. He'd already thought everything through. That morning, Ralf was the boss, the one making the speech and answering the questions. Unlike Christoph, he didn't move from his camping chair, walking around us, scanning our gazes or speaking to us in a professorial tone. He didn't have the manner of a leader but he had the confidence of someone who knew perfectly what he was talking about.

'We're not going to encrypt our e-mails or our phone calls or whatever anybody uses to communicate with anybody else. We're going to use something that anyone can see on the web, something public with no password or anything like that.

'You're going to create a blog and you're going to make it as real as possible. I recommend you choose a topic and stick to it, like photography or flowers... anything, as long as you have a good reason to put some pictures on your blog. All the messages we exchange will be encrypted in those pictures. I'm going to give you a bootable USB key that contains encrypting/decoding software that runs on the simple operating system within the key. You can boot up any PC with this key, even one with a broken hard drive.

'Once your blog is ready, you will have to upload one encrypted picture containing the address of your blog on an online photo-sharing website called GreenCat. I have assigned each of you a name for your picture. I'm going to give you a paper containing these names as well the address of my blog. To know the address of the other blogs you will have to go to GreenCat and look for the names of pictures on your list. Then download the pictures and decode them with the software. For security reasons, I recommend you download the pictures at an internet café. Just take a USB key with you and download them somewhere other than your home. And one last thing: we never use our real names in any communication. You have to decide today which name you plan to use. If we all respect this protocol it will be almost impossible to find a link between us.'

Christoph felt the need to add, 'Don't leave the USB key at home or even in your garden if you have one. Hide it somewhere that has no legal link with you. Don't forget that something can go wrong at any time and one day police officers could come knocking at your door. Never forget this.'

Once we all understood how we were going to communicate electronically, Christoph made sure that he had the last word. For the past few hours Ralf had been the guy with the skills and the ideas, the one who made our next step possible. Christoph had been the one to show he was the boss and that none of us would be here without him. He wasn't the person with the technical ideas, but he was the one with the plan nobody dared to question.

Standing in front of us holding a piece of paper in his right hand, he outlined to us what we were supposed to do after the meeting. His long speech could be summarised into five short points:

1. Setting and testing our communication system over the next four weeks.
2. Buying the necessary ingredients to build an incendiary device. A long and delicate task that Gordon and Christoph wanted to fulfil without even giving us a chance to consider it.

3. Sending lots of fake résumés with the hope of getting interviews within the headquarters of our future victims.
4. Collecting data on our victims and then preparing the arson attack.
5. Executing the arson.

According to him we could target several companies in the next four months. He was, just like the rest of us, full of optimism. We thought that we had the perfect plan and that everything would work as intended. And that was it.

We walked out of the tiny cave as if we were leaving a parallel world. It was only once we were outside we realised how pleasant the place we had spent the past hours had been. The sunlight hurt our eyes and the heat was unbearable. Our cars were like ovens, ready to cook us. Waiting for our cars to cool down, for the first and last time, we had some small talk. For a few minutes we could believe we were a group of friends, talking about the weather, our clothes, driving in the bush… I couldn't guess that it would be our last time together. Though we were supposed to see each other as little as possible for obvious security reasons, I had the feeling that we were going to meet up many times. Sharing secrets forges bonds between people.

Even today it all sounds so unreal to me. I have trouble describing it as my first step inside a terrorist organisation. Terrorists aren't like any other criminals. They always think they belong with the good guys, that they are on the right side of history. In the name of a nation, in the name of planet earth, in the name of God, most terrorists fight for a cause, not for money. It's why terrorism is so difficult to beat. I hate violence, I hate terrorism, but I did participate in designing an act of terror.

William was right. The first misunderstanding that you're victim to is the one that you have with yourself. We spend our time lying to ourselves, to trick ourselves into not seeing the obvious, inconvenient truth. I allowed myself to get into this situation because I denied the very nature of what I was doing. Why? Probably because I denied the right of the others to be the good guys. I thought I had understood William's story, but I hadn't.

Back home, I registered successfully at Sydney University to study geology. I discovered a real interest in the discipline. I made some new friends and had something that looked like a regular life. But I was never really comfortable with what should have been my official life. I failed to be normal. I couldn't enjoy the present. The 'right now, right here' was always offset by my vision of the world. You don't party on the deck of a sinking ship. You don't want to talk about the music that's playing or about anything not directly linked to the survival of all the passengers on board. I guess I was a boring student. Probably a boring friend as well. In fact, most of my 'friends' were men who probably found me physically attractive. Most men under thirty tend to be slaves of the testosterone in their blood. Thanks to that, I succeeded in giving the illusion of not being totally alone. I just looked like one of those very few young women who don't have much to offer apart from a good-looking body. That was nothing to be proud of, but at least the illusion worked. I have to emphasise that no one from my 'official life' was ever part of my eco-warrior's life. I lied and played a role, but I never used anyone.

While the 'official Helen' was building her new life, 'Helen the eco-warrior' did her homework. I created a blog about horses. I hadn't ridden for a while, but I could chat about horses for hours. Then I took one of my horse pictures to encrypt the internet address of my blog into it. I went to one of the numerous cyber cafés that Sydney offered at the time, and uploaded my picture with the cute name of RB456567. Then I searched for the others' pictures and downloaded them onto my USB key. Everybody already had a blog. Christoph's was about fuel-efficient cars, Gordon's about cattle stations in the Kimberley, Bruce's about camping and Ralf's about pocket PCs.

Communicating this way was far from smooth and to be honest, quite annoying. To be sure to get the latest messages, I had to go to an internet café every couple of days. To download and upload each picture took time and that wasn't the end of the process. I still had to decode every single picture back home. A conversation that normally would have taken an hour by phone took a week or two with this system.

At the end of October 2002, our group hadn't accomplished anything. Gordon and Christoph had all the necessary ingredients to build an incendiary device, but that was it. We had sent eighty-five résumés, got less than ten interviews and gathered none of the intelligence that we needed. We were no spies, we were just a band of amateurs. As far I was concerned, I hadn't succeeded in getting one single interview. We all agreed that we couldn't go on like this. We needed a new plan. We needed to meet once again in the desert.

But even before we decided on a date for our meeting, I received a phone call from WUM. I had an interview at their headquarters on the 8th of November at ten o'clock. I was not allowed to screw up. It was the interview that could change everything. Every member of the group sent me his little bit of advice and reminded me how important this interview was. But the biggest pressure came from myself. It was my chance to make my contribution to the group and to target the company that I hated the most.

On the résumé I had sent to WUM, I was Anabelle Smith, applying for the position of sourcing analyst. On Anabelle's résumé everything was fake, including the address that was just an unused mailbox with Anabelle's name on it in an abandoned building. The mobile phone number on the résumé was linked to a prepaid SIM card I'd bought in a shop that didn't make a habit of asking for ID. It was, I guess, impossible to make any link with the real me. Until now, no one has. The only real problem was my physical presence inside WUM's headquarters. To look and sound like Anabelle Smith, for someone who had never once tried to be an actor, was quite a performance. I did my best to look different, to hide the real Helen deep behind lots of make-up, a red wig and some ugly glasses that covered half my face. With my cheap suit, I looked like I'd come from another galaxy. I was fully aware that I was ugly and ridiculous, but that was of course the least of my concerns. As long as I looked like Anabelle Smith and not like Helen, I was fine.

On Friday the 8th of November 2002 Anabelle Smith was at WUM's headquarters being welcomed by Stefanie Kruger, the ambitious and competent forty-year-old in charge of the company's sourcing analysts. On the way to her office, going up the stairs and along several deserted corridors, Stefanie took the opportunity to start the conversation. Unfortunately, she knew the neighbourhood where my mailbox was quite well. Far better than me. It quickly got to the point when any answer from me would have proved that I didn't live where I was supposed to live. So, I pretended to feel bad, needing a drink of water immediately. She offered me a glass of water in a nearby kitchen and then the conversation switched to the topic of dehydration.

Once we reached her office, the real stuff started. She and I were face to face, and I had nowhere to hide, a situation that seemed to please Stefanie Kruger. She gazed at me in a way that made me very uncomfortable. I had the feeling that she was reading my mind, that she knew I was fake. She didn't get to ask me any questions, though, because I threw up everything I had in my stomach, some on her desk, the rest on the blue carpet. I was in a total panic. I couldn't speak. All I wanted was to go to the toilet and put some fresh water on my face. As I ran, Stefanie just had time to tell me where the toilet was. She didn't follow me. Alone in the toilet, I was able to calm down. I said to myself, 'You have to do it. It's an opportunity that won't repeat itself. This is it. You're inside WUM's headquarters. This isn't the moment to collapse. Think about William. Think about what they did to him.'

After ten minutes of talking to myself, I thought I was ready to face Stefanie Kruger again. But once outside the toilet, I was totally alone. I had no explanation to give, no story to tell, I could go wherever I wanted. I was calm as I'd never been before. My little misadventure inside Stefanie Kruger's office gave me the feeling I had already experienced the worst part of my journey in WUM's headquarters, now was the easy part. I wasn't afraid of meeting anyone in the hallway or having to explain my presence there. More than ever I knew what I wanted. I knew why I was here. I was determined.

Now, I wish somebody had challenged my determination and shown me the exit, but nobody stopped me. I was free to go almost anywhere. I stayed thirty minutes, but I'm sure I could have stayed longer. The thing is that in less than thirty minutes I had already gathered a lot of data. From the serial numbers of four photocopiers to the name of the guy who cleaned the toilets on the second floor, I took note of everything. I left WUM without any problems and with a great feeling that I'd accomplished a very difficult mission. I was so proud. 'I did it,' I repeated a thousand times, as if to persuade myself that all of this wasn't just a dream. Stefanie Kruger called me an hour later, asking if I was better and offering me a new appointment. I told her I was fine and made out the reception was bad, so I wouldn't have to continue the conversation. I then destroyed my phone and its SIM card as Ralf had told me to.

Back home I rushed to encrypt all the data. I couldn't wait to send it to the others. The messages of congratulation came fast. Everybody was impressed by the amount of data I'd gathered. But when the moment came to explain how I'd done it, the reactions were quite different. Christoph wrote:

It is not every day that somebody throws up on your desk. It isn't the kind of thing that you forget. Right now, you are probably a source of jokes at WUM, a story that travels from one office to another. The fact that you left the building unaccompanied without saying anything to anyone is probably a detail that bothers no one right now. But when the time comes for the authorities to investigate the arson attack on WUM's headquarters, be sure that Anabelle Smith's story will be told. Have no doubt they will look for her. An identikit of her will be made and it is possible that someone will recognise you. Less than two years ago, you made the headlines nationwide. Most people have probably forgotten who you are and what you look like, but not everyone. Therefore, I think that it would be wise for you to keep your distance from the rest of the group until our mission is fully completed. Of course, if you are uncomfortable with this situation, we could give up WUM as a target. I think that it would be fair to let you have the final decision on that matter. What do you think?

I couldn't believe anyone would recognise me from an identikit of Anabelle Smith. I thought Christoph had overestimated the risk of that, probably because he hadn't seen what Anabelle Smith looked like. But most of all, I saw my experience inside WUM's headquarters as proof of my determination. It was all about my ability to calm down, regain control of myself and be ready to face Stefanie Kruger once again. I thought I'd overcome my fear, I'd been brave. I was proud of what I had accomplished. I couldn't see it as a failure and definitely not as something preventing us from targeting WUM. I wanted the data I'd gathered to be used. I wanted to feel useful. So I told Christoph and the others not to waste this amazing opportunity.

It has been the biggest mistake of my life, or as William would have probably said, the biggest misunderstanding I have ever had with myself. I could have stopped everything. I can't deny my responsibility. I am a terrorist. I remember the last message Christoph sent: *We are all proud of you. Your job is done now. Don't try to contact us before our mission is over. It is time for you to be someone other than Anabelle Smith. Get on with your life.*

I didn't send any more messages and I didn't read the messages the others sent. I waited for something to happen, just as I was supposed to do. I waited and waited… and then on Tuesday the 4th of February 2003, at 11am, WUM's headquarters were evacuated. The building was on fire, and it made the headlines on every news channel. Two hours later came the communiqué from the Earth Soldiers:

We, the Earth Soldiers, have retaliated after years of attacks on the environment by WUM. The arson attack on their headquarters is just a warning. WUM must immediately stop any project in the Kimberley or we will strike again.

I was frustrated not to have been part of the action, but it didn't offset my happiness at seeing WUM's headquarters on fire. I thought I had taken part at last in something useful, something that would bring about major change. But then, at 5pm every national news channel reported the discovery of the dead body of a twenty-nine-year-old woman at WUM's headquarters. The death of this woman, Elisabeth Robinson, mother of a fourteen-month-old girl, was directly linked to the arson. She was a freelance accountant, not even an employee of WUM. The entire country was in shock; I was in shock. The news channels broadcast a picture of this woman smiling next to her daughter, and then she was on the front page of all the Australian papers. Wherever I looked, she was there, accusing me.

The government declared war on eco-terrorism, and Bill LaFleur got plenty of media time to play the victim and to describe how much his company cared about people. 'At WUM we care about people above everything. Nothing is more precious than a human life,' he loved to say.

The death of Elisabeth Robinson overwhelmed me. I stopped thinking about all the indirect deaths caused by WUM's rare earth mines in China, about the long-term damage to wild life, the pollution of the underground water... it was all about Elisabeth Robinson. I was deeply sorry for her and I cried for the poor little girl who had lost her mother. *All of this for that* went round my head in an infinite loop.

The future didn't exist anymore; it was dead, gone with Elisabeth and William. I'd tried everything. There was no hope for the future of this planet. The environment was a hopeless cause. My life was suddenly empty. I was deep in the darkness, lost, doubting myself, no longer the eco-warrior ready to fight the whole of humanity to save life on earth whatever the cost. Alone in my apartment, unable to share what was in my mind with anybody, in a long monologue full of self-blame, I reached the conclusion that the only thing I was still able to do was apologise to Elisabeth's daughter, explain to her why her mother had died.

I sat at my computer and started to write her a letter, before I realised that none of this made any sense. An anonymous apology was worth nothing. To surrender was the only honourable thing. Spending the rest of my life in jail didn't scare me at all. I thought my life was over anyway. But my monologue to myself was far from over at that point. What about the others? How not to expose them? What should I say to the police about my accomplices? For three days, I debated those questions with myself, eating almost nothing and drinking only enough to keep me alive.

I watched Elisabeth's funeral on TV. I liked the prime minister's speech and can write it down today word for word. 'We are a free country where free speech is encouraged and protected. We are a democracy where every citizen has his word to say about the future of their country. Australia follows no other path than the one that its citizens have decided to take. As citizens we have to remind ourselves that violence in a democracy like ours can't be used to deliver a message. Violence is the tool of people who want to impose their will on others.

'As citizens of this country we should ask ourselves these questions: Do we want to listen to what people who murdered an innocent mother have to say? Do we really want to listen to people who have no respect for our freedom, our will, our opinion? Why should their opinions matter more than those of any other citizen of this country? Today I'm asking you to think about Elisabeth Robinson and nobody else. Today I'm asking you to think about our democracy and our duty to defend it, and nothing else. Today I'm asking you to join me and send a clear signal to all those terrorists by telling them once and for all that we don't care about their demands, about their way of life, about their so-called political stance.'

And just a few minutes after that came another headline. Twelve mainstream environmental organisations released a common statement:

As environmentalists, we love life in every form. We cherish it more

I didn't take the time to turn off the TV. I ran out of my
apartment.

'What I have done?' I shouted over and over. Absolutely
exhausted and suffering from hypoglycaemia, I fainted in front of
my neighbour's door. She found me after some hours and called
an ambulance.

I woke up at the hospital twelve hours later in perfect physical
condition. I didn't even have a scratch. But I remembered nothing.
I didn't even know who I was. I had total amnesia.

A psychiatrist came to see me two days later. 'My neurologist
colleagues are clear on your case. Your brain is perfectly fine. This
fact makes me think that you are suffering from dissociative
generalised amnesia. It's not due to any medical illness. It's 100%
psychological. You and I will have to see each other regularly. But
first it's important that you see your family, the people close to
you. They will play a major role in your ability to recover your
memories. They are waiting behind the door. If you don't feel
ready to see them now, it's not a problem. You're safe here.
Nobody will impose anything on you.'

I agreed to see my family. The first minutes were quite a shock.
Seeing total strangers claiming to be your family is not a pleasant
experience even if they do seem to love you. My two brothers, my
sister and my parents, they were all there. They all wanted to talk
to me, to tell me who they were and who I was. It was too much
for me. The psychiatrist, who was in the room observing us,
interrupted this strange family reunion. He and I went into

another room, a very quiet one. We talked a bit about what I just had experienced and then he suggested I see just my mother, with him present. For an hour, my mother told me the basic information about who I was. She talked to me very slowly and gently. Things gradually got better from then on. A week later I was discharged from the hospital and I was back in the family hotel in Byron Bay.

You have ten years

Two days after I left the hospital, this announcement made the headlines all over Australia:

We, the Earth Soldiers, who burned down WUM's headquarters, have a short message to deliver to all the environmentalists who support non-violent action: You have ten years. Even though your actions have done nothing to save this planet over the last few decades, we give you ten more years to succeed. After that, it will be our turn to act.

I didn't understand what it was about, just like most of the news at that time. Emerging from total amnesia, I was like an alien discovering planet earth. But ten years later I remember this little text word for word. No doubt a part of my mind knew what it was about.

We had ten years. What have we done with it?

Amnesia

Helen the eco-warrior was wiped from my memory and had left no physical evidence of her existence. She was gone. But Helen the twenty-year-old student of geology living in Sydney couldn't be ignored. She was here, with her invoices, contracts, registrations… and friends. She was one of the visible parts of my past. But this Helen wasn't me. I wasn't comfortable with her. I felt that something was missing without knowing what. My family didn't like this Helen who had ignored them for almost two years. In fact, nobody liked this Helen, not even the ones who were supposed to be her friends. And there was Helen, Miss Free Enterprise. She was the one that appeared when I typed my name in a search engine. She was the one I could be proud of, the one I could love. She fascinated me but was uncatchable, like a ghost. She seemed to only exist online. There was no trace of her in my apartment in Sydney and no one was here to tell me anything about her. It was as if she had been a parenthesis in my life. My family didn't like this other Helen either.

'She wasn't you. She was a puppet controlled by people we've never met,' said my mother.

In fact, there was only one Helen I was comfortable with. This was the Helen my family knew, the Helen who had grown up with them, the Helen who had lived in a cattle station and in a hotel in Byron Bay. This Helen was loved. She seemed to me to be the only version of me who had a future.

I gave four months for the mysterious versions of myself to come back into my memories. Four months for Helen the student and Miss Free Enterprise to become something other than total strangers. Four months to recover. It didn't happen.

The fake Helen, the student of geology, the one with the normal life, died on the 5th of June 2003. My mother and my sister helped me to get rid of her. We went together to my apartment in Sydney and threw everything away. It wasn't rational, wasn't what my psychiatrist had recommended. I wasn't supposed to kill my past, to get rid of any object that had the potential to help me to recover my memories. But it felt so good. In less than a week, I managed to remove Sydney completely from my life. I had nothing left there. No work, no apartment, nothing to study. That was it.

I couldn't get rid of Miss Free Enterprise but I could ignore her. I could start with a blank page, letting the new Helen build her new life.

I decided to restart my life where I felt comfortable, in Byron Bay among my family. With my siblings, my parents and my grandparents, I felt I was in the right place with the right people.

The new Helen worked hard at her parents' hotel. Work filled my mind, stopping me thinking about the emptiness of my memories. From early morning to late evening, I always had something to do at the hotel. From cleaning the bedrooms to welcoming new guests in the lobby, I did everything. I had no free time and that was fine. I had the feeling that my daily routine healed me. I didn't allow myself to think about anything else.

When a man called Wolf Anderson visited our hotel in December 2003, any normal woman of my age would have noticed him. Wolf wasn't the kind of man you would ignore. Twenty-seven years old, tall with broad shoulders, a sculpted face dominated by impressive green eyes that seemed to shine in contrast with his dark hair, Wolf was a very attractive man. But it's a matter of fact that I ignored him for almost an entire week. The only words we exchanged during that time were 'good morning' and 'have a nice day'.

Wolf worked as a front-end developer for a software company with most of its customers in the tourism business, so quite a lot were in Byron Bay. His company had booked a room for him in our hotel for twelve days, which were filled from early morning to late evening, giving him almost no free time. Our chances to have any kind of interaction were theoretically close to zero.

But then an entire symphony orchestra came to the hotel. They were in Byron Bay to play a kind of best of classical music concert on the beach. Three concerts were planned, three evenings in a row. My parents and I promised almost everyone in this orchestra that we would go to their concert on the first evening, so we did. Wolf did too. We didn't sit close to each other, but I noticed his presence. I loved the concert so much that I came back the next evening. So did Wolf. This time we waved to each other but didn't exchange a single word. The third evening, I was there for the last concert. So was Wolf, once again.

After the concert, I felt the need to talk to him. Not that I was attracted to him. I just had to share what I felt about that music with someone who might have the same feelings, or at least might understand me. Wolf seemed to be the right person for that, even though I didn't know him at all. So right after the concert I approached him and said, 'I didn't know I liked classical music. What about you? Is this your first time or are you a real classical music lover?'

Wolf smiled and said, 'Just like you, I really enjoyed those three concerts. The orchestra is good, and the choice of music was excellent. But to answer your question, I don't know if I can say that I love classical music. It's like saying I love modern music. You can like hip hop and hate hard rock. You can even like one hard rock band and have no interest in all the others. Classical music is full of so many different genres that I'm quite sure very few people can say they love classical music. You can say I love Mozart's *Requiem* but don't like Camille Saint-Saëns' *Carnaval des Animaux*. You know what I mean?'

That was the start of a long conversation. I told him in detail what I liked about those three concerts. He listened to me carefully and most of all, he understood what I was talking about. This understanding pushed me to tell him about my amnesia. I told him everything about my current situation and especially about those mysterious two years.

Wolf's reaction was a game changer for me. He said, 'It's not about trying to remember something but more about betraying who you are. I can't believe that you're a boring geology student. You're far from boring. You shouldn't give up on your own past choices.'

I feared that my past years were the consequence of bad choices, driving me to the point where I was a lonely student, falling unconscious at her neighbour's door. I thought my brain must want to forget something very bad. Today I can say that I was right to think that. But Wolf was right too. I had a good reason for studying geology and today I can say that it was the right path to follow. There isn't an old Helen and a new one. I made some mistakes, but I have always been the same person.

Wolf told me, many times, that through time our vision of the world changes but who we are doesn't really. Our mistakes, our bad behaviour, have more to do with a misunderstanding of the world and ourselves than anything else. Wolf sounded like William. Of course, at that time I wasn't aware of it but no doubt, somewhere in my brain, it played a major role.

Wolf is a discrete, original, one-off person. A philosopher who doesn't pretend to be one. Nothing with him is about appearance. He doesn't show off who he is, what he has done, what he knows or what he can do. After our first evening, having talked for hours, I couldn't imagine my future without him. Neither of us wanted to end the conversation, to be apart from each other. Wolf extended his stay in our hotel and I took all the days off that I could, spending all my free time with him.

With Wolf, I felt I had something that looked like a life again. Suddenly there was something more than work and my daily routine. Laughter, joy, pleasure, entertainment, *love*... all these ingredients were now in my life. I was in love with Wolf, and he was in love with me, the entire me, the full me, the old and the new Helen. He didn't hide the fact that he was fascinated by Miss Free Enterprise and couldn't believe that my life in Sydney had been insignificant.

'You're not made to have a quiet life and work in a hotel owned by your parents. It's obvious that before getting amnesia you were up to something bigger than that. You're far larger than this life. You're somebody special,' said Wolf.

The truth was that I wasn't eager to let my old self come back. I was happy. I didn't need anything more from the past. All I wanted was to enjoy the present moment. 'Forget Miss Free Enterprise. Enjoy Miss in Love,' I replied.

In February 2004, I moved to Wolf's apartment in Sydney. Almost immediately I got a job as a receptionist in a hotel downtown. I didn't have time to question myself about the choice I had just made. Everything worked smoothly. It was the start of a very pleasant life. With Wolf, I had a social life, a real life. He was able to show me the beauty of humanity wherever it was. Architecture, music, movies, theatre, painting. 'We are surrounded by beauty,' he used to tell me. With him, I couldn't hate humanity. I was at peace with my own species. I felt at peace with myself. I thought I had overcome my amnesia, that I had removed its negative impact from my life.

Environmental issues were a subject of conversation, a part of the lyrics of a song, the subject of a movie, but not the main part of my life. With Wolf, I lived in the normal world where environmental issues were not an obsession. I was one of those passengers on the Titanic just after the iceberg struck. Everybody knew something had happened but very few were aware the boat was sinking. Why not enjoy life? Why not have fun? Are Brisbane, Sydney or Byron Bay on fire? Where is the emergency? We don't see it on the streets. At night all those shiny cities are an invitation to celebrate humanity in all its aspects. Meet some friends in a trendy bar, be amazed by the performances and the beauty of the Cirque du Soleil, laugh out loud at a comedy show... The world was not dying there, it was full of life. I wasn't at war any more, I was in love.

I married Wolf in January 2005. Our honeymoon was a road trip on the west coast between Perth and Exmouth. It wasn't about playing prince and princess in some expensive hotel or resort. It was about camping in the bush and sharing an adventure together. It was also about a mission. We had with us a small plastic box designed to be a 'time capsule'. This box, totally waterproof and airtight, was supposed to keep its contents intact for more than fifty years. In it was a letter Wolf and I had written to the future us and our future children. Both of us had written our own version of our love story and what we expected from our relationship in the future.

We could have buried it somewhere in the bush and taken note of the GPS co-ordinates. But Wolf and I thought that wasn't the right way to do it. We didn't want to keep a piece of paper with GPS coordinates on it. What we wanted to keep, and maybe share with our children, was a story. This box had to be buried, like treasure. At first, we thought of burying it on top of an escarpment we could see from our camp. But once there, we saw a wide, rocky plateau with almost no vegetation on it. There was no special tree or special rock. We thought about making a cairn by collecting stones together. But once we'd done it, we realised that it was a bit too obvious, like an "X" indicating the spot where treasure is located. We wanted something special, a sign that only people who look for it can see. Something with a bit of sophistication.

Looking at the scenery from the top of the escarpment, Wolf said, 'What if we make a marker that you can only see from here? Lots of small elements that don't look anything special when you're standing next to them but make a shape when you see them from above? What about an L for Love?' From this came the idea of making an L shape out of twenty piles of rocks spaced fifteen metres apart. Each rock pile was a kind of circle one metre wide.

It took us five long days to make this L visible from the top of the escarpment. It wasn't easy to see unless you looked for it. Once we were done with it, we buried our box at the bottom of the pile that made up the L's corner. It was the achievement of our honeymoon. Our faith in our own future is still there, materialised in a small box buried somewhere in Western Australia.

'See you in twenty years,' we both said in front of the pile of rocks. The future looked bright, we were happy.

Kyoto Protocol

I n 2005, my life seemed to be on the right track. I had what seemed to be all the ingredients of a happy life. I had a fantastic husband, a loving family, lots of amazing friends, a job that I really liked... everything was fine on the upper deck of the Titanic, but I had arrived at the point where I couldn't ignore any more that the ship was sinking.

2005 was the year when our prime minister, John Howard, reaffirmed more strongly than ever his government's opposition to the Kyoto Protocol. It had been signed by 141 countries and was the first baby step on the long journey to fight climate change. It was more about starting a process than accomplishing anything. The Kyoto Protocol was full of flaws but had the advantage of existing and being agreed on by many.

But our prime minister saw things differently. He told Southern Cross Broadcasting, 'The reason I won't ratify the Kyoto treaty is: the existing Kyoto treaty doesn't cover countries like China, and we could be at a competitive disadvantage.'

The president of the United States of America at that time, George W. Bush, had used the same kind of rhetoric, saying that he was opposed to the Kyoto Protocol because, 'It exempts 80% of the world, including major population centres such as China and India, from compliance, and would cause serious harm to the US economy.'

It was about promoting an ideology based on the false dichotomy that you couldn't protect the environment and support the economy at the same time. As if letting China and India burn coal, like the US and Europe had done for the past hundred years, was going to give them a serious competitive advantage. Coal, the energy of the nineteenth century, emitting polychlorinated dioxins, hydrochloric acid, oxides of nitrogen, fine particulates, heavy metals like mercury and of course tonnes of CO^2. Air pollution produced by coal combustion in power plants can affect the respiratory and cardiovascular system as well as cause abnormal neurological development in children, poor growth of the foetus before birth, and can cause cancer. What sort of competitive advantage is that? How does it make sense for rich countries like the US or Australia to burn coal? Is it economically wise to damage your environment and endanger your own population when you could do otherwise? Should we burn coal just because China and India do?

Global warming and the protection of the environment in general isn't about costs or competitive advantage. It's about our future on this planet. Global warming is probably the greatest moral challenge of our generation. Why had somebody as clever as John Howard, someone who had proved his ability to consider environmental issues over the past decade, come to this point? Why was his party, defenders of entrepreneurship and the free market, so eager to defend the coal industry, this old and obsolete part of our economy?

I didn't have answers and I was really disturbed by that. In my head, the Australian Liberal Party represented too many people to be ignored or simply despised. My need to understand what was going on in this party quickly became an obsession that I couldn't explain, even to myself. I had no interest in the Greens or the Labor Party. I had no interest in the people who shared my opinions. I needed to confront the people I disagreed with. I had to get out of my comfort zone, to test my own limits, to see what kind of environmentalist was sleeping inside me. I needed to feel who I really was.

So I became an active member of the Liberal Party. I went to every meeting, reading all the documents available, meeting as many people from the party as I could. I wasn't there to hide who I was. On the contrary, I was looking for myself. I used to be Miss Free Enterprise, someone who claimed to be a Liberal, someone who seemed to be comfortable in front of the cameras. I tried to be her, just to see how it felt. The day I had the opportunity to deliver a speech in front of an audience, I didn't hesitate.

It was the 14th of May 2005, a Saturday afternoon. The Sydney University Liberal Club had invited all the young Liberals of Sydney for their annual speech workshop. For most young Liberals, this was an event you could easily skip, but for active members who planned to have a future in the Liberal party, this was a big deal.

As a new member, I wasn't really the kind of person who was expected to come to this workshop. In fact, I belonged in the category of members who were least expected. Unlike most of the participants, I wasn't a student at Sydney University and had absolutely no liberal culture. I was a complete ignoramus, the kind of person that needed to read *The Liberal Party for Dummies*. At every meeting I apologised for my ignorance, reminding the people around me I was the former Miss Free Enterprise, the young woman who was trying to remember who she used to be. Nobody expected me to be a leader or to play a major role within the young Liberals.

The speech workshop took place at Sydney University in the David Harland seminar room. There were forty people in a room that could have welcomed at least another twenty. Grey carpet, grey fake ceiling, white walls; this rectangular unimpressive room was full of grey chairs and grey tables, all aligned in the same direction. Nothing seemed to have been modified for the workshop. Everybody was seated as if a regular course was about to take place.

At the beginning, it really looked like a course. Harald, around sixty, short and overweight, wearing an expensive black suit that fitted perfectly with his ego, taught us the right way to write a speech and to read it in public. Harald claimed to have written many speeches for high-level liberal politicians. He was the one who knew everything about speeches. Everyone in the room seemed to venerate this guy with his chubby round face. I hated him from the first word he pronounced. You could tell he was in advertising. We weren't talking about sharing ideas or ideals but about reaching a target. What I hated the most was the way he described the audience. 'They will remember less than 10% of your speech. A few sentences, maybe a slogan. But no more,' he repeated over and over. For him the electors were a band of idiots who never read the manifesto or policies of the party they voted for. Winning an election was all about communication.

'People don't vote for the best. They vote for the one who appears to be the best. A speech is like a song. You don't necessarily need good lyrics to have a summer hit. It's all about the right vibes at the right time. I want you to write your speech like a pop song. I don't care about the profound meaning behind what you say. Put one or two sentences in my head that I won't forget in the next five minutes. Give me a hit! You want me to dance and have a good time!'

I didn't want him to dance. I refused to bring politics down to a good slogan. I wanted to write a speech that was Politics with a capital P. I dared to protest, to question the big master, the God of the speech. I heard almost the whole room snigger. What I was doing seemed to them an act of extreme stupidity. One of them said, 'Did you understand what this workshop is about? It's all about communication. If you want to have an ideological debate you're in the wrong place.' Then two more tried to explain how wrong I was, but Harald interrupted them.

'I remember you. You're Miss Free Enterprise. You were yourself a pure object of communication. Without you saying, "free enterprise" you wouldn't ever have made the headlines and I wouldn't remember you. Whether you like it or not, politics has a lot to do with communication and you're the very last person in this room who can deny it.' He continued teaching us about the art of the speech.

I didn't interrupt him a second time. I hated what I had just heard but I couldn't yet express it in words. I was still looking for the Helen that I used to be, waiting for Miss Free Enterprise to somehow rise from my inert memories. I couldn't have been just a slogan. It wasn't me.

If I hadn't been able to write a speech that sounded like it came from Miss Free Enterprise I'd probably have left the room very quickly. Staying here meant hearing lots of insignificant speeches that Harald never seemed happy with. No one had fun or seemed satisfied with his own work. I was. I could have waited my turn for ten hours if I had to. I felt very satisfied. I didn't know who I had been, but I knew in great detail who I was. It was as if my amnesia didn't matter anymore. When my turn came to read my speech in front of everybody, I showed my confidence with a big smile. I was proud of my speech even before I pronounced the first word of it. I didn't care about Harald's opinion or how the audience reacted. It was all about being fully myself. I didn't remember Miss Free Enterprise but I felt I was her. My speech was her speech. That Saturday afternoon, she and I were reunited. Her words were my words.

'As a liberal, I imagine a world where the state is limited to the minimum and taxes are as low as possible. Free enterprise should be our everyday slogan. Let people do business and make this country richer. The taxpayer should pay just for the basic functions of a central state like justice, health, defence, and so on. This means a world where taxpayers don't have to pay for the environmental damage done by companies. A free world is a world that can take care of itself. Every company should take care of the damage it does. Not the state, not the taxpayer. A free market needs responsible actors so that there is no need for a strong state. A good economic system should be able to grow and be sustainable. In other words, a good economic system should take good care of the environment. Air, water and ground pollution have a cost.

'By not taking care of our environment today, we create the taxes and disruption of tomorrow. Renewable and sustainable are the two magic adjectives for a long-term healthy economy. Environmentalism doesn't belong to the left. As a concept, it doesn't belong to people who think central government should control everything. On the contrary, I believe true environmentalism belongs to people who want to empower individuals. We are those people, the ones who trust citizens more than a central state that decides for all of them.'

These last words attracted everyone's attention. I was watching them watching me. I folded the piece of paper on which my speech was written as an act of defiance against all those people who'd been trying to tell me what a speech should be about. For hours,

I'd been listening to their hesitation, their lack of passion. Now it was my turn to give them a lesson. So I continued, gazing at each one of them, my eyes supporting every single word that came out of my mouth.

'I know lots of you think a green economy means extra costs or complications for business. But what kind of economy are we living in? Is our current system stable and sustainable? The answer is no. The way we produce our energy and the way we manage our resources will get us into trouble soon. So yes, I do understand that oil is cheaper than any kind of renewable energy but is oil a sustainable source of energy? Is the future made of oil or coal? Are we still in the nineteenth century? Nobody believes that coal is the future. Nobody believes that the future of cars has any link with petrol or internal combustion engines. Is it reasonable to base our economy on those old technologies, those sources of energy that endanger life on our planet? Does all of this make any sense? I don't think so.

'We're supposed to be the flexible ones, the ones open to new ideas, the ones supporting innovation and entrepreneurship. We're the political party of the start-ups, not of the status quo for the benefit of a few big companies. We don't believe in state intervention because we hate those bureaucracies, those governments that limit individual initiatives. This vast coal industry, coming from the past, unable to evolve into anything else, is a perfect analogy for the heavy and bureaucratic state, killing innovation, any initiative to bring any kind of change.

'The green economy, the economy of tomorrow, is very disruptive, just like the industrial revolution was in its time. It requires us to change everything, to invest a lot of money in new technologies but the potential for return on investment could be phenomenal. Why do we let people think that this green, sustainable, innovative future belongs to the left? Why do we let the people see us as the ones who defend the status quo, good old coal? In 2005, we should be ashamed of even saying the word coal. It's time to get the future back on our side. It's time to get environmentalism back into our vision of the future and not let the left create a world where environmentalism is a pretext to bring more state control into our economy.'

Almost everybody applauded, except Harald. His gaze expressed the same disapproval he'd had for all the other speeches. Once the applause stopped, he said, 'You played Miss Free Enterprise once again. It won't work all the time. You shouldn't trap yourself into a character.'

'I didn't play a character. It was 100% me. I meant what I said. I didn't play any role,' I said with confidence.

'You did play a role. What we've just heard is one of Miss Free Enterprise's speeches from 2000. I remember you because I studied your case. In 2000, you played a role written by William Brotsky for the John LaFleur Organisation. He was a talented guy when it came to writing speeches. I am sorry to say this, but at that time you were just his puppet. I'm quite disappointed to still hear his words coming from your mouth. This workshop is about helping you to write good speeches, not to recite speeches written by others years ago.'

'Bullshit! It's all bullshit! I don't know what your problem is but your little story doesn't work, because due to my amnesia I can't remember anything before 2003. What you've just said is full of shit!' I said with an aggressiveness that I have never expressed before. Harald, undisturbed, responded calmly.

'Helen, all Miss Free Enterprise's speeches are on the internet. You can insult me as much as you want, it won't change the fact that your little speech today had a deep taste of déjà vu. But if you really are suffering from amnesia, I suggest you investigate Miss Free Enterprise just as I did. Have a look at the pictures the various media took of you in 2000. Have a close look at them. Look for the Indian woman in the background. She's almost always there. Her name is Salima Gunning. Today this woman is the head of the John LaFleur Organisation. I think it would be interesting for you to contact her. But now, I think it would be good for everyone that you leave. Your aggression isn't welcome here and I can't say I'm a big fan of the John LaFleur Organisation. I believe in political parties, not in strange underground organisations.'

I was stunned. Salima Gunning. Those were the only two words in my head. Why didn't I know about her? Was all this true or a product of Harald's sick mind? I left the room without saying a word, ignoring the eyes that were scrutinising me.

Back home, I did a search for all the pictures of Miss Free Enterprise. The Indian lady was there, almost always behind me in the background. Picture after picture, the same silhouette, the same gaze. Salima Gunning. I typed her name in every search engine on the internet and I always found the same picture on the website of her law firm. This was her. There was no doubt. Now nothing was more important than meeting Salima Gunning, the woman who had known Miss Free Enterprise, this mysterious part of myself.

A quiet militant

On the morning of the 6th of June 2005, I called Salima's law firm. 'My name is Helen Flowers. I'm an old friend of Salima.' A few seconds later, Salima was on the phone. 'I'm so happy to finally hear from you, Helen.' It was that easy.

Two days later, I sat next to her in her office. Salima was very nice to me, acting like an old friend. She had only positive words to describe what I'd done and who I'd been before my amnesia. In her story, I was a great person who fitted in perfectly with the John LaFleur Organisation. She didn't mention the fact that I had cut any contact with her in 2001. According to her, I was a peaceful student of geology, looking forward to becoming an active member of the John LaFleur Organisation. It was the kind of fairy tale that I needed to hear, it made me feel I was on the right track. I hadn't got my memory back, but I felt I had a past once again.

Meeting Salima soon became a necessity in my life. My amazing private life with Wolf and my great friends weren't enough to make me happy. Not in this dying world. I wasn't made to be a spectator. I was, and I am still a militant. Salima did more than tell me what kind of environmentalist I had been, she gave me a purpose, a cause to fight for.

As if time had made a four-year jump, Salima reintroduced me to Lenny Bedford, the now sixty-year-old old geologist from the heart of the Kimberley who I'd already met in 2001. The story hadn't changed, Salima hadn't changed, Lenny hadn't changed, but I had changed or, should I say, my vision of the world had changed. Without any past, you're like a small kid discovering the world. You don't judge; you observe, you try to understand this new world that surrounds you. Nothing is evident, you want to understand why things are as they are. When you're four years old, you're still a tourist, discovering a brand new world, seeing no normality, no self-evidence in anything that surrounds you. You want to know why the world is like it is. Whether something has been as it is for one minute or for two millennia makes no difference to you. It's only the 'why' in either situation that's relevant.

The new Helen was better able to understand the world because she was free of any kind of prejudice. There was no past to filter my views. So, when I met Lenny Bedford and heard once again about his mining project in the Kimberley, my reaction was totally different from in 2001 when I had met him for the first time. A rare earth mine in the Kimberley owned by the native Njarinjin of the region didn't seem at first sight to be exciting for an environmentalist, but it did make a lot of sense. By having their own project, the people of the region could prevent anything coming from the big mining companies.

'We can't stop the rare earth of our region being extracted, but we can be the ones in charge. We love our region. Nobody can protect it better than us,' said Lenny, after telling me what was at stake. But in 2005, just like in 2001, Lenny wasn't at the head of a company exploiting a mine in the Kimberley. He first had to win a legal battle against WUM who claimed to have exclusive rights to rare earth extraction there.

It was a matter of fact that WUM was the company that had discovered rare earth in the region in the first place. Without Lenny's intervention, WUM would have long had a mine at the heart of the Kimberley. Lenny's fight was a noble one. I don't know why I didn't understand it in 2001. Maybe I hadn't understood that his project was the only alternative to WUM's presence in the Kimberley. It's always important to understand the world that surrounds you before you even think of changing it. In 2001, I had the arrogance to think that I knew the world. In 2005, I knew that I knew nothing.

I didn't become a noisy militant going to demonstrations, distributing flyers or going to meetings. I became a quiet militant, updating Lenny's internet blog or helping him to feed his YouTube channel. I wasn't impatient, I didn't expect immediate results. I accepted how slow a long legal battle could be. I had changed. I wasn't Miss Free Enterprise or an angry eco-warrior. I wasn't a full-time militant obsessed by the cause. I had a real, private, happy life with a husband I loved, and that changed everything.

Spending time with Lenny and Salima soon made me want to be more than a hotel receptionist. I was fascinated by their expertise. I could have followed Salima's example, studying law, but I thought that geology made more sense. It was a fresh attempt to reunite the old Helen with the new one.

Wolf supported this idea. 'You shouldn't give up on your own past choices,' he always said. So I re-registered at the university. In September 2005, I was officially once again a student of geology.

. . .

There followed years of happiness when I had everything you can dream of. A great husband, a great family, some great friends, a cause to fight for, and the chance of one day having a very interesting job. I have nothing to confess about this period of my life. Nothing else that needs to be shared.

Tadarida

In April 1999, WUM had conducted an unauthorised two-week reconnaissance near the Tadarida escarpment in the Drysdale River National Park. The company's chief geologist, Christian Toledo, who knew the region quite well, had suspected for many years that the area contained large deposits of rare earth. Geological maps, rock samples, geophysical and geochemical surveys – everything pointed towards it.

In June 1999, WUM applied for mineral rights. The Liberal government in Canberra gave a positive answer, defining the potential presence of exploitable rare earth deposits on Australian soil as a great opportunity for the Australian economy.

A legal and ideological battle began between the federal government in Canberra, backed by the government of Western Australia, and the Kimberley Land Council, an Aboriginal political land rights organisation. It was all about who was entitled to award WUM the mineral rights to the Drysdale River National Park. The Kimberley Land Council, concerned by environmental issues, was totally opposed to any mine in the Drysdale River.

For six long months, the Kimberley Land Council did its best to demonstrate in court that no mineral rights in the National Park could be granted by the federal government, since it was surrounded by Aboriginal land under the control of the Kimberley Land Council. Besides, the Council pointed out that allowing mining activity in any part of the Drysdale River National Park would change the status of the area. The question was then: can a mine be considered part of a national park? For the Council, it was clear that the moment a part of the Drysdale National Park became a mine, then this area could be claimed as Aboriginal land under the Aboriginal Land Rights Act. For the Kimberley Land Council, the Wanjina Wunggurr Wilinggin people were the rightful owners of the entire area. A claim on that matter had already been filed in the Federal Court.

In December 1999, the Federal Court suspended the mineral rights that had been granted to WUM in the Drysdale River National Park, arguing that the case clashed with a claim of native title rights filed by the Wanjina Wunggurr Wilinggin people. Though WUM hadn't yet lost its mineral rights in the Kimberley, this was seen as a victory for the Kimberley Land Council and the environmentalists.

This court decision irritated the federal government, who considered rare earth minerals too strategic to be simply left untouched in the Kimberley subsoil. The interest of the local community couldn't override the national interest. In January 2000, annoyed by the attitude of the Kimberley Land Council and by the recent court decision, the government threatened to pass a law that would forbid any landowner to refuse rare earth mining on his land. The government gave a six-month ultimatum to the Kimberley Land Council to come up with a solution. For many commentators and experts of that time, there was little doubt about the determination of the government to pass the law.

In March 2000, Lenny presented to the Kimberley Land Council his idea of creating a mining company, owned by the native people of the region who would operate the rare earth mine within the Drysdale River National Park. At first the Council refused the idea. Many members thought it would be giving up everything they had fought for. But as the months passed and the deadline set by the government drew closer, Lenny's idea seemed more and more reasonable. But it wasn't till June 2000 that the Council took the decision to support Lenny's project.

In July 2000, Lenny and two members of the Kimberley Land Council founded Tadarida Inc., the first mining company owned by the native people of the Kimberley. The company, with the support of the Kimberley Land Council, immediately claimed its rights to exploit the subsoil of the south-eastern part of the Drysdale River National Park near the Tadarida escarpment. From that moment, the long dispute began between WUM and Tadarida Inc., the two companies claiming to own the same mineral rights in the same area. This was the moment when the John LaFleur Organisation came to help Tadarida Inc., both financially and legally.

'Without Salima and the John LaFleur Organisation we would have had no chance of beating WUM,' Lenny said. 'It was too complicated and too expensive to fight alone against a huge company like that. They had an army of lawyers exploiting every single loophole in every document that we produced. And they fought us in the media and online, trying to find any way to strip us of our credibility.'

For more than six years, I witnessed Lenny's strength, never giving up, never losing hope. I doubted we could beat WUM. The work I was doing on the internet for Lenny wasn't enough to compensate for what WUM was doing. They spread rumours and fake news about Tadarida Inc., stuff we couldn't stop. But in December 2012, Tadarida Inc. beat WUM in the Federal Court. It was the final victory, the one that Lenny had been awaiting for more than twelve years.

Lenny didn't waste any time. At the end of December 2012, he recruited his first employee, planning to start exploring at the beginning of the dry season in April 2013. Banks were ready to finance Tadarida Inc.'s expenses as long as the company demonstrated its credibility. It had to show it could deliver. The first exploration needed to happen fast and be successful, bringing in the important data everybody was waiting for.

Meanwhile, Tadarida Inc. had to deal with the opposition of environmentalists who didn't want to see any mine in the Drysdale River National Park. For them we were the bad guys, the polluters who were destroying one of the world's most beautiful national parks. I have to confess I wasn't comfortable with that, even if I did believe that Tadarida was the best way to preserve the environment in the region. Tadarida was the story of a compromise. There was no passion, it was all about pragmatism.

Lenny always told me to welcome the critics. 'We don't want to do the wrong thing,' he said. 'None of us ever dreamed of digging a mine in the middle of a national park. So, if there's one single good reason to not do this, I want to know about it. If there's another way to stop WUM coming here, then I'm ready to support it. It's good to doubt now, because it's still not too late to stop everything. The past twelve years, Tadarida was just words on paper; that was the easy part of the fight. But now, everything is going to become real. The biggest challenges are ahead of us.'

Facing reality, that was all the exploration was about. There was no better reality check than this. This was what Lenny feared the most. It was strange to see a guy like him show so much doubt. He was the guy who had spent the past twelve years trying to persuade anyone he met that Tadarida Inc. was the solution. He was the guy who seemed to know what he was doing.

But in March 2013, while I was spending my last months at university preparing a thesis on rare earth, Lenny invited me to join his exploration team. He confessed he needed someone on his side who understood the deep meaning of what this project was about. 'When we're there, in that beautiful landscape, there have to be at least two people who know why it makes sense to build a mine there. There's nothing pretty about a mine,' he said.

I didn't mind facing up to the reality of this project. On the contrary, I wanted to experience it. This exploration at the heart of the Kimberley was the ultimate test of all the theories in my head. I needed to know if I was the kind of environmentalist who could focus on the big picture and not spend all her energy on the small details. Lenny's project was about to give the native people of the Kimberley the financial means to protect their land. The rare earth mine was the detail making it possible… at least in theory.

In the Kimberley

I remember the 8th of April 2013 very well. It was a Monday. Early in the morning, around 6am, Lenny and I, and another geologist called George, were at Sydney airport. An hour later we got on a flight to Broome. Five hours after that we arrived in Broome. The airport was quite small, and the terminal looked like a big house with palm trees all around. Roger, the pilot of our next flight, was waiting for us at the terminal. He told us we should hurry because we had to reach Wyndham before nightfall. He said, 'I don't have a jet plane and Wyndham airport isn't equipped for night landing. In fact, I don't know what this airport is equipped for!'

So here we were, in a small plane, a Cessna 172. The flight was noisy and bumpy, and Roger never stopped talking the whole time. His favourite subject was horse racing. Roger claimed to be the president of the horse racing club and he pretended to be an important person in Wyndham. Listening to him, I imagined Wyndham was a big modern city with an airport, a harbour and a hippodrome. In reality the population of Wyndham is around eight hundred and the airport looks like a place where a Cessna 172 might just possibly be able to land without any damage.

What Roger didn't tell us about was the beauty of the landscape around Wyndham. On one side were the Cockburn ranges, a spectacular sandstone escarpment that stretched for kilometres. On the other side, a flat area with some boab trees and burned grass that looked like gold in the light of the setting sun. Then a many-coloured estuary came into view. Far away was the blue of the sea; closer, the brown water of the estuary. On either side of the estuary the dry brown earth was cracked into a billion pieces. Then we saw a flat zone with no trees and almost no grass, just red dust and thousands of small red rocks. In the middle of this was something that looked like an old road. Roger said, 'Wyndham airport straight ahead! Be ready for landing!' The landing was a bit bumpy, but we got down all right and at the end of the landing strip three Aboriginal men were waiting in front of two Toyota four-wheel drives, fully equipped to drive in the real outback.

The three men, John, Keith and Dwesmond, none of them more than thirty years old, worked for Tadarida Inc. Lenny knew all of them very well. None had studied geology or had any experience in the mining business, but Lenny had trained all of them in exploration techniques and they had a very precise idea of what they were going to do with us. But most importantly, they were all very experienced outback drivers.

That day we didn't have time to get far from Wyndham, but we still spent our first night in the bush. There wasn't much opportunity to talk. We needed a good night's sleep before the long journey waiting for us over the next two days.

We hit the road at 6.30am, enjoying the pleasant fresh air of the early morning. An hour later we were on the Gibb River road, facing the Pentecost River and a vast area with almost nothing in it except spindly trees and spinifex, or triodia, a kind of grass that you need to keep away from. From a distance it looks green and inoffensive but, if it pierces your skin, its leaf tips can break off and lead to infection. We crossed the river without any difficulty and had a smooth ride until the junction with the road heading to the Home Valley station. After that point, the dirt road was in very bad condition. The ruts were shaped like waves, making the ride really uncomfortable. Before noon we reached the Kalumburu road, which was in even worse condition than the Gibbs River road. Then we had to drive very slowly indeed.

Three hours later we reached the Silver Valley road, heading to our final destination of the day, the Silver Valley cattle station. The thirty-five-kilometre road had been damaged by the previous day's rain so our speed never went over thirty kilometres an hour. Sometimes it was easier not to drive on the road at all. Our drivers were experienced. They knew it was stupid to try to rush in those conditions.

It was after sunset when we finally reached the Silver Valley station. The full station team, about fifteen men and women, was eating out in front of one of the bunkhouses. They were all very friendly and I talked to most of them, but I couldn't tell you their names or what they looked like or even what we talked about. It was dark, and I was very tired; I didn't really pay attention to anything. All I wanted was to go to sleep. But there was one person I did notice. This was an Aboriginal man of around sixty with long hair and huge snake tattoos on both arms. I had the feeling that I knew him. I asked him if we knew each other.

'No. But you do look like an old friend I haven't seen for a long time,' he said. This didn't satisfy me. His face, his voice, awoke something inside me. Something that I couldn't describe or understand. It was there in my head, disturbing me, but I couldn't translate it into words. Totally exhausted by our journey, I couldn't think any more.

We all went straight to bed after a very quick meal. The next morning, Lenny pushed us, giving me no time to think about anything. He didn't want to waste any daylight. We had another long journey ahead of us. At 6.45am, we were ready to hit the road, or I should say, the grass, rocks and streams. All morning we drove through the bush, sliding among the trees, checking for rocks on the way. We went at about the speed of a horse walking at an average pace. Our goal was a huge grassy plain on which we hoped to drive faster. At noon, we still hadn't reached that plain.

We didn't get to our destination till 5pm. We were in the middle of a flat plain with a few small trees about ten metres apart. Between the trees was a bit of high grass burned by the dry season, not enough to cover the red earth and billions of small stones wearing their cloaks of red dust. On the eastern horizon, big escarpments ran up to a high plateau. Those escarpments were the only relief in the flat landscape that surrounded us. After five, the low sun, blowing a yellow-orange light over the red earth, made those trees and brown grasses look like gold. With no wind, this scenery was static, like a gigantic picture. It was beautiful. Once again, we were exhausted and none of us was eager for conversation. We busied ourselves setting up the camp and making dinner. At eight we were all in our tents, ready to sleep. My mind was busy thinking about the man I thought I had recognised at the station but that night the fatigue won once again.

The next day at 5.50am we were already on our way heading north-east, approaching those escarpments. The path got rockier and rockier, making our progress very slow. Before noon, we were between two huge escarpments, in a kind of rocky valley between two plateaux. After two kilometres, the valley started to look more and more like a gorge. We were only 500 metres from the escarpment now.

Keith, who was driving the car I was in, said, 'On the map this gorge looks like a dead end. What the hell is Lenny doing?' We stopped for lunch in this impressive gorge, canyon, valley… even geologists like us couldn't decide what to call this rocky formation. It was a dry mineral desert where even the toughest species of grass had trouble surviving. There was absolutely no wind, and the fifty-degree heat was really difficult to handle. Keith, John and Dwesmond spread out a topographic map on the bonnet of one of the cars, trying to figure out which way to go.

'Put that map away,' Lenny said right away. 'I know exactly where we're going. One of my closest friends explored this area with WUM. He told me everything. Not far from here we should find a path going up to the plateau. Our cars can handle it. Let's go. I want to get to the other side of the plateau before nightfall. There's a nice spot to camp there.' After a forty-minute drive, we finally reached this natural path. It looked almost like a road going up the side of the escarpment.

Once on the plateau, we found much greener vegetation with small trees and grass almost everywhere. It got more and more dense, making it difficult to drive through. The trees got closer together until we were in something that looked like a forest of very special palm trees. Keith said they were similar to the species you see on the Mitchell Plateau, 100 kilometres from where we stood. We couldn't go any further with the cars, but Lenny didn't seem surprised. 'We camp here tonight and tomorrow we'll walk to the end of this plateau to do our first exploration with the spectroradiometers,' he said.

We set up our camp and had dinner. That evening, it was the same story. I was disturbed but not to the point of being obsessed by this disturbance. Something was there in my head, but it didn't go as far as the next level. I slept almost normally.

The next morning at 7.30am, we were ready to penetrate the mysterious palm tree forest, with our lunch and spectroradiometers in our backpacks. It was dense, but not like a tropical rainforest. There was enough space to walk. Lenny said the best way to see it was on the back of a horse.

Then we heard the sweet sound of water. We found the stream and followed it until we reached its end. From there, the stream became a beautiful hundred-metre-high waterfall, filling a freshwater rock pool surrounded by a green carpet of thousands of different kinds of vegetation. The pool down there was at the far end of a green gorge, its source was a stream of water, filling pool after pool. We walked a kilometre along the top of the gorge, admiring its beauty, until we reached the end of the plateau.

From there we found a path to take us safely down a hundred metres. Once off the plateau, we were on a plain filled with grass and beautiful boab trees. The grass was so high and so dense that it was exhausting walking through it. The plain was enclosed by massive escarpments all around it, except for two places where streams ran between two different canyons. We were in the middle of two great plateaux. Our destination was the one in front of us with massive 200-metre high cliffs.

At the bottom of this plateau we used our axes and spectroradiometers for the first time. We spread out along a one-kilometre line, each making our own measurements and notes even though the whole area appeared to be geologically uniform.

After our long journey, Lenny did his best to make this day as relaxing as possible. We had a lot of breaks, a long lunch and a half-hour nap in the shade of a cave. There were plenty of opportunities to go over things in my mind. Partial memories came back to me, like pieces of a massive and complicated puzzle.

None of the pieces seemed to fit together. But the nap in the cave was the point of no return. Here were thirty minutes in the middle of the day with nobody to distract my crazy brain. This was when I realised that I knew the man I'd seen at the station; it was Gordon. I had memories of him though I couldn't clearly say who he was.

The day was over for me. I couldn't do anything. My mind was one hundred per cent focused on those memories. My hands were shaking, my legs hurt and my heart felt close to exploding. Lenny noticed immediately that there was a problem. It took me a while to make him understand it wasn't anything physical. It wasn't about the heat, a spider or snake-bite. It was my memories coming back in a big mess. Lenny helped me get back to the camp. I talked to him the entire afternoon, describing all the blurred pictures, the strange sounds that I had in my head. What I said probably didn't make any sense, but Lenny was a good friend. He took care of me that day. I needed someone to listen to me. When the night came, when my crazy monologue had to stop, he gave me his MP3 player and his big noise-cancelling headphones.

'It's time for your mind to go on a little journey,' he said. 'On my MP3 player I have hours of beautiful classical music. Music from heaven. It's going to help you feel better, I'm sure of that.'

I went to my tent, put the headphones on and pressed play on the MP3 player. *Das Wohltemperierte Klavier* by Johann Sebastian Bach, Mozart's piano concerto no.23, Handel's *Lascia Ch'io Pianga*... hours of beautiful music that almost succeeded in calming me down. But then came Fauré's *Requiem*. I recognised it immediately. I remembered listening to it in my room in Byron Bay. I remembered William giving me the CD. I remembered William's story. I remembered everything. My amnesia was completely gone.

It was like waking up from a ten-year dream. It was far from pleasant. I didn't like what I remembered. The positive parts of my past didn't offset the negative ones. Over the last ten years I had fantasised almost everything about my past. My imagination had built up a positive image of myself. I woke up, not from a nightmare, but from a very nice dream, to find myself in a darkly disappointing reality. Nothing made sense any more. I was in total panic, unable to stay still. I needed to move, get out of the tent, to be away from everyone.

I left my tent and walked into the bush without thinking about where I was going. All I needed was to walk. If nothing had stopped me, I could have walked all night and been completely lost. I wasn't scared. I didn't listen to all the little noises around me, or to the dark grey scenery in front of my eyes.

But this didn't last. Fear is a strong feeling that can easily overcome all the others. Normally, I wouldn't have been afraid of seeing a horse in the bush, but not in that context, not in the middle of the Drysdale River National Park. Not in the middle of the night. What I heard wasn't the sound of one horse coming towards me, it was at least five horses following each other. I stayed still, making no noise. I wanted to hear every sound. I had done enough horseback riding during my childhood to recognise most of the little sounds a horse makes. I had no doubt these horses were wearing horseshoes. And there was this other noise, a leather noise. These horses were, without any doubt, saddled. Some people were out here riding in the middle of the night, right here in the Drysdale River National Park, far from everything.

I was terrified, unable to do anything except keep quiet and hide behind a tree, still as a stone. They stopped ten metres away, close enough for me to be able to hear them murmuring. I couldn't understand what they were saying but it was crystal clear that they wanted to be discreet. Thousands of thoughts crossed my mind at that moment, trying to figure out who they could be and what they were doing here.

But the answer came soon enough. I heard them getting down from their horses and getting rifles out. My father had a rifle at our cattle station. I knew that sound very well. They came closer and closer. Now I could understand what they were saying. There were five men. They weren't here to hunt. They were here to murder us, the whole exploration team. It didn't take me too long to understand that. There were two names and two voices that sounded more than familiar in my head: Gordon and Christoph were here, a few metres from me, holding their rifles.

I can't describe what went on in my head in those few seconds when they were standing right next to me. I understood the situation perfectly, but I was unable to make a move. It was like a part of my brain was switched off. I could have talked to them, slowed them down, giving Lenny and the others time to see what was happening. I wasn't just anyone. Gordon and Christoph knew me. I had a real chance to talk to them, maybe to stop them. I don't know. It was only when I heard the first shot, the first cry, that I came to. I shouted Gordon and Christoph's names. But it didn't stop the rifles. Hearing more cries and more shots, I ran towards the camp. I wasn't rational. I'd been so terrified that I was unable to move a few minutes before, and now I was running towards the danger, looking to face the aggressor.

But before I even reached the camp, the cries and the shots stopped. Everything was suddenly calm. Torch lamps were scanning the camp. I stopped running, slowed down, trying to make as little noise as possible. Then I heard Gordon saying, 'Helen! We know you're here. You have nothing to fear from us. You're one of us.'

Then silence. Nobody was moving. The torch lamps were still scanning the area. I didn't see Lenny or the others, but it was obvious to me that it was too late to help them. I was now the prey, the one those lights were trying to catch in the middle of the bush.

The adrenaline had switched my brain to its most basic mode. It was focused on right now, right here. Second by second, they were getting closer to me, reducing my chances of escape.

I didn't think too long before running. I just ran as fast as I could. I didn't know if they were behind me or not. All I thought about was their horses. I knew where they had left them. They were my only chance of escape. I didn't think about the fact that one of them might have stayed with the horses. It was my only plan and I couldn't think of another one. Thankfully, they'd left their horses alone.

I got on the first horse I found and left as fast as I could. After ten minutes of galloping on terrain I didn't know and without looking behind me at any time, I let my horse rest. Standing still for a few minutes, I looked around me, listening out for any unusual noise. Nobody seemed to be there.

I rode all night, following an imaginary straight line, to give myself the feeling I was going somewhere, far away from this madness. At dawn, I allowed myself a pause, something my horse probably appreciated. I took the time to check inside the saddle's pocket, looking for something that could help me with my journey. Unfortunately, I couldn't find a satellite phone or a satellite navigation system. All I had was a sleeping bag, a flashlight, a pair of binoculars and a one litre-bottle of water. Not really enough. Of course, I could easily survive without eating for a few days, especially with a horse carrying me, but no more than two days with only one litre of water. Besides, my horse needed to drink as well.

The good news was that the Kimberley is full of streams, rivers connected to each other. Finding one of them was more than finding water; it was like finding a route. I wasn't from this region, but I had studied enough maps of the area, including satellite pictures, to have an idea of which river I had to find to make my way out of here. I didn't know how to get back to the Silver Valley station but I did know how to cross the Gibb River road. It was at least a 70-kilometre journey, but with a horse it was not impossible to do it in two or three days. A stream, a river, was all I needed to find. I knew I was east of the Drysdale River and that it crossed the area from south to north. So, by going west I had to cross it sometime. The only problem was that I didn't know how far I was from it. Ten kilometres would be all right but thirty could be lethal. I needed to be lucky.

All morning, hour after hour, I saw the same landscape. The same dry grass, ready to be ignited by the smallest spark. All those small trees, metres apart, no use for shade but giving you the illusion you're in a place where there is water. They are so green, and the ground so dry. This was not a desert, not a savannah, not a tropical forest either. This was something in between.

At noon there still was no river in sight, not even the least trickle of a stream. On the contrary, the landscape looked less green and more mineral. Rocks, more and more, replaced grass and trees. At 2pm I really started to get worried. I was facing a space of cracked earth so big that I could see no end to it. In the middle was a large rock with trees on it, looking like an island in the middle of a dry lake. No doubt this place would look like a lake during the wet season. It must be beautiful then. But now it was the end of the dry season. The water levels were at their lowest everywhere in the Kimberley. I stayed there, in the heat, for at least ten minutes, thinking that maybe this time this was it, this was the end of my journey. But that thought didn't last too long. With the heat, my brain probably wasn't working as well as it should, but I was still able to think rationally. A place that could collect so much water must be connected to several streams. I followed the shore of this dry lake and after only half an hour I heard the sweet music of water finding its way through the rocks. It was a very small stream coming from the top of a fifty-metre-high plateau that was only twenty metres from the dry lake's shore. My horse and I drank all the water we could drink. I decided that was enough for the day. My horse and I were exhausted. We needed to rest.

I'd survived the night and most of the day, but I was still in danger. To get out of here alive was one thing, not to be found by Christoph, Gordon and their accomplices, was another. I needed to do more than look for water, find food and head west. I had to look around me constantly, be prepared to run away at any time. At the bottom of this plateau, I couldn't see anybody coming. Anyone could surprise me at any time. So, I went up to the top of the plateau with my sleeping bag and my bottle of water. I was very hungry, but I wasn't in the mood to look for food, especially with my lack of skills. I wanted to rest in a place where I would feel safe. On the plateau, I could see for kilometres around on a 180° angle. If somebody came, I would have enough time to get away.

All day I had dreamed about the cool of the night. I thought everything would be better at night, but when it came, things didn't turn out as expected. The previous night, I had been running away. Strangely, I hadn't felt an easy target then. But here, on this plateau, immobile on a lump of rock, I felt vulnerable. I needed to observe my surroundings, to be attentive to every noise. The problem was that by night it is, of course, far more difficult to observe anything. Any noise sounds far more suspicious at night than during the day. At night, your imagination replaces your eyes, and keeps you alert.

But that night it was reality that made the headlines.

At 11pm a bright light appeared several kilometres away. It wasn't the kind of light that comes from a truck or a car. It was like there was a city just a few kilometres away. It was so spectacular, so incredible, that for a few minutes I thought I was dreaming. But it was real. I hadn't dreamed it. I needed to know what it was. It could be my chance of survival. I had forgotten to take the binoculars with me, so I walked down to fetch them from the saddle pocket.

The problem was that I used my flashlight for this little walk. I made my presence obvious hundreds of metres away, to not say kilometres. Back on the plateau, using the binoculars, I still couldn't tell what the source of the light was. I watched it for half an hour, paying attention to nothing else, not realising that far closer to me a weaker light was shining in the middle of the dry lake. When I finally noticed it, my heartbeat reached a record high. And when I took the binoculars to look more closely at it, I thought I was going to have a heart attack. There were two flashlights on the ground lighting something written on the cracked earth: *HELEN*.

It was probably done to scare me, to push me to panic. As if they were saying, 'Hey, we're here, looking for you. Please make some noise, don't stay calm, don't stay hidden in silence.' It worked perfectly on me. First, I panicked. Again, I had this strange idea that it was safer to move than stand still. My greatest fear was losing my horse. To leave this area without him and without any food or water would be seriously problematic. I needed to keep him, at any cost.

I left the plateau and saddled up as fast as I could. Once on my horse, I had a little moment of hesitation. I had one choice to make. Going back to the dry lake or going on the top of the plateau? I didn't hesitate too long. God knows what was on the other side of this plateau. A cliff or a gentle slope? I had no clue and I didn't want to find out in the middle of the night. To go back to the dry lake was risky but at least I knew what to expect in terms of landscape. Besides, I thought that the dry lake offered the advantage that my horse could gallop safely if necessary.

Riding a horse by night without using a flashlight is of course totally different from riding during daylight. You and your horse are more attentive to each other, interpreting any movement, any sound. The advantage is that your horse is likely to react more quickly to any directions you give him than during the day. The down side of this is that the smallest signal can have big consequences. A slow pace can become a fast gallop at the wrong time. I had to be fully in control. My brain, my body, still exhausted from the previous hours, had to give it everything it had. I was close to my limit, close to making a stupid mistake. My horse walked slowly, but of course not silently, masking a lot of the surrounding noise, including the sound of somebody coming in my direction.

Every couple of minutes I stopped to look around. Night-time in the bush isn't like at home. In the wild, especially in a dry landscape like this, you can always see something. But beyond five metres you're not really seeing, you're guessing. Among those small trees, those rocks, everything looked suspicious.

Then I heard a horse neigh 200 metres behind me, maybe less. It was very difficult to say. But it was close. My own horse neighed too. Horses like to talk to each other, they always do that. A few seconds of silence, then I heard several horses trotting, heading in my direction. I didn't move straight away. I couldn't see them, and I concluded they couldn't see me either. I wanted to know where they were coming from before I decided what to do. A wrong move could have terrible consequences. But suddenly they stopped. They were probably looking for me, listening for any sound coming from my direction. I didn't move, trying to keep my horse as still and silent as possible, but with horses, you're never really still and silent. I could tell they weren't far from me;

probably a hundred metres. It was difficult to guess the number of horses or see their outlines from such a distance. The moment I picked up the binoculars, I heard the horses start walking again. I asked mine to walk too. It seemed we were all going at the same pace. However, slowly but surely the nature of the sound changed. I could still hear horses walking but the sounds weren't coming from the same direction any more.

There was going to be a chase. It was a question of minutes. I knew I had to be a bit clever if I wanted to survive. Go to the shore and hide behind one of the small trees in silence or gallop straight across the dry lake? I quickly concluded I had to do a bit of both. I needed to be on the move, keeping my distance from them, and I needed trees, rocks, hills, escarpments. I needed to be a shadow among the shadows, a confusing sound reflecting itself onto the escarpments.

I had to leave the comfort of the dry lake. They were close. I had to gallop to get rid of them, but I had to go where it was risky, where the ground wasn't flat and safe. I had to trust my horse. I had to take that risk. I hesitated.

But then they came. Their horses galloped fast. I saw them – they saw me.

'On the left!' one of them said. I turned away from the lake and pushed my horse as fast as he could go. Every step on this rocky ground was ten times noisier and more dangerous than the dry lake. We soon found ourselves on a rocky slope that grew harder and harder to climb. My horse was exhausted, he couldn't gallop any more, he fell and I fell. He lay on the ground. I didn't know whether he'd be able to get up again or not. There was no time to find out. They were here, just a few metres away. I ran as fast as I could, going straight up where the slope was steepest. No horse could follow me there. I climbed until I reached the top of the hill. I was more than exhausted; I had difficulty breathing. But I couldn't stop. I could hear them behind me. I went as fast as I could, but I knew I couldn't win this race. I had to stop, to hide myself somewhere.

On my right was a rock at least five metres high. In normal circumstances I would never have tried to climb it, and especially not at night with no flashlight and no food in my stomach for over twenty-four hours. But when your life is at stake, so much more seems feasible. Besides, I didn't have lot of time to think. I climbed up as fast I could, giving it everything I'd got. I nearly fell three times, but I didn't give up. I was on the top by the time they thought of walking all around the rock to look for me.

They kept calling my name and Christoph shouted, 'We don't want to harm you, Helen. We just can't leave you alone. We have to leave this place together. You're one of us. Stop denying who you are. Your amnesia didn't erase who you are. It can't have.'

They were there an hour, scanning the area with their flashlight, looking for me everywhere except up the rock. I'm not sure any of them could have climbed that rock. I still don't know how I managed it. Before they left, Christoph gave me a last opportunity to show myself.

'This is your last chance to save your life, Helen. We're going to leave and then you will be alone here, with nothing. Soon the sun will rise. It will be hot. You will be thirsty first, before you get hungry. You have five minutes, Helen. Not a single minute more.'

I knew I had no chance of survival here. But this time, I didn't want to be Christoph's accomplice. I didn't want to go back to the past. Just remembering it was already painful enough. I knew which side I was on. I stayed on that rock for more than an hour before I thought about leaving. *What I have done?* I asked myself.

But then I saw the bright light on the horizon again. This time it seemed closer. I thought I could walk there. What was it? I didn't know. I took into consideration that the light might have something to do with Christoph and his team, but I had a feeling that was not the case. It was simply too bright for people travelling with horses and wanting to be discreet. This was like an industrial light. There must be a lot of people there. I made a way down from my rock and walked in the direction of the light. I walked all night without a break. Walking in daylight wasn't an option. I had to get to my destination, wherever it was, before sunrise, before it got too hot.

At dawn, I was still nowhere. There was no bright light on the horizon to lead me. I just walked straight ahead hoping that at some point something would appear. Then at last, in front of me like a mirage, I saw vegetation so dense it was difficult to pass through. There was water here, I was sure of it. I accelerated my pace as fast as I could, like a kid that can't wait to open his Christmas present. Step by step, the sound of a waterfall got closer. I descended a slope that became steeper and steeper until I stood in front of a beautiful natural pool, dominated by a fifty-metre-high waterfall. I laughed, and shouted, 'Thank you, God!'. I was happy, even if my stomach was still empty and my chances of survival were still very slight. I hadn't even noticed that I'd been walking east all night, making my future journey back to civilisation even longer. I was just happy to be out of the danger of dying of thirst.

I was drained. My body had used up all its reserves and my strength was ebbing. I lay down beneath a tree, at last able to relax. Here in the shade and with the sweet music of the waterfall, nothing really mattered anymore. I could close my eyes.

Aisha

I opened my eyes. It was night-time. I could feel the cold air moving on my face, but the rest of my body was comfortably warm, covered by what seemed to be a sleeping bag. Under my head, I could feel the softness of a pillow. For a few seconds I thought I was dreaming. 'Maybe I'm dead. I'm waking up in paradise,' I told myself. But then a sound attracted my attention. Someone seemed to be moving plastic boxes around. It was close. Five metres away, not more. It was here behind dense vegetation, where artificial light was glowing. I stood up and walked through the vegetation, heading to the source of the light.

The scene seemed surreal. A woman, fortyish, looking middle-eastern or Arabic, was having dinner, seated at a large wood table. There was a cave nearby, which seemed to be her home. Everything was positioned for a long stay: a bed, a kitchen, a portable toilet and even a laptop that lay on a large camping table.

'Here you are! You woke up at the perfect time. Have a seat! I made dinner for both of us,' said the woman with a big smile. It was a bit too much for me. Barely awake, I kept still and stayed quiet. The woman stood up, took my right hand and led me to the table. 'Everything is fine. You are safe here. Have a seat. You are probably hungry,' she said in a very soft voice. Once I was seated she said, 'My name is Aisha, by the way. And you are…?'

'I'm Helen. We need to call the authorities. They killed the entire team… they wanted to kill me… Where is your satellite phone? We need to call the authorities now. Call them now. NOW!' I said, suddenly overwhelmed by my recent memories. Neither thirst and hunger, nor anything else related to my direct survival was keeping my mind busy anymore. The door was open for all the rest. Confusing memories were free now to take up all my attention and throw me into a state of panic.

'Where's your phone? Where is it?' I repeated over and over, each time more aggressively. I found her absence of reaction suspicious. I was here, shouting at her that people had been murdered, but she was impassive.

'Calm down, Helen,' she said in her soft voice, annoying me even more.

'Something is wrong. You're one of them, aren't you?'

'I don't know what you're talking about, Helen. Please calm down.'

'Where is your satellite phone? Tell me where it is and then I'll calm down.'

'I have no satellite phone. I'm sorry, Helen.'

'It's impossible. How can you live here without a satellite phone? Why are you lying to me?'

'I'm not lying to you. I'm here to experiment with total isolation from the outside world. My colleagues will be here in four days. But before that no contact is possible with anyone who isn't physically here.'

'What kind of bullshit is that?' I stood up and searched the entire cave, looking for a satellite phone or any kind of long-range radio. I opened all the boxes, moved everything that could be moved. I couldn't believe that someone living in such comfort in the middle of nowhere could not have something as essential as a satellite phone. Aisha didn't move at all while I transformed her place into a complete mess. Once I was done, she got up and stood next to me.

'You see. I didn't lie to you. I don't have a satellite phone or radio transmitter. I do understand that you've experienced something terrible. You have the right to panic or to be confused. But you do need to calm down. You need to tell me what happened and where it happened so then we can figure out what we can do. So please have a seat.'

She and I sat at the table. She offered me something to eat and then guided me through my story, asking questions. She didn't let me digress or skate over the chronology. She asked a lot of questions, making it hard for me to hide the truth.

'You just said that one of the aggressors is from this region. How do you know that?' she asked.

'It's a long and complicated story,' I answered before crying, 'What have I done? What have I done? It's all my fault. What I have done?' I shouted. Then came the moment when I felt the need to tell everything. I had to tell the story that had been wiped from my mind for ten long years. I needed to speak, to let it out. I really wanted to hear someone telling me what I had done. I wanted to be judged.

For three long hours, I told Aisha everything. She listened carefully. I wasn't disturbed by the fact she was a complete stranger. On the contrary, I think it helped me to feel free to speak.

Once I was done, Aisha said, 'You don't sound like a bad person, Helen. Far from it. I do believe the world would be better if it were full of people like you. Indifference is what's killing this planet. You are the opposite of indifferent.'

'But I could have stopped Christoph and the others years ago. People died because of me.'

'I know it's going to be hard for you to believe, but I do know what you're experiencing right now. I went through that too. I've had a complicated life. I'm not going to tell you my own story right now; it would bring you more confusion than anything else. But I do want to share with you what's been the cure.

'I wrote my memoirs, as if I was telling the story of my life to strangers. Doing that gave me a perspective on my own life that I'd never experienced before. Writing your own story is far more powerful than just telling it orally to someone. It's like watching your life from the outside. And trust me, it changes everything.'

'Thank you for your advice, but I doubt that you ever thought people had died because of you. There's no cure for that.'

'I used to think that my sister and her husband died because of me. Trust me, your life isn't more complicated or disturbing than mine. But we'll continue this conversation tomorrow. A few hours ago, you were alone in one of most remote places on earth, with nothing more than the clothes you were wearing. Look where you are now! It's a miracle. Right now, that's the only thing that should be occupying your mind.'

Aisha insisted on giving me her bed and refused my help when it came to clearing up the mess I'd made. 'You are my guest, Helen,' she repeated, many times. It was all so disconcerting I found it hard to believe any of it was real. I thought maybe I was in a coma, having a strange dream, probably the last one of my life.

Once in Aisha's comfortable bed I told myself that if this wasn't a dream, if I wasn't in coma, then yes, I could say that it was all a miracle.

'It's a miracle,' I murmured, before closing my eyes and falling asleep.

Day one

―――――――――

I opened my eyes. I was fine. I'd slept well, the sun was up, the air was warming up and the waterfall nearby was playing its lovely music. Aisha was already about, preparing breakfast. It was nice... for a few seconds. Then reality made a comeback. This wasn't a peaceful morning in one of the most beautiful places on earth. Lenny was dead. His entire exploration team had been murdered. Some people, my ex-accomplices, were after me. It wasn't a nice morning. It couldn't be.

Yesterday's questions were still there. Nothing had changed. I couldn't accept the idea that I was stuck here for the next four days. I couldn't believe Aisha had no means of communication with the outside world. So, we had the conversation once more. Aisha remained totally calm. She invited me to search the entire cave again, allowing me to open all the boxes, all the bags... everything. There was no phone. Then the conversation resumed.

'Helen, you have only two options. The first one is to walk to the closest station. It could take you four to six days. I have all the gear here you need to do that. But, I have to warn you, it won't be an easy hike. The second option, probably the most reasonable, is to wait here until my colleagues come in a helicopter. They will be here in four days. Four days here to think calmly about your future, or four to six exhausting days walking through the bush. You decide,' said Aisha in an appeasing voice.

'It's not about my future. It is about stopping Christoph and his band. People have died! It's not about me. I have to stop them.'

'How are you going to stop them? By telling the whole truth? Then you won't only stop them – you'll stop yourself. As I just said, these four days could be useful for you to think about what comes next in your life.'

'There is nothing to think. I am a murderer. I could have stopped these people ten years ago. I don't want to think. There is nothing to think. People died because of me.'

'No. They didn't. You're confused because you're only focusing on little bits of your life. You don't see the big picture. Yesterday you told me about this arson. But what happened before? What led you there? Definitely not craziness. You did follow a path. Your life probably makes more sense than you think, and you're probably not who you think you are. You're not a murderer, Helen. So, let's start at the very beginning; long before that arson. Have you always been an environmentalist?'

I didn't answer the question. But Aisha insisted.

'Do you think your life would have been better if you'd never become an environmentalist?'

I didn't respond.

'Who would you be if this world weren't so self-destructive?'

I didn't respond.

'Do you really think that you're here because you're a criminal?'

'It doesn't matter who I am or why I'm here. I've failed in everything I've done. Who cares about the intentions? At the end of the day, only the results matter.'

'A little more than twenty years ago, my sister killed herself. For months, I blamed myself, ignoring the complexity of the truth. I thought I knew everything until someone asked me to describe in detail what had happened. Not just part of the story, but the whole thing. What was my life like through all those years; my childhood, my relationship with my sister? What were my dreams? Everything.' Aisha paused for a few seconds, staring at the empty blue sky.

'It isn't only about what you do or how you do it, it's also about the context you do it in.' Aisha paused again. She gazed at me, seeing that she'd got my attention at last.

'You know what? Let's go up to the plateau. It's a great place to tell you a bit more about… all of this.'

We packed our breakfast in a backpack and took two folding seats and a small camping table with us. The path to the top of the gorge was challenging, giving me no time to think about anything, apart from the right here, right now. The top of the gorge was a flat mineral world devoid of any vegetation, offering a stunning view in every direction. We walked few minutes until we reached the eastern edge of the plateau and installed our table and two chairs just two metres away from the cliff. In front of us there was a vast plain where boab trees thrived. On the distant horizon, there was an escarpment, drawing the limit of what we could see.

Once we were set up, Aisha didn't grant me a single second of silence. She probably didn't want to leave me alone with my own thoughts. Watching the horizon, she said, 'I'm from Saudi Arabia and when I was a kid I loved it when we went to the desert. Our parents, like many Saudis, liked to drive far away from the city to enjoy the nice fresh evenings. In the desert the temperature drops right down at night. You don't need air conditioning. All you need is a comfortable tent.

'But I didn't enjoy the desert because of its night temperature.

Facing a vast horizon, clear of any kind of human presence, just like here, made me feel good. It was the only place I felt free. There I could do whatever I wanted. There were no religious police, no strangers, no neighbours, no one to remind me that as a female, I had no rights. I loved to run as far as possible from our camp and then remove my headscarf and feel the wind in my hair. I shouted, sang, danced, lay down on the sand, ran for long minutes… There I experienced a complete freedom.

'Once the sun had gone down, the desert had something more to offer to me. There was this glow, a hundred metres away from our camp. It was the light coming from my uncle Amin's tent. He'd been in Australia for years and he wasn't like a normal man living in Saudi Arabia. He was tall and thin, always perfectly shaved and he wore elegant clothes – he looked like a British explorer. My father used to call him Lawrence of Arabia even though he had no idea of who Thomas Edward Lawrence was. Divorced from an Australian woman, and with no kids, my uncle Amin didn't feel comfortable in Saudi Arabia and so he visited us only twice a year, and he always pitched his tent a hundred metres away from the rest of us.

'During the day, my parents did their best to stop me talking to him. But at night, they couldn't stop me running towards the glow coming from his tent. Listening to Amin's words made the world far larger and brighter. I loved to hear him talking about his travels around the Pacific in his sailing boat, or about astronomy, describing the great somewhere else above our heads. With him, I learned to look further, beyond the horizon, dreaming not only about the great somewhere else but also about the great tomorrow.'

Aisha paused for a few seconds. 'The future.' She sighed. 'In Saudi Arabia, women have just one possible future: to be an obedient wife and the mother of many children. Dreaming about alternatives to such a future is in itself a challenge. We women don't have freedom of movement. We can't meet who we want when and where we want. Men decide almost everything for us.' She sipped at her tea and remained silent a few seconds.

'I have four brothers, all younger than me and with whom I share almost nothing. Boys learn very rapidly in Saudi Arabia that they can dominate the girls, that their future is far more open than ours. Though my parents taught them to respect their sisters, they always liked reminding us what our place would be in the near future. I hated that and always liked to show them that I was physically and psychologically stronger than they were. I was three years older than my oldest brother, so as long as they were under twelve, they were manageable. But in the end, with the help of my father, they always had the last word. A sister couldn't be allowed to dominate her brothers. My father wouldn't accept that. The lesson was more for my brothers than for me. "Don't ever let a girl have the last word!" he told them in front of me. I always protested and was always reprimanded. But thank God, I had a sister. Two years older than me, Naima was the eldest and somehow the jewel of the family. Everybody loved her, especially me. Whatever happened, she was able to smile at the right time and make me feel better. I was the rebel who complained about everything and received absolutely nothing. She was the smiling girl, obtaining everything she wanted in any circumstances. God had given her more than a permanent smile. She was physically beautiful. "The kindness and the beauty of an angel," my father used to say when he talked about Naima. She wasn't the tall, thin kind of woman you see in the fashion magazines. She had a generous, well-proportioned body and a lovely round face with beautiful, glittering blue eyes. She was the physical expression of kindness. Just by watching her, you wanted to hug her like a teddy bear.

'She made everyday life bearable. She was the person I could talk to and she was always there to calm my father down when he was angry at me. With her, everything seemed all right. She had this optimism that was very close to naivety, shining like a lamp in the middle of darkness. For years, I refused to see the reality, to admit that her optimism, her "joie de vivre" would reach its limits one day. She was my sunshine, but for Saudi Arabia she was a weak candle burning its last reserve of wax. The angel of the family couldn't escape her fate as a woman living in that country.' Aisha drew in a long breath.

'Unfortunately, our father was an ambitious and successful businessman who had made our family extremely rich. We had enough money to live very comfortably for the next two hundred years without the need to work, but for my father, who had no other purpose in his life than to get richer, what we had wasn't enough. He wanted more, always more. Naima, the jewel of the family, the one that no man could resist, had only one possible future: marry a very rich man. So one day our father returned home with a twenty-three-year-old man called Nasser, the son of another rich businessman. Naima smiled at Nasser, as she would have done with anyone else. She barely exchanged a few words with him before being invited to leave the room with all the other females present. A few days later our father met Nasser's father and then it was decided: Nasser was going to marry Naima. "Even their names sound good together," said my father, full of joy. Naima couldn't help being optimistic about it. I wasn't.

'I was going to lose my sister, my daily sunshine; this couldn't be good news. What I didn't know yet was the fact that Nasser was a violent and disrespectful person who was totally incapable of kindness. My sister was his trophy, his good-looking piece of meat, nothing more. The expensive wedding with its two thousand guests had more to do with public relations than the celebration of a union between a man and a woman.'

A strong wind blew for a few seconds, stopping Aisha from telling her story.

'It happens a lot here. During the dry season, it lasts just a few seconds but during the wet, you don't want to be here. Where did I get to? The wind confused me.'

'The wedding.'

'Ah yes! The wedding… It was spectacular but then, after that, nothing. And when I say nothing, I mean that I didn't have any contact with my sister. She didn't visit us. She was gone. She wasn't a part of my life any more. I was alone in this insane world. Without her, life at home was unbearable. I had an argument with my father almost every day. I spent most of my time jailed in my own bedroom. My father, who told me many times that he'd had enough of me, made it clear that the only way I'd get out of the house was to get married. For me it meant only one thing: get out of Saudi Arabia as soon as possible.

'Such a thing was unimaginable without the help of my uncle Amin. Without any money, no passport and unable to drive a car, my chances of escape from that country alone were close to zero. So, I waited and waited until Amin visited us. Once in the desert, it wasn't my uncle who immediately attracted my attention, but my sister. She was there with Nasser and their army of servants. She wasn't shining anymore; she looked sad and weak. She didn't need to say anything to make me realise something was wrong. As long as the sun was up, it was impossible for me to even think about approaching her. Nasser's parents were there, and my father didn't want any dramas in front of them. During dinner, although I was ten metres away from her, I kept staring, trying to make eye contact, but she seemed to be somewhere else, as if she'd been drugged. It was only after dinner, when all the women had been invited to go into the tent reserved for them, that I was finally able to talk to Naima.'

Aisha took a deep breath. 'Naima… hmmm… she wasn't a little light in the darkness anymore. She was now part of the darkness. Those days when she had been the jewel of the family, the one nobody could say no to, were gone. She didn't shine anymore. She was Nasser's wife now. He beat her, he'd raped her several times, he talked to her like he would probably do to an animal… her life was hell. But she was here, talking about it all, as if it were a normal topic of conversation. My mother and three aunts were here, giving her advice about how to calm Nasser down. "How can you accept such a life?" I asked her loud and clear. "You aren't married. You can't understand," answered my sister, in unison with my mother and my aunts. It was a nightmare. I couldn't believe that my lovely sister, the queen of kindness, could tolerate being treated so badly. From my point of view, Naima was dying and needed to be rescued. But don't be mistaken into thinking you know where this story is going. My sister didn't kill herself in Saudi Arabia. She did it here in Australia. But telling you only what happened here in Australia wouldn't make any sense. The truth is a long and complicated story. What I've just told you is the beginning of what I wrote in my memoirs.' Aisha stood up.

'I wrote my memoirs as if I wanted it to be published. As if I wanted the entire world to understand what had happened. As long as your memories are trapped in your mind, they remain confused. They're like the pieces of a puzzle that your mind only allows you to look at one by one. But once your memories become words, sentences, paragraphs, chapters, then you start to see the big picture. It took me some time to realise that everything had started with that.' Aisha pointed to the horizon with her left arm.

'Me, watching the vast horizon, looking for the somewhere

else. A book about my life couldn't start any other way. What about you, Helen? How would you start your memoirs?'

I did answer this question. I did search through my memories, to where my journey had started. Just as for Aisha, it had to do with a landscape. The gidgee trees, the golden grass, this plain that seemed to have no end… my grandparents' cattle station. And then WUM came… It all started from there.

'Write all of this down before you bury it somewhere in your subconscious,' Aisha said while I was describing the landscape of my childhood to her.

Back in the cave, Aisha gave me her laptop and I started to write. It felt good to think about that distant past and to transform it into words. It was exactly as Aisha had told me. It was like doing a puzzle. My memories were in small pieces. Alone, none of them made sense. But together in the right order, forming sentences, paragraphs, chapters… suddenly everything became clear.

I wrote the first thirty pages of the memoirs that first day. It was magic. Everything was clear in my head. My life story wasn't as complicated as I had imagined. Everything, through its imperfection, made sense. What a feeling!

Only hunger and thirst stopped me writing that day. Lunch was quick. Aisha let me eat in front of the computer, doing her best to not interrupt my writing. At dinner things were different. By then I was eager to talk about what I had written. From the little girl in Quilpie to 'Miss Free Enterprise', there was a lot to tell and Aisha had lots of questions. Our conversation went on for two long hours until I said, 'What about you, Aisha? How long did it take you to write your memoirs? How many pages?'

'It took me one night to write it. I was sixteen. I didn't have much to tell.' Aisha paused, staring at her glass of water.

'It wasn't far from here. Just few kilometres east, on the top of a hill… My God, I can remember every single detail of that night.'

'What were you doing here?'

'To answer this question I have to tell you the rest of my story. Let's go back to the top of the gorge. There's no better place to tell you a bit more about me. I love drinking tea at night up there.'

Once on the plateau, we sat once again on the east side, a few metres away from the cliff. Aisha glanced up at the starry sky as if she was looking for something.

'The starry sky always makes me think about my uncle. He's millions of points of light glowing in the dark sky. He's the light that leads you to tomorrow. And he always had his head up at night, watching the stars. "You belong to the generation that will walk on Mars," he said to me when I was eight, watching the red planet for the first time through the telescope he'd brought to the desert.' Aisha smiled and was quiet for a few seconds, then she stared at me, covering my left hand with her right.

'There are some great people on this planet, Helen. Some great people. Never let yourself feel overwhelmed by mediocrity. Always look for the light glowing in the middle of the night.' Aisha removed her hand and stared at the horizon as if something was going on there.

'My uncle Amin had always told me he'd help me leave Saudi Arabia whenever I wanted to. That day had come. My life in Saudi Arabia had become unbearable. But I couldn't imagine myself leaving Saudi Arabia without Naima. I couldn't leave her. Giving up on her was like killing a part of myself. I couldn't let an angel become the slave of the devil. It couldn't be like that. Not in my world. My uncle Amin wasn't against the idea of helping Naima even though he'd never had a good relationship with her. Once he said to me, "Naima sees the future as an extension of the present, as if the future has something to do with current reality. I don't see it that way. The future is a dream where everything is possible. Human history is full of achievements that previously seemed impossible to reach." For my sister, Amin was someone who had failed to build a family, a dreamer who couldn't accomplish anything in the real world. She was so wrong.'

Aisha sipped her tea. 'All my life, I had wished to leave Saudi Arabia. Not Naima. Every time I brought up the idea she said she wanted to stay in Saudi Arabia. She didn't like the idea of leaving everything behind and being away from our family. But despite everything she said, I couldn't believe that she was fine with Nasser. I couldn't believe she wanted to stay with him. For me it was totally unimaginable.

'Amin hadn't told me how and when he would help me leave Saudi Arabia. The only thing he said was, "I'll take care of everything. I promise you'll be out of this country in the coming months." He kept his promise. I can never thank him enough for that.'

Seeing me watch a plane twinkling high in the sky Aisha paused for a few seconds and said, 'That's the Singapore-Perth, operated by Qantas. You can observe it every evening. I know. It feels strange to be here and to see this little piece of the outside world flying over our heads. You're stuck here and those people up there will be at Perth airport in just a few hours.'

Yes, it did feel strange. But that feeling was soon replaced by another one. I felt sorry I'd interrupted Aisha's story by staring at that stupid plane. 'So, how did you leave Saudi Arabia?' I said to push her to continue.

'My last hours in Saudi Arabia…' Aisha took a big breath.

'It was in the desert. A big family reunion like the last time. Everybody was there except Amin who had chosen to stay thousands of kilometres away in Australia. There was no sign that anything was going to happen. On the contrary, everything had the feel of a déjà vu. I hadn't seen Naima for three months and I hadn't been able to have any kind of contact with her, but the expression on her face showed her situation hadn't changed.

'During dinner a servant, a young woman of around twenty, whispered to me while she was filling my cup of tea, "This is the night. Look for the glow at 1.30am." From that moment, my attention was on two things only: my wristwatch and my sister. I had just a few hours to find a way to persuade Naima to come with me. The problem was that I didn't know how I could have a private conversation with her. At a family event like that, you're never alone.

'I waited and waited for the right moment, but it didn't come. At half past eleven, Naima was in her tent with her husband. I thought it was all over.

'At twenty past one, I was outside: I was ready to leave. Just ten little minutes and that was it, I was going to leave this country. But there was Naima's tent, just ten metres away. The light was on and I could distinguish my sister's voice. I thought maybe this was the chance I'd been waiting for all evening. Maybe now, right at the last-minute, I'd have a chance to talk to my sister and help her leave with me. I had ten minutes. That's all I needed. So I walked towards the tent. I stood at the entrance, trying to understand what I was hearing. Heavy breathing, stifled crying, the sound of skin on skin. I didn't want to do anything to compromise my escape. I knew it wasn't really the moment to be impulsive.' Aisha paused and sighed before getting up.

'I can't tell you any more without moving. I can't stay still. Are you alright if we have a little walk?' I welcomed the idea of moving a bit. The nights are cold in the Kimberley and standing still for too long can be uncomfortable. So we walked, and Aisha continued her tale.

'I don't know how long I stayed in front of that tent. I don't know. But what I do remember perfectly, like it happened just a few hours ago, is the agonising voice of my sister saying, "Please stop". I glanced quickly at the horizon. There was a glow. This was it. It was happening. Our chance to get out of there. My chance to rescue my sister, to get her out of this nightmare. So, I entered the tent. I wasn't there to have a conversation but to end something.'

Aisha turned away and covered her face with her hands. I could hear her breathing heavily. I asked her if she was OK. After a few seconds of silence, she removed her hand from her face, took a big breath and answered me in a trembling voice, 'I'm fine.'

'Are you sure?' I asked.

'I'm fine. I'm fine,' she said, in a voice that this time seemed more confident.

'My sister was half naked on the floor. Her face, her lovely face that once smiled all day long, showed only suffering. It was unbearable. I didn't think. I jumped on Nasser and started beating him with all the strength and energy I had. I gave it everything and I managed to free my sister. Now he focused on me. It took him less than a few seconds to turn things round. Lying on top of me, he hit me in the face. Stunned, I wasn't able to react. He started to undress me, to touch me… and then there was a loud noise. I remember him howling. A second loud noise. He howled so much. I could feel warm blood running on my chest. He tried to stand up. A third noise. A fourth. A fifth. He collapsed on the floor. The only thing I could hear then was my sister breathing. I got up and saw her holding one of those awful gold candelabras that were everywhere in the tent. She stood there still and silent. One branch of the candelabra was covered in blood. Still stunned, I stayed quiet and motionless for a few seconds, hardly able to understand what had just happened. When I saw Nasser lying on the floor in a pool of blood it was like an electric shock. Then my mind focused on one thing. Get out of here with my sister as fast as possible. I said to Naima, "We run away now, or we die here." She didn't respond. I grabbed her clothes from the floor, took her by the hand, and led her outside.

'Nasser's howling had woken almost everybody up. We could hear people coming. I said to Naima, "run towards the glow over there as fast as you can." She ran with me, giving it everything she had. We reached the source of the glow in less than five minutes. Two people were waiting for us there; Fatima, the young servant who had told me about tonight and Jamal, a young man who turned out to be our driver. Both were Saudis like us, and wanted to leave the country. We just exchanged names and that was it. We weren't really in the mood for a chat.'

Aisha gave me a little push with her hand on my back, signalling it was time to resume our little walk.

'We drove for four hours through the desert and on narrow deserted roads. No one said a word until we reached our destination. It was a small beach. A woman was waiting for us next to a rowing boat. Around thirty, this athletic woman spoke to us in English with a French accent. "Get on the boat and be quiet," she whispered to us. This Frenchwoman, Anne-Marie, rowed for fifteen minutes without interruption until we reached a beautiful twenty-metre-long sailing boat flying a French flag. On board, a man who looked about thirty and also had a French accent, introduced himself briefly. "I'm Laurent and this is my ship, *Trégastel*. Here, I make the rules and I expect you to respect them. Right now, the most important rule for you to respect is to stay inside the cabin. As long as we're on the Red Sea, you don't come out. This is for your own safety."

'Unable to do anything and totally exhausted, we should have slept. But our minds were too busy for that. I didn't know how, but I felt a great need to say something to my sister. This silence between us was terrible. It had to end. I wanted my sister back.

The one with the smiles. The angel who had made my life in Saudi Arabia bearable. I wanted her to feel that she was a good person, that she'd done nothing wrong. Nasser was the monster, the bad one who should have been haunted day and night by his own crimes. Naima and I should have been happy together on this boat. We should have celebrated our journey to freedom. "You saved my life, Naima, more than once. You're my angel," I said, trying to catch her eye.'

'She looked away from me. "When you came into that tent, you ruined my life. You pushed me into doing something that nothing can repair. Everything's gone. You made me a fugitive. You brought disgrace on our family." She shouted, "Why did you come into my tent? How could you be so disrespectful? Leave me alone! You understand me? *Leave me alone!*"

'I must have reminded her a million times what Nasser had done to her; it didn't change anything. Her answer was always the same: "I didn't ask you to rescue me. You or anyone else. I didn't want to leave. I had a life there. A family, a husband, honour." It hurt me so much to hear that. So much. I was too young to deal with something so complex. I couldn't understand.'

Aisha stopped once again.

'It doesn't take days or weeks processing something like that; it takes years. It wasn't going to happen on that boat. My sister and I learned to hate each other. We couldn't distance ourselves from what had happened. The simple presence of each other kept the scar open, as if the drama was still developing.'

Aisha sighed.

'I think that's enough for tonight. I don't want to confuse you too much with my own story.'

Aisha hadn't confused me at all. On the contrary, she'd distracted me from my own misery. That evening all the questions on my mind were about her.

Day two

____

I opened my eyes. I was somewhere I knew. The cave, Aisha, the sound of the waterfall. I stood up knowing how my day was going to be. It was to be my memoirs and nothing else. I wrote just like the day before, page after page, rediscovering my own life.

That evening Aisha and I were once again on the plateau, watching the vast, dark horizon in front of us and drinking hot tea. I didn't think at all about the outside world. My new normality, my daily routine, was here and nowhere else. I didn't think about leaving this place. All I wanted was to hear Aisha's story.

Aisha seemed to welcome this new routine as well. She didn't make me feel odd about being there. She acted as if we were old friends who had decided to live there. With her, I felt I was in the right place with the right person. The outside world, my past, her past, were just stories that we told each other.

I was fascinated by Aisha's life. Listening to her was like watching a brilliant and addictive TV series. I couldn't wait to hear the next episode.

'So, what happened on that boat?' I asked, impatient for her to tell her story.

'On *Trégastel*, my sister was silent. She was cooperative with Laurent and Anne-Marie, she took part in every meal but she never entered into a conversation with anyone. Her eyes never met mine, and she avoided being in the same part of the boat as me as much as she could.

'We were on *Trégastel* for three weeks. It was in the middle of the Indian Ocean, a few kilometres away from the French island of La Réunion, that we met Megan. She had a twelve-metre sailing boat which proudly flew the Australian flag. Naima and I boarded Megan's boat, *Wyndham's Star*. Jamal and Fatima, who had helped us leave Saudi Arabia, didn't go with us. France was their final destination. They stayed on *Trégastel*.

'Megan welcomed us very warmly. She was a tall blonde athletic Australian woman. Things on *Wyndham's Star* were very different from on *Trégastel*. This time we didn't need to hide. On board there was nobody except us and Megan. We weren't just encouraged to participate; we had to.' Aisha paused, looking briefly at her watch.

'From the very beginning, Megan made Naima and me work together. There was no way for us to avoid each other. She and I might have had terrible arguments all day long but it didn't happen. The weather didn't give us the opportunity. We didn't encounter a storm or any other sort of extreme weather. No, we had to deal with the unpleasant weather that lasts for weeks. The kind that pumps out all the energy you have until there's none left. A light rain that never stops, and a swell working in concert with a moderate wind. Can you imagine being seasick for four weeks? Being unable to stay dry the whole time? '

'It must be hell, I imagine.'

'Yes, Helen. It was hell. After four weeks, I thought I couldn't experience anything worse. I thought I'd reached the ultimate limits of my body. But then came the storm. The real nasty one.

Thirty hours experiencing yet another level of hell. You're seasick, wet, extremely tired and you're needed all the time.

'Our sailboat was dismasted and the hull was severely damaged. We had a leak that we couldn't repair. The only thing we could do was pump water, over and over. There was no coast in sight but Megan knew we weren't far from the Kimberley.

'"We can make it," she told us, in a convincing tone, and switched on the diesel engine. Naima and I did everything Megan told us. For an entire night we pumped out water that had leaked inside the boat. We couldn't risk stopping. Any additional litre of seawater inside the boat made it slower. With only forty litres of diesel left and unfavourable currents, Megan didn't hide from us that it was going to be a challenge to reach the Kimberley's coast.'

Aisha had a brief look at her watch once again. 'At dawn, the coast was in sight, but we had no diesel left. When the engine had burned its last centilitre of diesel, we packed everything we could onto the rowing boat. Food, first aid kit, radio… everything essential for the coming hours on that tiny boat. Every additional minute on *Wyndham's Star* was moving us away from the coast with the current. So we hurried. We all rowed; we fought the current for five long hours. Then we saw huge red cliffs, as far as the eye could see, a vast, endless cliff wall, impossible to climb. But Megan wasn't pessimistic. On the contrary, she scanned the landscape with a broad smile. "Koolama Bay!" she said with unexpected enthusiasm. Megan knew the place from the King George Falls. It's one of the wonders of Australia. Planes fly low over the site, several times a day all year round. Seeing the King George Falls from above is a must for anyone visiting the Kimberley.' Aisha again looked at her watch.

'Why are you checking the time? Is there a programme on TV tonight you don't want to miss?' I asked with a smile.

'No TV show, but something that will probably get your

attention. But until then let's go back to the Kimberley coast. We rowed along the coast until we reached the King George River. Then we rowed upstream to these amazing waterfalls. Imagine two massive streams of water falling from 100-metre-high sandstone cliffs. It was so spectacular that we took time to watch it in silence from our rowing boat for at least ten minutes. Then we spent at least an hour looking for a way to get to the top of the gorge.

'We climbed, we walked, and we climbed again. And we finally got to the top, but it still wasn't time to rest and set up camp. We weren't regular people who needed to be rescued. We couldn't simply draw an S O S on the ground and wave at the first plane to fly over us. Megan insisted on reminding us that my sister and I were illegal immigrants and that she was the one who had broken the law by helping us. For her there was only one plan possible. She had to be the one waving at the first plane that would fly over. She was Australian. She had the right to be here and could tell a credible story to the authorities. My sister and I had to follow another path. We had to wait for Megan to inform our uncle about the situation and then rely on his capacity to rescue us as fast as possible. According to Megan, it could all happen in a single day. "Your uncle has the means to act fast," she said with confidence.

The direct consequence of all of this was that we couldn't camp near the waterfalls. We had to hide. We walked for an hour through the bush until we found a small cave that was a good shelter and a place to hide. We took the time to eat some of the food we had with us and then we had a good long sleep. My God, I slept so well that night. I was so exhausted.' Aisha stretched her legs while having a look at her watch.

'At dawn, Megan left, leaving me to deal with Naima who didn't want to exchange a single word with me. Three hours passed before we heard a plane flying over the area in circles. An hour later another one came, making more noise. And then nothing. Just the sound of the wind that grew stronger by the hour.'

Aisha leant forward, grabbing a handful of earth. She took my left hand and poured the earth into it.

'Feel how dry it is. From April to November, it rarely rains here. And if by any chance it does rain, it's unlikely to last more than a few hours. That's why our uncle had made sure we arrived here in the middle of July. But of course, some years are exceptions. We experienced one of these exceptions. It was as if the bad weather was following us. A heavy rain like I had never experienced before. All this dry landscape was soaked in a matter of minutes. By nightfall, our cave looked like a small swimming pool. We had nowhere to shelter from the rain. We were wet and cold.

'At dawn, totally exhausted, we still had no relief. The rain hadn't stopped. The King George Falls, fed by so much water, made a terrifying background noise. There was no way to rest. Everything around us put us on constant alert. Naima and I had reached an extreme level of fatigue. Nothing logical came out of our brains. Everything irritated us. The only thing that my sister and I were able to do was to shout at each other. You know this kind of fatigue, this constant stress that doesn't stop. I saw it in your eyes the first minute we met. Two nights you hadn't slept, running away from people who wanted to kill you. You know what I'm talking about, don't you?' I nodded briefly without making any comment. Seeing that I didn't want to talk about it, she continued her story.

'Naima and I were arguing about where was the best spot to shelter when suddenly we heard the noise of a small plane circling over the falls. Without telling me anything, Naima ran towards the falls. I ran after her as fast as I could, willing her not to be seen.

With the wind and the noise of the waterfalls she couldn't hear anything I said. The events of the past weeks hadn't changed the fact that I loved my sister. Her insults, her silence, nothing could change that. I was scared that, once in the hands of the Australian authorities, she would be sent back to Saudi Arabia. There, only death was waiting for her. So I ran as fast as I could, using what little energy I had left in my body.' Aisha paused few seconds.

'I couldn't stop her. I only just had time to hide myself. Naima made it clear she needed to be rescued. They flew over her at least five times before they disappeared over the horizon. I didn't know how long it was going to take for them to get there but I knew I couldn't waste a single minute. It was my last chance to persuade my sister to hide in the bush and I had to be fast. But Naima didn't want to talk. She said, "I won't allow you to interfere in my life. Not anymore. This is my life, not yours. If you want to hide in the bush and hope that Amin is going to rescue you, do it. But do it alone. It's your choice, your life. Go and leave me alone, once and for all." And that was it. That was the last time I heard the sound of her voice.'

Suddenly a powerful light appeared on the horizon. It looked like the one I'd seen near the dry lake when I was running away. Aisha didn't seem surprised.

'What's that?' I asked immediately.

'My home for more than twenty years.'

'What do you mean by that? You've lived in the bush for twenty years, or what?

'Let me finish my story first. It's important. My sister was rescued by the authorities. My uncle rescued me a few hours later and brought me right here, to this gorge.'

'So you really have lived in the bush for twenty years?'

'Let me finish, Helen. Some details are important. Saudi Arabia had issued an international arrest warrant against my sister and me. We were both accused of murdering Nasser. Even though Australia had no extradition agreement with Saudi Arabia, and the risk of being deported was close to zero, Naima still had to answer the accusation against her. As a judge told her, the absence of an extradition agreement between Australia and Saudi Arabia isn't a licence to kill. Naima told the whole truth. Not a single lie came from her mouth. Not even a single one by omission. She told everything. *Everything!*'

Aisha stood up, staring at the light.

'Thankfully the authorities found nothing against Amin. It could have been the end of everything for us.'

Aisha turned around and gazed at me.

'Telling the truth and only the truth didn't help my sister at all. It made her an enemy of our Uncle Amin and anyone else who had helped us, including Megan who had to testify against my sister to defend herself. At the end of the day, the truth didn't serve anybody's interest at all. It didn't satisfy Nasser's family, nor most members of our own family. It didn't even help the cause of women's rights in Saudi Arabia.'

Aisha walked a bit away from me, putting her hand to her face. I heard her take a long breath and then she came back to me.

'My sister was a great person. She was an angel. If she'd lived all her life in Australia, none of this would have happened. Context does matter.'

Aisha shoved her hands into her pockets and stared at the light in silence for a few seconds before coming back to me again.

'A newspaper reported that Naima had said to the authorities, "I could have stopped hitting Nasser. He was neutralised. My sister and I could have run away. But I wanted to go on hitting him. I couldn't get it out of my head, everything he'd done to me. I couldn't forgive him." Naima felt bad about what she had done to Nasser. She isn't a violent person. She's an angel. She couldn't accept the idea that it was alright to beat this son of a bitch. She thought she had to pay for it. "I'm a murderer," she kept saying. And then… one morning… she committed suicide.'

Aisha remained silent for a few seconds before sitting down next to me and sipping her tea.

'Meanwhile, I was living here, in this gorge, in this cave, totally ignoring what was going on outside, with no idea about what my near future could be. I was just stuck here, waiting for a visit from my uncle. Bernadette, a woman around sixty, was my only company. She cooked, cleaned the dishes, cleared up the mess and disappeared into the bush for four hours each afternoon. Speaking no Arabic and barely speaking English, she and I couldn't have any kind of conversation. The only thing that I knew from her was the fact that she was French.

'After two long weeks my uncle finally visited me. It was only then I learned what had happened to Naima. I was devastated but not only that. I was very angry. Angry with myself. Angry with my uncle. What if I'd never gone into her tent? What if my uncle had rescued us earlier at the King George Falls? What if I'd stayed with her, and been rescued by the authorities? What if…?' Aisha sighed.

'I couldn't stay in this gorge anymore. I needed to tell the world my sister wasn't a criminal, that she was an angel. I had to be there to defend her honour. Her story couldn't finish like this. I couldn't let Nasser's family think that Naima was the problem, that she deserved to die and go to hell for eternity. My sister was an angel and now she is in heaven for eternity.'

Aisha stood up. 'Let's have a walk. I need to walk.'

I stood up and walked slowly with her, without saying anything. I listened carefully because I felt her story was soon going to meet mine.

'I told my uncle I wanted to leave, to go to where my sister was buried, abandoned by her own family. He didn't say no. But he told me that the only way to go back to the outside world was to walk through the bush. He said, "We will give you everything you need. It's a four-to-five-day walk. It's more exhausting than difficult. You can do it." I was stunned to hear such a thing. He, Bernadette and I hadn't walked to this gorge. A helicopter had brought all of us here. I didn't understand what his problem was. But then he invited me to have a walk with him, right here along the east cliff. It was night time, around ten, just like right now.

My uncle Amin remembered what I used to dream when I was a kid. The hidden magic world in the desert. A place where girls have the same rights as the boys. "You can only access it at night, when the glow appears on the horizon," I used to say to Naima. "Magic worlds don't exist," she said, every time I brought up the subject. But then one day my uncle said, "I know this world. I've visited it many times. It's in the future." Naima responded immediately, "No one can go to the future". My uncle laughed and said, "Everybody can. The future exists only in your head. The future is a dream where everything is still possible." Naima wasn't the kind to give up. "Dreams aren't reality. Dreaming about a magic world doesn't make it real," she said to Amin. He replied, "There's no great accomplishment in this world that doesn't come from a dream. We experience today what seemed impossible yesterday. Do you even know what a magic world could be? Can you define it before you deny its existence?" This kind of conversation could last forever. God knows how much I annoyed Naima when I talked about this magic world. Do you know the song Xanadu?'

'No. Why?' I answered, a bit annoyed about this digression.

Aisha sang the beginning of the song:

'I used to love that song without knowing it came from a mediocre movie. Because of that song, I named my magic world Xanadu. Naima was so annoyed every time I sang it. Have you seen Citizen Kane?'

This time, I really had had enough of her digressions. Too many questions were building up in my mind. A few minutes ago, I'd had absolutely no thoughts about tomorrow. I was in the right place, here and now, trying to deal with my past. But now I really wondered what this place was, and if Aisha's so-called colleagues were going to take me out of the bush. I didn't want to hear stories anymore, I wanted some answers, real ones.

'Aisha. Get straight to the point, please. What is this light? And what is your current situation? Have you been living hidden in the bush for twenty years? Is that what you're telling me?' I said, annoyed.

'The answers are coming, Helen. But they aren't easy, and details do matter. Sitting right here next to me, my uncle reminded me of Xanadu. He reminded me of the glow in the desert. "Xanadu doesn't exist yet, but it already shines in the night," he used to say about the little light he'd put on top of his tent. This was his way of supporting me. He pushed me to dream. And then this light came. I was just like you, right here, wondering what it could be.'

Aisha took a deep breath. 'Amin said to me, "Behind you, there is the world that you know. You walk four, maybe five days through the bush and you're back there. And believe me, it's easier than it sounds. The question isn't about the journey through the bush but more about the very nature of the destination. Do whatever you want. But don't lie to yourself. You know what to expect over there."'

Aisha pointed to the light with her left hand. 'He pointed his left hand at the light and then said to me, "It isn't Australia over there. It's the somewhere else that you, I and many people have always dreamed about. It isn't a self-destructive world that we're trying to fix. This is a clean slate where history is still to be made. The dream has become a reality. We have the means to dream, to imagine the future without limits. We made it, Aisha, we made it. This is the light you looked for in the desert. It's right here, shining for the first time. It's just a three-kilometre walk."

'I asked him to tell me more about this light, this dream, whatever you call it. He answered, "If I told you what we're doing there you wouldn't believe me. The only way for you to find out is to walk there and see for yourself. You walk towards the light or you walk the other way where your sister was. Whichever path you choose, you will walk it alone. Once you've reached your destination there will be no way back. So, think twice." And that was it. End of conversation. He left me here, watching this light without knowing what it could really be. What he had said about my childhood, my dreams, the light in the desert, had reached a part of my mind but it couldn't offset my will to restore the honour of my sister. I couldn't give up on her. It was morally unacceptable for me. It was decided. I was going to leave this place.'

'You're still telling me stories, Aisha. I don't want to know what your uncle said or what you did. I just want to know what it is, what you're really doing here, and if anyone is going to take me out of the bush anytime soon?' I said, in an aggressive tone.

Aisha stayed very calm. 'My story is your story. Don't you see it? We're almost there. You're going to know what kind of choice you're facing.'

She took a deep breath. 'The next morning, Bernadette gave me a backpack. In it was all the gear, food and the instructions to follow for my five-day journey to the outside world. I took it badly at first. I imagined my uncle saying to me, "You want to go! So, go now. Don't waste a minute. Get out of my way!" But I changed my mind quickly and saw it as a positive thing. I couldn't stay in this situation, living alone in a cave without knowing what my future was going to be. So, I read the instructions carefully, inspected the contents of the backpack and at 10am I was already out of the gorge, heading to the outside world.

'Around 3pm, I got to a huge place made of cracked earth that fills up with water during the wet season. This is where you were. How did you call it? You gave a name to it? It was…'

'The dry lake. Please get to the point. I don't want to hear stories anymore. I want to know what's going on here,' I said impatiently.

'Patience! We're almost there. After an exhausting day of walking, I camped at the top of a plateau, just like this one. From there, I could see kilometres around. And then, while I was watching the horizon, the light appeared. But it wasn't especially bright anymore. I had walked away from it. It was all I'd done that day: walked away from my uncle's light. It didn't sound right. It didn't match what my life had been so far. I'd always walked or run towards this light. The fact that this time I didn't know what it was didn't bother me. This light looked more than ever like the one of my dreams. This wasn't a glow on the top of a tent. It was a powerful light in the middle of one of the most remote places on earth. It might sound ridiculous but just watching this light made me dream. There was something mysterious about it, something that excited my imagination. It resonated like the Xanadu of my childhood. There, alone on the top of that plateau, staring at the light, I had the feeling that I was once again outside my sister's tent, facing the same choices. My sister was dead, but I was still trying to rescue her. This time it wasn't about her life but about her honour. Like in Saudi Arabia, I could walk alone towards the light. For the first time since I'd left home, I considered the idea that maybe helping Naima had been a mistake. What if I hadn't gone into her tent? What if I'd run alone towards the light? Maybe my sister would still be alive. Maybe not. Maybe Nasser would have killed her. I didn't know anymore why I was here or what I was doing. From this confusion came the idea to write down what my life had been so far. I needed to see the events of my life in their chronological order, to see the facts in their crude form written down on paper.'

Aisha glanced at me, seeing my patience reaching its ultimate limits. The story had to finish now. She had to tell me if she had ever left the bush.

'OK, I'm not going to tell you everything that crossed my mind that night, even if I think it would help you to understand your own situation. So here we are! I didn't leave the bush. I came back here and walked those three kilometres towards the light. What would I have been in that crazy world? What could I have accomplished? Saving the honour of a dead sister? And then what? You know this world well, Helen. You tried to fix it. You tried very hard. But it doesn't matter how hard you try the results are always the same. In front of you, there's no world to fix. There's a world to build. A place where people aren't trying to save this civilisation but are doing their best to create another one, a far better one, a sustainable one. There are lots of people like you there. Some great personalities who did their best to make this world better, trying to save it from its own self-destruction. Just like you, they tried hard. Very hard.'

'Are you telling me that nobody is going to get me out of here? Everything you told me the first day was just bullshit.'

'The first day, I told you what you needed to hear. You were confused and panicked. Instead of focusing on my little lie…'

'Your little lie! I've been here two days waiting to be rescued by your so-called colleagues. I'm still here because you lied to me. Without your lies, I'd be on the Gibb River Road by now.'

'Without me, you'd be nowhere, Helen. This is the truth that you should consider before talking about my lies.'

'Alright! I owe you so much. So, you can lie to me. No problem. Sorry to be so ungrateful! All you want is to keep me here forever. Not a big deal! Why am I complaining?'

'Helen, don't be like that. Don't you see the beauty of all of this? It's a miracle! You and I weren't supposed to meet. We're in the middle of nowhere. No one comes here. No one. I was supposed to be alone for a couple of days. And here you come with nothing but the clothes that you're wearing. You, an environmentalist with a story to tell. Normally, anyone from the outside world coming here is really bad news. But you're different. You're a pleasant surprise.'

'My friends were murdered a few kilometres from here. My presence here has nothing to do with a nice surprise. At dawn, I'm gone, Aisha. Thank you for everything.'

'Gone to go where and to do what? Confess your past to the police and spend one, two, maybe three decades in jail? Or maybe you prefer to lie and get back to your life where you left it.'

'This conversation is over. Tomorrow I'm gone.'

'That's what I said to my uncle, right here twenty years ago.

Tomorrow, I'm going to give you a backpack with everything you need. You will walk and then you will think about your memoirs, about what you wrote, your life so far. Then the night will come and you'll think about this light. The somewhere else, the unknown, the adventure…a place where you could finally achieve something. This conversation is not over, Helen. You will come back, just like I did.'

Day three

―――――――

I opened my eyes. Aisha was already up. My backpack was ready waiting for me in front of the cave. The moment I stood up, Aisha said, 'You should go now before it's too hot. It's the best time of the day for a walk.'

She explained the way to the Drysdale River Station, and showed me the contents of the backpack. Water filter, dehydrated food, first aid kit, a compass… everything I needed was there. But then she gave me her laptop and a USB stick.

'You aren't done with your past. Tonight, when you're alone in the bush, you will probably want to read what you've already written and then you'll write more. Twenty years ago, I didn't have a computer with me, but I did have a pen and a diary. You'll be busy tonight.'

'Stop comparing your past with my life. There's nothing to compare. Keep your computer, I don't need it.'

'Yes, you need it. It's fully charged, by the way,' she said before she put the computer in the backpack.

'Adieu, Helen.'

'Adieu, Aisha.'

Then I left.

I walked and walked… thinking about nothing more than keeping the right course and staying hydrated.

At sunset, I was busy preparing dinner.

At night, I was in my sleeping bag, watching the starry sky. I had nothing to do. Nobody to speak to. I thought about Wolf, my parents, my sister and my brother, my friends. I thought about my life back home. I couldn't imagine it. How to live with my past? How was Wolf going to react? What about my criminal past? Did I have to confess it? How many years in jail did I risk? And if I chose to lie, what kind of future did I have? After everything that had happened, what could an environmentalist like me do? William was dead, Lenny was dead, what would be my next step this time? So many questions going in every direction leading me to a state of total confusion. I didn't have any answers. I didn't know.

So, I took the computer and read what I'd written. Here, everything was in chronological order, following a logic. Here, my life seemed to fit together. I resumed my writing. I had to finish these memoirs. The past had to meet the present. The whole thing had to make sense.

I wrote and wrote… I couldn't sleep or think about anything apart from writing my memoirs. Page after page, it was the same story repeating itself over and over. Before everything else, I was an environmentalist. Nothing else drove my life. I was a militant… a militant going nowhere. All the paths I'd followed had been dead ends. Could I be something else? Could I stop being a militant? Could I have a so-called 'regular life' with Wolf? Could I go back and become a geologist working for a mining company? No, I couldn't. I had no plan B back home. I couldn't be other than what I'd always been. I couldn't stop being a militant and acting for the planet. Nor could I hide my real life from Wolf. I was an outlaw and he was going to find out. He would have four options:

- Accepting fully who I am and being my accomplice, keeping my secrets and letting me be the militant that I've always been, exploring other paths, maybe some bad ones.
- Having a wife who had chosen to confess everything to the authorities, spending her next years in jail.
- Denouncing me to the authorities and ending our relationship.
- Divorcing me and staying quiet. Letting me become whatever I want to be.

That only produced more questions:

- Do I want Wolf to become my accomplice?
- Do I want to confess to the authorities what I've done?
- Could I survive a divorce from Wolf?

NO! I didn't want any of this. My future looked darker than ever. This time I didn't know how I was going to get out of the dead end. I missed my amnesia. I missed that feeling of starting from zero. When I met Wolf for the first time, I was a woman facing a wide open future where everything had still to be invented. Everything remained possible. I wanted all of that back.

The future

Here we are, I'm in front of this computer, in the middle of the Kimberley, facing my past. Here is the complicated truth, demanding the time to be understood and, perhaps, judged. I could hide it all with an easy lie that would bother no one. Nobody would ask me any complicated questions.

Politicians and even companies tend to choose the easy lie. And who can blame them. In this world of social networks, easy ideas circulate faster than ever, leaving almost no chance for the complicated truth to be heard. I remember a cartoon showing a movie theatre with two queues in front of it. The short queue is for the documentary *An Inconvenient Truth* and the long one is for another documentary, *A Convenient Lie*. I remember when I saw it telling myself how true this was. But how can I change the world if I think that most of us are cowards or stupid, preferring to hear lies rather than face the truth? William used to believe in this world, in its intelligence. For him, there were no idiots, no cowards, no selfish people; there were only misunderstandings between us all. I want to believe in our world. I want to believe in all of you, in your ability to understand the meaning of what I have done. I am not asking you to forgive me or to make excuses for me. All I ask is for you to look at the complicated and inconvenient truth. The one that makes us all responsible for the current situation.

Aisha told me that the future is a dream. You can visit it at any time, it's right here in your mind, in your imagination. William had many dreams, Lenny had a wonderful dream. I shared their dreams, but they are all gone now. Back home, right there where you live, I can't visit the future. It's all blurry and sad. I can only see darkness. I see a world travelling to its extinction and behaving as if nothing is going to happen. It's business as usual on the Titanic. There is no dream, no future, just a routine that nothing seems to stop.

Where is the future? Where are the real dreams, the crazy, wonderful ones, the impossible ones? Where is the other way, the alternative? Where is the bright light?

Right here. I'm facing it. What are these people doing? What is this light? I don't know. But I do know Aisha's story. I do know that without her, I would probably be dead. I want to believe that they do something amazing over there.

In the middle of the bush, in one of the most remote places on earth, this powerful light does have an effect on you.

Aisha and all the people there, they may pretend they're building another world, but they're still a part of humanity, a part of us. I don't run away from you, I don't stop believing in us. On the contrary, I want to visit our future. A place where everything is still possible. This light on the horizon could be anything. That's what makes it special. It switches on your imagination, makes you dream… I am going there.

To you, Wolf

Not having so much time, I didn't build an L like the one we built together on our honeymoon. This one is way smaller, but I do believe that you'll find it and know where to dig.

It's our L, not an S O S. You're the addressee and I'm not asking to be rescued.

Please don't let me be misunderstood. I'm not leaving you, I'm leaving this so-called civilised world. I wish you were here, right next to me. I hope you find this message as soon as possible. Look for the gorge and then go east. I'm sure there is a way to find these people and so to find me. You and I aren't done. This could be a new chapter of our lives, not the end.

Of course, I do understand that it's a very complicated situation for you. You have the right to be angry with me and to wonder why I didn't choose to come back to you but decided to join some people I don't know. I know that what I wrote in my memoirs can't be enough... I know that it hurts... I know you could hate me... I know, and I am sorry.

I wish I could talk to you right here, right now and wasn't

writing this. I struggle to find the right words and I know that everything I'm writing risks bringing about even more confusion.

The computer battery will soon be totally flat. So, I must hurry and get to the essentials. I have to foresee the worst-case scenarios. It could be that you fail to find me or that I die, or that you simply don't want to find me. In these cases, please share my memoirs with everyone. Make sure that this didn't happen for nothing. People deserve to know the truth about the WUM headquarters' arson. I don't want to hide myself behind lies. I apologise to all the people I hurt. I'm not looking for excuses. All I want is to be understood. I know it will be difficult for you to share this document but please do it. It's only through the truth that my life can find its meaning. But please keep the part concerning Aisha to yourself. Whatever she and her uncle are doing, it has to be their decision to make it known.

In my memoirs, I didn't say much about our happy life together. True happiness is difficult to translate into words. My love for you has always been real and profound. There is no explanation to give, nothing to analyse, nothing to confess. I have always loved you. There is no minute when I don't think about you. I am deeply sorry to have brought this upon you.

I love you.
Helen.

You should now be reading the end of the novel I wrote at Digger's Rest. I deleted that ending. To understand why I did such a thing, first we have to go back to September 2016. After spending four fantastic weeks at Digger's Rest, I was at the Novotel Hotel in Darwin. I had a comfortable room that I planned to leave only occasionally in the coming forty-eight hours. My aim was to rest before the long flight back home.

Though the Digger's Rest station had wireless internet around its main homestead, I hadn't checked my e-mail or visited any webpages. There, I was in paradise. I had no interest in the outside world. But in Darwin, things were different. I wanted to reconnect myself with what could be a regular life. First, I checked the news, interested to know what had been happening in this world over the past weeks. After an hour, browsing through different websites of US news outlets, I finally decided to check my e-mails, without expecting anything.

Among the hundreds of newsletters I never read and the advertisements that had succeeded in getting through the antispam filter, there was one e-mail from the Flowers, asking me to call them before leaving Australia. I did call them.

'We would love to see you before you leave Australia. We can drive to Darwin. It's not a problem at all,' said Abigail in a very friendly voice. We agreed to meet in front of the hotel the next day at noon and then to have lunch together. 'We can't wait to see you again,' she concluded before hanging up.

I didn't meet the Flowers again. This was a ploy, telling a journalist from a local newspaper where and when to find me. This journalist did find me in front of the hotel. Christiane Cambray, thirty-one, dressed as if for a wedding, didn't need to say much to show me how motivated she was to get an interview. She was the last journalist still writing about the Flowers and probably the only one who believed that Rachael's memoirs were authentic. I had every reason to be annoyed by this little surprise. God knows how angry I was with the Flowers that day, but Christiane had the antidote to this anger. She smiled at me and talked to me like I was a rock star. Yes, me, the seventy-year-old guy who'd thought a few weeks ago he had absolutely no future. She made me laugh so much, I couldn't resist her. So instead of pushing her away, I invited her to lunch with me and gave her the interview she wanted so much. From my first encounter with Andrew's story to Scott's office in Sydney, I told her everything about my little adventure in Australia. But Christiane wasn't here to hear that. She let me tell my little story so I wouldn't realise she was only here to ask me about Rachael's memoirs.

Christiane knew what she was doing. I didn't. After what looked like an interview, she started the real conversation, telling me about her passion for the story of the missing exploration team. Her knowledge of that was far greater than mine, with one major exception: Rachael's memoirs. Though she had an excellent relationship with the Flowers, they had always refused her the right to read it, fearing she would share everything.

'They're maybe right on that matter. I don't want to read the memoirs and then keep everything to myself. I've always thought they should've shared everything from day one,' she confessed, then said she hoped my future novel was really close to Rachael's memoirs.

But then she used her knowledge to make me speak. She wanted to make me feel my novel contained nothing that she didn't already know.

'I hope there's something about the role Rachael plays within the Earth Warriors.' she said, staring at me, watching for my reaction. But I didn't react.

'It would be unfortunate if you didn't mention her political involvement,' she said. I didn't react.

'Think about Scott and the role he played in her life through that strange environmental organisation.' Once again, I didn't react; I was starting to get annoyed with her little game.

'But you and I wouldn't be here talking about Rachael if those two sisters from Saudi Arabia hadn't succeeded in reaching the Australian coast.' I did react. My gaze said what my voice didn't. I couldn't hide my surprise. How could she know about this? How could she have made the link between Rachael and those two women? It was in the most mysterious and incredible part of Rachael's memoirs. The part you couldn't guess. The part that fascinated me the most.

'Oh, my God. So, it's true. It's all true. Rachael met her. What about the uncle? He's there too, isn't he?' she said immediately.

I wasn't comfortable with this situation. Within me were two opposing feelings. I was craving to know more, to ask Christiane how she knew about those two women from Saudi Arabia. I wanted to find the missing pieces of the puzzle. But on the other hand, I was angry with myself. I felt I'd revealed too much. I wasn't supposed to talk about Rachael's memoirs.

But what finally pushed me to leave Christiane behind was the professional author living within me. I was writing a novel flirting with a complicated reality. I knew that with Aisha's story I was right at the edge. One small step further and the border would be crossed. Christiane was a journalist, I wasn't. I hadn't done any investigating. I was writing fiction. Helen, William, Salima, Aisha…they were all characters that came from my imagination. I didn't want a visit from them, even though sometimes reality can take you further than fiction. So I left Christiane, and twelve hours later I was heading back home.

After having spent almost twenty hours up in the air and four hours in transit at Singapore airport, I was happy to be home.

During my screenwriting career, I'd got into the habit of isolating myself inside my house for the final check of my manuscripts. I didn't leave home for days, sometimes even for weeks; didn't watch TV, didn't read a newspaper, switched off all my phones, disconnected all my computers from the internet… I separated myself from the rest of the world, away from its distractions and its influence. More than ever, I needed to return to this habit. The only way to complete this book was to remove myself from the real world.

The internet was switched off, the entrance doorbell disabled, all the curtains were closed, the fridge was full… nothing could stop me completing this book. Reminding myself of some good memories from the time when I was a screenwriter, I said to myself, 'I'm back in business!'

By the fourth day I was already checking the end of my novel.

The one that you won't read. In this ending, Helen was hallucinating. Her last hours were a dream. A dream containing a woman from Saudi Arabia who lived in the bush and asked her to live with her, somewhere the light shone in the middle of the night. All of this was a dream. The Earth Soldiers were the reality. They'd let her walk alone in the bush without water. The book finished with Helen's death. The screenwriter, who was still living inside me, was satisfied with this ending.

But then someone knocked on my door. At first, I ignored it. But they kept knocking. 'Go away!' I shouted three times from behind the door, extremely annoyed. But the person kept knocking. So, I finally opened the door. Behind it was a woman, fortyish, middle eastern looking. A bit short, a curvy body and with a round face showing a large smile, I found her likeable at first sight. The fourth 'go away' that I wanted to shout didn't succeed in getting out of my mouth. I fell silent, and she did the talking.

'Hello, I guess I'm a character in the novel you're writing. You and I have to talk. It's about Rachael. May I come in?' she said with a sweet voice.

'Are you Aisha?' I asked, as if calling someone by the name of one of my characters made some kind of sense.

'Is that the name you gave me? I like it!' she said as she came into the house and closed the door.

Then everything went very fast. With no time to think about anything, I was in my own living room, sitting on the couch, facing her in the armchair.

'What I'm going to tell you is pure fiction and shouldn't be considered otherwise, but it doesn't mean that you should take it lightly. It's more than a story. It's a message and I do hope that you will deliver it properly,' she said in her sweet voice.

'Who are you? And how did you find me?' I asked, still confused by the situation.

'You know who I am! I'm Aisha! I'm here because you said too much to a journalist. Some people are going to believe I'm real. They're going to look for explanations. They'll want a story. So, let me feed your imagination a bit.'

'But why do you want to tell me your story?'

'Does my character say in your book that the future is a dream?' Since I didn't answer she said, 'You did write that. You wrote fast. Four weeks. Is that correct?' I nodded.

'I don't say you wrote an exact copy of Rachael's memoirs. But you and I wouldn't be here together if you hadn't liked what you read in Sydney. The real me is not in your novel. But I guess Aisha and I are not so different from each other. And to answer your question, I want to tell you my story because the future is a dream and there is a dream that I would like to share.'

I don't know how long she stayed here. Five, six hours, maybe more. I wasn't wearing my watch that day. 'You will hear from me,' she said, before she disappeared into the darkness of the night. Alone, I went back to the couch and read all the notes I'd taken. I couldn't get to sleep. My mind was too busy. But exhaustion rapidly took over. The next morning, I woke up on the couch with the strange feeling that the previous day had been a dream. 'Was this woman real?' I wondered, looking for any trace of her visit. An empty glass here, a dirty plate there, the armchair not in its regular spot… somebody could really have been here… or not. It could just be my imagination. But my notes were real. I'd written plenty of them. The story of this woman was here. A long and fascinating story. At the top of the first note was written:

Helen doesn't die in the Kimberley. She is still alive!

Helen's story is far from over.

To be continued in

in the Name of
Tomorrow

Contents